W9-API-068

Enemies on the Battlefield

Faye M. Benjamin

This book is a work of fiction. Names, characters, places, and incidents either are products of the author's imagination or are used fictitiously. Any resemblance to actual persons, living or dead, events or locales is entirely coincidental.

All rights reserved. No part of this book may be reproduced in any form or by any means without the prior written consent of the author, excepting brief quotes used in reviews.

Copyright © 2015 Faye M. Benjamin

All rights reserved.

ISBN-13: 978-1518645617

ISBN-10: 1518645615

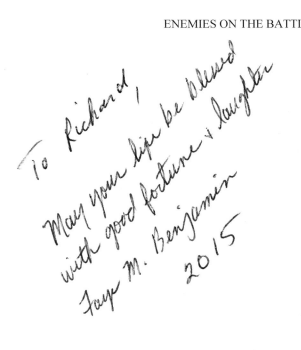

To Richard,

May your life be blessed
with good fortune & laughter

Faye M. Benjamin
2015

DEDICATION

Dedicated to the re-enactors from the 10th Kentucky Infantry Regiment and 33rd Alabama Infantry Regiment for educating our present and future generations about their past that was changed forever by the Civil War.

Also, dedicated to my cousin, Ryan Hamm from Indiana.

ENEMIES ON THE BATTLEFIELD

BOOKS BY FAYE M. BENJAMIN

Freestone Series

Book 1 - <u>The Terrible Three and Murder</u>
Book 2 - <u>Judgment Leads to Murder</u>
Book 3 - <u>Shower Curtain Killer</u>
Book 4 – <u>Murdered by Mistake</u>
Book 5 – <u>Who is Stalking Me?</u>
<u>Book 6- Barn of Terror</u>

<u>Civil War Novels</u>

<u>River of Tears</u>
<u>Lost Drummer Boy</u>
<u>Frozen Fields of Fire: Fredericksburg</u>
<u>Enemies on the Battlefield</u>

ENEMIES ON THE BATTLEFIELD

ACKNOWLEDGMENTS

Special thanks to Wikipedia, National Archives, and
Library of Congress for the use of
their photos, maps, and illustrations.

LIST OF CHARACTERS

1. Abraham & Florence Waverly
2. Randolph & Alice Kramer Waverly
3. Edwin & Eleanor Waverly Burdette
4. Austin/Albert/Kramer/Laura/Michael/Sally Waverly
5. Gordon/Matthew/Tess Burdette
6. Zeke/Sophie/Jupiter Green
7. Overseer Grady
8. Dr. Mills
9. Toby Wilder
10. Myrtle Higgins
11. Madeline Sawyer
12. Household servants
    Asa/Leroy/Beulah/Daisy/Trudy/Freddie
13. Leaders of the slaves
    Oscar/Calvin/Jerome/Sidney
14. Sgt Warren Taylor
15. Rosie Harris
16. Sammy
17. John Baker
18. Robert Baker
19. Judge Canby Anderson

CHAPTER 1

In 1833 on a fine spring day, Abraham Waverly looked over his beloved Evergreen Manor plantation with great pride. He had turned his land in Alabama by the Chattahoochee River into one of the largest cotton plantations in the state. Of course, now, he was a member of the southern aristocracy entertaining rich planters, lawyers, and politicians. His plantation became the place to be for parties, political discussions, and elaborate meals. His wife was an elegant hostess and the envy of many women.

Florence had given him two children any man would be proud of. Their son, Randolph, was nineteen years old and was learning what he must do to continue his heritage, because one day he would be the master of Evergreen Manor.

Their daughter, Eleanor, was attractive and charming. In his opinion, she would make a perfect mistress of a large plantation. However, Eleanor was only twelve, so she had more growing up to do before thinking about marriage.

This evening they were entertaining the aristocracy to fine wine, food, dancing, and games. He was hoping at this party Randolph would meet a southern belle worthy of Evergreen Manor and end up marrying her. It was time to hear grandchildren laughing and playing all over the mansion.

As the guests started arriving at Evergreen Manor, the household slaves were doing everything possible to insure the party would be a complete success. Massas Waverly wouldn't tolerate anything less than perfect. When he was happy, the household slaves were rewarded.

Randolph asked, "Is anyone new coming to the party, Poppa?"

"Yes, there's a new doctor coming with his wife and daughter."

"Have you seen them before?"

"I've only met the doctor and talked with him. I'm so thankful he's taking over Dr. Wilson's practice, so Wilson can take it easy. His health has been failing over the last two years."

"His daughter probably looks like a cabbage."

Abraham laughed and replied, "I hope not."

"Remember Poppa, you don't want to get the senator all riled up over his campaign. The man doesn't know when to shut up."

"Don't worry; I don't want him to ruin my dinner, either."

Randolph asked, "Who's that getting out of the carriage over there?"

He responded, "That's the new doctor, I assume that's his wife, and that must be his cabbage."

As his father kissed her hand, Randolph couldn't take his eyes off of her. She was simply gorgeous with beautiful black wavy hair, light blue eyes, and long eyelashes to get lost in.

Abraham greeted them and said, "Dr. Kramer, I'm so glad you could come this evening with your lovely family. This is my wife, Florence, and my son, Randolph."

Randolph kissed the mother's hand and asked, "Welcome to Evergreen Manor ma'am, and who might I ask is this lovely woman?"

"She's our daughter, Alice."

"Well Alice, you are a picture of perfection. Let me be your escort for the evening and introduce you to our other guests."

She responded, "If you're an honorable man, I suppose that will be alright."

"Why Miss Alice, my middle name is honorable."

"We shall see, Mr. Randolph."
Abraham thought, "I like her, because she has spunk."

When the guests sat down for their dinner feast, Randolph sat next to her and worked his magical charm. He didn't give another single male, of which there were many, a chance to woo her.

They danced the night away in each other's arms not noticing the people around them. Both were quite smitten with each other which lead to a whirlwind romance.

The following year, Alice Kramer married Randolph and became the future mistress of Evergreen Manor. Both Abraham and Florence loved her, dearly. Randolph's sister, Eleanor, became a very close friend to Alice. Eleanor would talk to Alice about her problems and fears when she wouldn't go to her own mother.

In 1835 Alice gave birth to twin boys named Austin and Albert. Now, Randolph could pass on his legacy to his sons. He was bound and determined to improve the plantation like his father had done before him.

During the years leading up to the Civil War, Randolph buried his beloved father and mother and Alice's parents in the family cemetery. He was glad all of them were proud of his family, and the improvements he had made by adding 250 more acres and a gristmill to Evergreen Manor. He was growing corn on the new acreage and grinding it into cornmeal for their needs and selling the rest in Eufaula, Alabama and Columbus, Georgia.

The Fugitive Slave Law was not being enforced in a lot of northern states, because law enforcement refused to return runaway slaves. The abolitionists that opposed slavery were setting up the Underground Railroad to help runaway slaves reach freedom.

The Kansas-Nebraska Act stated the citizens of these territories would determine whether they became a free or slave state. Now, pro-slavery and anti-slavery settlers were flocking to the area, and it was just a matter of time before this would erupt into violence.

All the planters near Randolph were angry and worried about the political uproar concerning new territories becoming free states or slave states.

Randolph was worried about the gridlock in the Capitol. He thought, "Senators and representatives argued day after day and didn't get anything accomplished. Shoot fire! Some of the politicians resorted to violence when they lost their tempers." Randolph prayed cooler heads would find a compromise both sides could live with.

Randolph had hired a new overseer named Grady to keep the plantation running smoothly. He was getting top dollar for his cotton crop, and he wanted that to continue.

He was the proud father of six children in 1847. Alice had just given birth to his second daughter, Sally. He had to laugh, because three of his children looked like their mother with the black wavy hair and light blue eyes. The other two children had reddish hair and green eyes like him. The baby had reddish-brown hair, so she would probably look like him. One thing for sure, all his children had a loving mother. Even after five pregnancies, Alice was still gorgeous and elegant.

Randolph's third son, Kramer grabbed his fishing pole and headed for the slave quarters. He and Jupiter were going fishing today, because it was Saturday. During the week, Kramer and his brothers and sister had to study hard with their tutors. Now, it was his day to have fun.

The two friends headed for the river to fish and enjoy a swim to cool off. The boys laughed and talked about all sorts of things. Today, the fish were biting, and the boys were rewarded with a large mess of fish for Jupiter's family to enjoy.

After they played in the water, they stretched out on the river bank to dry off.

Kramer commented, "I wish we could do this every day, but I have to get lots of book learning."

Jupiter asked, "Do you wants to have a big plantation, Massas Kramer?"

Kramer fired back, "Don't call me massas! Just call me by my name. I don't want to run a plantation."

"What do you wants to do, Kramer?"

"I want to be a doctor like my grandfather. That's my dream, so I can help people feel better."

"That's a mighty fine dream."

"What do you want to be?"

Jupiter answered, "I don't wants to be a slave no more."

Suddenly, Kramer looked at Jupiter as if he had two heads.

"You can't dream and be something other than a slave! That ain't right, Jupiter."

"Kramer, you knows how plantation life is."

"I promise you, my friend, that one day I'm going to buy your family's freedom."

"You knows that ain't goin' to happen."

"Yes it will, and I'm going to teach you how to read and write."

"I want to read and write, but both of us could gets into lots of trouble."

"We'll do it in secret up in my tree house."

"I hopes nobody catches us, because I could gets beat to death."

"I won't let that happen."

Kramer was good to his word and taught Jupiter how to read, write, and figure numbers. No one on the plantation caught on to what was happening. Kramer's sister, Laura, felt the same way he did, so she always let them know when somebody got too close to the tree house. She was kind of like a lookout for them.

In 1854 Kramer happened to stumble upon their overseer whipping Jupiter's father, Zeke. He ran up and grabbed the whip out of Grady's hand.

Kramer yelled, "Don't you ever hurt Zeke, again, or I'll use this whip on you!"

"This is none of your business, boy!"

"I'm making this my business, you brute! I never have liked your attitude, because you have a mean streak a mile wide. Now, get out of here!"

"I'll speak to your father about this!"

"Go right ahead! Zeke needs help, and I'm going to patch him up! Get out of my sight!"

Grady stomped over to his horse and took off towards the Waverly mansion.

"Massas Kramer, bless you."

Kramer helped Zeke get back to the slave quarters and helped Sophie clean his whip marks. Kramer was angry enough to knock a building down as he bandaged Zeke's back.

"Zeke, why on earth was Grady whipping you?"

"Because I lets a basket of corn fall off de back of de wagon."

"Sweet Jesus, if Grady comes after you again, send Jupiter to tell me. This is not right, because nobody deserves to be beaten like this!"

"Your Poppa is going to bes real mad."

"It's time I had a talk with my father, because he needs to open his eyes. I will not let this happen, again!"

Laura appeared at the door and gave Kramer some ointment to put on Zeke's back.

She remarked, "I overheard Grady telling Poppa what happened. That man is mean as a cottonmouth snake. In my opinion, he's lower than a snake. You know whose side Poppa is going to take."

Kramer replied, "I know, Laura. This showdown has been building for a long time. It's time to stand up against the status quo, because this injustice is eating away at my soul. I can't let this happen anymore!"

Laura walked with her brother towards the elegant mansion knowing their father would be mad. When they walked inside, their father stormed into the foyer, grabbed the whip from his son, and yelled, "Get in my office, son!"

Laura took off to find her mother, because she wasn't sure what her father was capable of doing to her brother when he was really mad. She had never seen him this angry.

Randolph slammed the office door shut and threw the whip on his desk.

He roared, "You are forbidden to interfere with the overseer's job! You can't go around the slave quarters or Zeke's family anymore! Do you understand me, son!"

Kramer fired back, "Whipping anybody's bare back is cruel! Grady is a mean snake who enjoys whipping the slaves! How can you stand by and let this happen, Poppa?"

"That's the way it is on a plantation."

Kramer shouted, "Then, that way is wrong! Zeke's back is a bloody mess, because a basket of corn fell off his wagon! What's wrong with your conscience, Poppa?"

"Do not question my authority!"

Kramer shot back, "I'm questioning your soul, Poppa! Grady tells you what you want to hear. He slaps and hits the colored children for no reason. I can't stand by anymore watching one injustice after another happening on our plantation. Open your eyes, Poppa! You have to listen to your heart!"

"You are lucky I'm not using this whip on you!"

Kramer took off his shirt and yelled, "Go ahead, Poppa, beat me to a bloody pulp like the slaves!"

Randolph stepped back, blinked several times, and asked, "Do you think I would beat you like that?"

Kramer shot back, "I don't know. You let Grady do it to the slaves! Will you take a whip to me, too?"

Laura and her mother were listening outside the door when Alice decided it was time to intervene. She gently opened the door, stepped in front of her son, and picked up the whip.

She ordered, "Kramer, put your shirt back on."

"Yes, Ma'am, but I'm not going to let these injustices happen anymore, Poppa! Zeke's blood is on the whip!"

"Leave your father and me alone, son."

"Yes, Mother."

She turned towards her husband and suggested, "Sit down, Randolph, before you explode! I have never questioned the way you have run this plantation, but when it involves our children, I will speak my mind."

"Don't interfere, Alice!"

"I'll speak my mind, my dear. What has happened to you, Randolph? Have you fallen so low that you're willing to whip your own son for coming to the aid of a wronged slave?"

"Alice, you don't understand what it takes to run a successful plantation."

"Oh yes, I do. Running a successful plantation doesn't go hand and hand with whipping slaves. We're making more money than we've ever made. Has money and greed turned your heart into stone?"

"You don't understand the problem."

"I know exactly what the problem is. You aren't the same man I married."

"People have to change with the times, Alice."

She fired back, "Not when that change is for the worse."

"Kramer can't interfere with Grady!"

"Randolph, you know Kramer is not like the twins. He wants to be a doctor in order to help people."

"I can't have Kramer causing trouble with the slaves! We can't have this plantation in a constant uproar!"

"Kramer is helping the slaves; the trouble is coming from Grady! You are the master of Evergreen Manor, not Grady! Would you have whipped Zeke over a basket of corn?"

"No, I won't have."

"Do you understand what I mean? The whipping has to stop!"

"I can't have two abolitionists in my own family! Kramer and Laura can't live here and cause trouble with the slaves."

"It grieves my soul to think you're willing to send two of our children away, because they oppose an injustice."

"Then, they must keep their opinions to themselves. Two of our children have turned their backs on our way of life, Alice."

"No, Randolph, they're turning their backs on an injustice. If you send them away, it will be on my terms, because you know Kramer and Laura won't let these injustices continue, nor will I. You most stop the whipping! You must change, Randolph."

"And what are your terms concerning Kramer and Laura?"

"Contact your sister and see if she'll take them, and we will pay for their keep and education."

"Alright Alice, I'll do that for you, because I love you, Kramer, and Laura very much. Just remember, I'm walking a fine line here."

"Stop the whipping, because you love me, Kramer, and Laura."

"Alright Alice, I'll stop it for any reason."

Alice left and took the whip with her. Randolph had calmed down, so she knew she still had some control of the situation. In the back of her mind, she feared Kramer and Laura would force the issue on slavery, and now, they had to do something.

She saw Laura and could tell her daughter overheard the argument.

She asked, "Where is Kramer?"

"He went to his tree house, Mama."

"Let's go get him, because we have a lot to talk about. Your father will walk around a bit and think about the situation."

"He should see what Zeke's back looks like!"

"Trust me, honey; your father will go see Zeke. He needs time to think things through. He's not an evil man."

Slaves picking cotton

CHAPTER 2

Alice didn't know her twin boys had talked to Grady and decided to teach their younger brother a lesson. Austin and Albert had found Kramer near his tree house and had beaten the crap out of him. When his mother and Laura found him, his eyes were swollen shut, his nose was bleeding, and he had been kicked several times.

"Sweet Jesus, who did this to you? Was it Grady?"

"No Mama, it was the twins. I can't get up."

Alice ordered, "Laura run to the house and get Leroy and Asa to help me get Kramer to the house!"

Laura was angry as she raced to the mansion to get help. She hated her brothers, because they had turned into cruel brutes just like Grady. Oh, how she wished her Grandpa and Grandma Kramer were still alive. She just knew in her heart they would have taken them in, and then, this nightmare would be over.

Laura got Asa and Leroy and between all of them they got Kramer back to the house. As they were carrying Kramer up the spiral staircase, Randolph came into the house and wanted to know what all the commotion was about.

Laura stomped up to her father and yelled, "Austin and Albert beat up Kramer some kind of bad. They are mean monsters just like Grady, so are you happy now, Father?"

Randolph stared in shock as Leroy helped Alice take Kramer's bloody shirt off. Alice wanted to scream when she saw how black and blue he was. As gently as possible, she cleaned her son's bloody nose, face, and lip.

Leroy commented, "Ms. Waverly, Massas Kramer has bruises on his legs, back, and bottom."

Randolph looked at his son in horror and saw the tears running down his wife's face. That was it! Things would have to change at Evergreen Manor in a hurry.

"Alice is there any laudanum left in the house?"

"It's in my top dresser drawer."

Laura fired back, "Why should you care, Poppa? You've always let Austin and Albert do whatever they wanted. Did you tell them to do this to Kramer? Are you going to have them beat me to a pulp with a whip?"

Alice shot back, "Laura, that's enough!"

Randolph answered, "I'll punish the twins, because this was uncalled for and cruel. This is an outrage I will not tolerate! I'll get the laudanum, Alice."

She mentioned, "You have always handled the discipline of our children in a fair manner. I will not accept anything less, now."

He nodded and left to get the medicine.

Randolph thought as he was getting the medicine, "Maybe, Alice is right. If Grady put the twins up to this, then, I must fire him. Grady has to go, today. I'm the master of Evergreen Manor, not Grady. Also, I will punish the twins, because they need to know they aren't running the plantation, yet. I'm furious at this brutal attack!"

He gave Alice the medicine, because he knew Kramer was in a great deal of pain. Today, Kramer, Alice, and Laura had stood up to him. He didn't agree with all their beliefs; however, he couldn't help but respect their spunk.

He looked at Asa and said, "Go find the twins and have them meet me in my office as soon as possible."

"Yes sir, Massas!"

"Alice, I'll have Velma sit with Kramer for the next few nights. I'll have her bring up some cool water from the root cellar, so she can put cool cloths on his face."

"That would please me very much, Randolph."

He turned to his daughter and said, "When Austin and Albert get to my office, and I take care of the situation, I'll tell you and your mother what I decided to do."

Laura shot back, "Make sure Grady stays away from Kramer and me!"

"He will Laura, because I'm getting rid of him."

It wasn't long before the twins walked into the mansion laughing like they didn't have a care in the world. They went into their father's office and sat down knowing their father would be proud of them.

Randolph asked, "Have you seen Grady today?"

Austin answered, "Yes, sir. He told us what Kramer did, so we decided to teach our handsome brother a lesson. Zeke is always doing something stupid, so he needed to be whipped."

"Did Grady tell you to teach Kramer a lesson?"

Albert answered, "Not exactly. Our brother and Laura have turned into abolitionists, and we can't have that, Poppa! The slaves need to know their place. Kramer can't be stirring them up."

Randolph's face turned blood red, his fists slammed down on the desk, and he yelled, "No one disciplines one of you children except me or your mother!"

Austin added, "He's stirring up the slaves with that abolitionist propaganda, and he's a traitor to our planter aristocracy! He deserved that beating to teach him to leave abolitionist lies alone!"

"Your brother is upstairs beat to a pulp. When he can open his eyes, you better pray he can see. If he dies, I will turn both of you over to the sheriff for murder!"

Randolph got up, grabbed both boys by the neck, and marched them upstairs to Kramer's room. Alice was startled when the door flew open.

Randolph pushed the twins next to the bed and scolded, "Look at him! I'm outraged and angry that you two are capable of this kind of violence! Your mother and I are ashamed of you. Just because Kramer and Laura don't agree

13

with everything we believe in, it doesn't give you the right to beat either one of them to a pulp!"

Alice got up, looked the twins in the eyes, and said, "I never thought two of my children would be capable of such cruelty. You two are forbidden to get anywhere near Kramer and Laura, again!"

"Poppa, tell mother to shut her mouth, because it's none of her business!"

"Don't you dare think I will tell your mother to shut her mouth! What she has to say is important! What you did to your brother is very much her business!"

Randolph continued, "Starting tomorrow, you two will be in the fields picking cotton or corn along with the slaves for two months. When we entertain guests, you will stay in your rooms for the next two months."

Alice went on, "Until Kramer has recovered, both of you will eat all your meals in your rooms."

Randolph reminded, "Just remember, if your brother dies, you go to jail. I'm firing Grady, so I'll be the overseer until I find a suitable replacement. From now on, no one is whipped unless I say so."

Alice suggested, "I'm ashamed of both of you, and you better pray your brother recovers. Your father and I will make sure his dream comes true. Now, go to your rooms and stay there, because I don't want to see your faces until tomorrow."

Both boys said they were sorry, but that fell on deaf ears.

Laura spoke up and said, "Both of you make me sick, because neither one of you is really sorry."

She walked over and slapped both of the twins across the face. Austin raised his hand to hit Laura, but his father grabbed his arm and warned, "Don't you dare lay a finger on your sister, or I'll break your pathetic arm!"

Austin knew better than to challenge his father, because he was as strong as a bull.

Randolph ordered, "Go to your rooms, now! Don't get near Kramer or Laura, again!"

The twins were ushered to their rooms, and then, their father went to his office to think. He knew he would never be able to trust Austin and Albert, again. Also, he knew Kramer and Laura would not be safe at Evergreen Manor. As soon as Kramer recovered from his beating, he would send them to Eleanor in Louisville.

Later, Alice walked into the office, kissed her husband's forehead, and said, "Thank you, Darling."

"I'll never be able to trust Austin or Albert. That kind of violence comes from an uncontrollable temper, so Kramer and Laura won't be safe here."

"I know, because the twins will figure out some way to hurt them."

Randolph suggested, "As soon as Kramer can travel, I'll send them to Eleanor. I know she will be more than glad to have them. I'll pay for our son's education and provide an inheritance for Laura. They'll have whatever they need."

Alice added, "I know our son, and he'll demand you let him take Zeke's family with him. Do that for me."

He replied, "Alright, I'll have their freedman's papers drawn up and signed. I want you to know I'm changing our will and leaving Michael Evergreen Manor. The twins don't deserve this land our ancestors worked so hard to clear and farm."

Alice asked, "Are you sure, Darling?"

"I'm very sure."

Alice remarked, "Jupiter wants to visit Kramer."

"He can visit any time. I'm going to check on Zeke later and make sure he has what he needs to recover. Dr. Williams should be here tomorrow morning to examine both of them."

"That's good to hear."

"Alice, maybe Laura was right about the twins. Maybe, I

did treat them differently. What concerns me the most is which twin is the leader."

"I have a feeling Austin is the one. Laura told me once that she saw Austin drown a kitten in a bucket of water, and he thought it was funny. I confronted him about it, but he denied killing the kitten."

"That sure makes sense. Mother told me once that if a person was cruel to pets and animals, they'd be cruel to people."

Alice agreed, "Your mother was a wise woman."

Over the next few weeks, Kramer and Zeke slowly recovered from their wounds. Eleanor had sent a telegram saying she would be very happy to have Laura and Kramer come live with her family. What the brother and sister didn't know yet, was their Uncle Edwin had paying jobs open for Zeke and his family.

Randolph had hired a new overseer and had made it perfectly clear no one was whipped unless he gave his consent. The twins were having a hard time working in the fields along with the slaves, but they knew if they didn't accept their punishment neither one of them would inherit Evergreen Manor. Neither one could understand why their father was so hard on them. Abolitionists had no place on their plantation. Kramer could turn their lives upside down and talk the slaves into revolting.

Austin and Albert figured as soon as Kramer and Laura were gone things would get back to normal, and their father would ease up on them. One thing for sure, they had to be very careful around their parents, because they wanted Evergreen Manor and be part of the southern aristocracy. There's where the power was, because powerful friends in high places were always very important and necessary to climb the social and business ladders.

Albert said, "It was your idea to beat up Kramer, so now we're picking cotton and corn right along with the stinking slaves. My hands are killing me, my back hurts, and every muscle in my body is sore. It's your fault we're in this mess!"

Austin fired back, "You didn't seem to mind punching that traitor in the face while I was kicking him."

Albert shot back, "I wanted to mess up his handsome face, because all the single women who come to Evergreen Manor flock to him like he's the Fountain of Youth. From now on, I'm doing my own thinking, because trouble seems to follow you around."

Austin suggested, "Do whatever you want, but just remember I know some things you've done that our parents would go crazy over."

"You wouldn't dare tell them I messed with the judge's stupid daughter!"

"Oh yes, I would."

"You haven't been a saint either, Austin. You know how Poppa feels about messing with the slave girls."

He responded, "It kinda looks like we're both not saints."

Albert went on, "I'll be glad when Kramer and Laura leave. We won't have any trouble with Michael and Sally, because they're nothing but dumb little kids."

Austin suggested, "They won't be preaching abolition from the pulpit. At least, Poppa is getting rid of the trouble makers."

The brothers laughed and headed home to eat their supper in their rooms. Both would be glad to get back to the dinner table like normal people.

Randolph and Alice called Kramer and Laura into his office. Asa brought Zeke, Sophie, and Jupiter to the office and closed the door behind them. Zeke had no idea what was going on and prayed Massas Waverly wasn't going to sell them.

Randolph started by saying, "Kramer and Laura, you aren't safe here, because I don't trust Austin and Albert after they beat you to a pulp, son. They showed me a violent side I didn't know they possessed. Your Aunt Eleanor wants you to come live with them, so you can follow your dreams without looking over your shoulders every minute of the day and night. Kramer, I want you to become a doctor and fulfill your dream. Laura, I want you to finish your education and follow your dream. Your educations will be paid for, and both of you will receive your inheritance to help you get started in life."

Kramer asked, "Are you sending us away, because we don't believe in a planter's life?"

"No son. You want to take a different path in life, and I respect that. I want you and Laura to be safe."

Alice remarked, "Michael, Sally, and I will visit you several times a year. Your father doesn't want to leave Austin and Albert alone on the plantation, because Lord knows what they'll do."

Laura asked, "Aren't you afraid the twins will hurt you, Poppa?"

"They won't, because they want to inherit Evergreen Manor, and I control my will."

Randolph looked at Zeke and said, "Your family has a special bond with Kramer and Laura. All of you are good friends, so I want you to go with Kramer and Laura to Louisville to take care of them for me. Will you take real good care of them, so I will know they are safe?"

Zeke replied, "Yes, Massas Waverly, we'll takes the best care of them."

"Thank you. Zeke, all of you will be leaving for the train five days from now. You'll need to help Kramer and Laura pack and pack what you're going to need."

Sophie went on, "Massas Waverly, we'll be ready."

After Zeke's family left, Kramer commented, "I want you

to free them, Poppa."

"Listen to me, son. When you arrive in Louisville, you can give them their freedmen's papers. Trust your mother and me and think about this as a masquerade. One must keep the cats in the bag, right now."

Alice asked, "Do you understand, son?"

Finally, he knew what was going on and answered, "Yes, ma'am."

When it was time to leave, Kramer took Zeke and Jupiter to his room, so they could change into brand new clothes. Laura did the same thing with Sophie who was so excited she could barely talk. Laura told Sophie there were three boxes in the wagon with more new clothes for all of them.

Sophie mentioned, "Ms. Laura, these clothes are too fine to be slave clothes."

"Poppa and Mama want you to look real nice."

Sophie asked, "Can we keep these here clothes, Ms. Laura?"

"Of course, you can!"

When everyone was near the wagons, Randolph pulled a few envelopes from his jacket and gave them to Kramer.

He looked at Zeke's family and said, "I just gave Kramer your freedman's papers and money, so all of you can get started on your new life. Your papers come with two conditions."

Kramer asked, "What are the conditions?"

"First, they will go to Louisville with you and Laura. Secondly, your aunt and uncle have jobs for all three when they get there."

Sophie burst into tears and asked, "Do you mean we ain't slaves no more?"

Randolph replied, "Yes, Sophie."

Zeke responded, "Massas Waverly, this is the happiest day of my life. Praise the Lord!"

Jupiter asked, "Are they paying jobs, Massas Waverly?"

"Yes. Edwin's freight company is growing quickly, so he needs teamsters and warehouse workers. Eleanor is a seamstress, and she needs more help. Are you willing to take the jobs?"

Zeke responded with tears in his eyes, "Yes sir, Massas Waverly!"

Jupiter asked, "Where is we going to live, Massas?"

"Edwin has a large space above his office you can live in, and you can eat your meals with his family."

Laura spoke up and said, "Oh Poppa, you have done a wonderful thing!"

Kramer hugged his mother and said, "Laura and I promise to make you proud of us."

Alice mentioned, "I know you will."

Kramer hugged his father and said, "If the twins harm Mama or you, I will find them."

"I don't think that will happen. We wish you Godspeed on your journey."

The parting was bittersweet for all of them. Kramer and Laura knew they wouldn't see Evergreen Manor, again, as long as the twins were around. Both of them understood their father had to walk a narrow line concerning them and the running of the plantation. A planter's life was all he knew, and now he had to watch two sons like a hawk to make sure they behaved themselves. He still had two young children to raise, but they knew their mother would be right there by their father's side. She was the quiet one that could outwit a pack of wolves. The twins feared their mother far more than they feared their father.

That night, Randolph held his wife in his arms and tried to make sense of the last several weeks. His family was turned upside down by a way of life he was part of.

"Alice, I see the violent storm clouds of conflict building over our nation. I don't believe compromise is going to win out."

"Do you mean a war is coming between free and slave states?"

"Yes, and I fear Eleanor's family, Kramer, and Laura will choose the free states."

"Of course, Austin, Albert, and maybe Michael will choose the slave states."

"I believe there will be a lot of fighting in Kentucky, Tennessee, Virginia, northern Alabama, and along the major rivers. The army that controls the major rivers like the Mississippi, Ohio, Tennessee, James, and Potomac will win."

"Do you think the railroads will be important?"

"Oh yes, and the factories will be very important."

"Then, that means Evergreen Manor will need to feed itself and make do without help from anywhere."

"That's right! I'm going to increase our livestock of cows, pigs, chickens, goats, and horses a great deal, because we'll need them to stay alive. I want you to buy extra clothes, shoes, material, yarn and things like coffee, tea, sugar, salt, spices, wax, and wine."

"Randolph, how much extra do you mean?"

"I would say for at least a year or more, and I'm going to hold back more of our cornmeal, too."

"You are really worried aren't you, Randolph?"

"Yes, because I have a bad feeling about our future, so we must do as much as we can to protect our plantation."

"The next time I visit Kramer and Laura; do I have your permission to give them the money I inherited from my mother and father?"

"Of course, you do! If the South loses the war, that money will help us. In fact, I'll move some of our money, too."

Causes of the Civil War

- Underground Railroad- early 1800's
- States' Rights 1820
- Sectionalism due to disputes over slavery 1830's
- Abolitionist movement 1830's
- Wilmont Proviso 1846
- Missouri Compromise 1820

- Compromise of 1850
- Uncle Tom's Cabin 1852
- Kansas Nebraska Act 1854
- Dred Scott decision 1857
- Harper's Ferry 1859
- Lincoln elected 1860
- South Carolina seceded 1860
- Battle of Fort Sumter 1861

Slaves picking cotton

CHAPTER 3

By 1860, Randolph's bad feeling about the nation's future was coming true. He had a feeling the next presidential election would determine war or compromise, because the North and the South were pulling further and further apart.

Kramer had studied hard, gone to the Kentucky Medical School, and studied in England for a year. Now, he was working with a surgeon in Louisville to sharpen his skills as a surgeon.

Laura finished her education and was training to be a nurse in the hospital. Eventually, she wanted to work with Kramer in his own practice.

Zeke and Jupiter were doing well at the Burdette's Freight Company. They worked in the warehouse some of the time and other times as teamsters.

Sophie was a very talented seamstress and had a large number of loyal customers. Between Eleanor and Sophie, they had all the work they could handle. Eleanor's daughter, Tess, was learning to sew as quickly as she could in order to help them.

Eleanor's two sons, Gordon and Matt, were working for their father, because his business was booming.

Alice, Michael, and Sally visited Kramer and Laura four times a year, and Alice was pleased with the life they were carving out for themselves.

Zeke's family was happy and enjoying their freedom. Of course, they still ran into people that didn't think they should be free. Kentucky had its fair share of slave owners.

Edwin told his family Kentucky was one of those states that could side with the South or the North. If war should come, the state government would have to decide which way Kentucky would go. He expressed his concern that Kentucky might split over the slavery issue.

During the years between 1854 and 1860, Randolph Waverly's twin sons did everything they could to get back into their father's good graces. Of course, Randolph and Alice knew what Austin and Albert were up to, and they weren't fooled for one second.

Austin romanced one woman after another, but couldn't find one that would do exactly what he said and would stay out of a man's business. The last thing he wanted was a woman like his mother, because he believed, mother dear, had too much influence over her husband. He wanted a wife who was a good hostess, kept her mouth shut, and had babies. Of course, she had to be pretty and docile.

Albert didn't share all his brother's opinions about a wife and her duties as mistress of a large plantation. However, he didn't want a wife just like his mother, either. He was able to find a woman that fit his requirements by the name of Dora Purcell. Her father was a lawyer and a member of the southern aristocracy. They were married in 1857 and had a son named Thomas in 1859. So, Randolph and Alice had their first grandchild to divert some of their attention away from the twins. However, Alice and her husband knew exactly what each snake was doing at all times.

Michael and Sally benefitted from their trips to visit Kramer and Laura. They could see how each side was living and come to their own conclusions. Unfortunately, Michael and Sally could feel the tension gripping the nation as they traveled from one state to another. Tennessee was a slave state they felt comfortable traveling through, but Kentucky was a different kind of slave state, because it had a strong pro-Union population. If war was declared between the North and the South, Kentucky could go either way or remain neutral.

Alice didn't know how much longer the three could visit Eleanor's family before it became too dangerous to travel.

The nation would elect a new president in 1860, and Randolph thought this would determine whether the nation went to war or not.

So many events kept fueling the fire between the North and South such as the Compromise of 1850, Bleeding Kansas, the Dred Scott Decision, Harriet Beecher Stowe's book *Uncle Tom's Cabin*, and John Brown's raid on Harper's Ferry, Virginia.

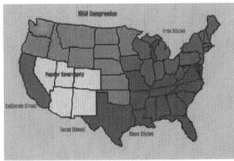

Compromise of 1850   Bleeding Kansas

In Kansas, pro-slavery settlers were murdered by John Brown's fanatics. So, Kansas became a powder keg ready to explode.

Dred Scott

The Supreme Court ruled that Dred Scott was still a slave even though he fled to a free state.

John Brown captured the federal arsenal at Harper's Ferry hoping to arm runaway slaves to revolt against their masters.

John Brown at Harper's Ferry

One of Randolph's neighbors stated he was glad John Brown was executed, because abolitionist fanatics like him weren't welcome in Alabama.

Around Randolph's dinner table, the election dominated the conversation.

Austin stated, "If that backwoods, ugly lawyer gets elected president, the South will secede!"

Albert added, "I think the South should have seceded a long time ago, because none of the presidential candidates will protect southern interests."

Michael asked, "If Lincoln is elected, will he let the South secede and leave us alone?"

Austin fired back, "Are you serious? He's not going to let us go without a fight!"

Michael asked, "What happens to all the forts and arsenals in the South?"

Randolph answered, "In my opinion, the federal troops will stay put."

Albert piped in, "Then, the South will take them over and run the Yankees out."

Alice remarked, "Let's hope things don't come to that."

Sally asked, "Are the Yankees going to take our plantation away from us?"

Austin blabbed, "Don't worry; the South will raise an army and beat the Yankees in less than a year."

Sally replied, "Good, because I don't want Yankees killing all of us."

Michael asked, "Austin, are you and Albert going to join the Confederate army?"

Albert responded, "You bet we are! No Yankee can beat an army of southern boys!"

Randolph commented, "Maybe, cooler heads in Washington will prevail."

Dora remarked, "I think Albert will look dashing in uniform."

Alice steered the conversation away from war by asking, "Has the gristmill been repaired?"

Michael answered, "Yes Mama, and it's working well."

Randolph asked, "How is the irrigation system working on the acres by the river?"

Albert responded, "I'm surprised at how well it's working. As long as the Chattahoochee River has water flowing in it, we can irrigate about 35% of our fields and the orchard."

Randolph looked at Austin and said, "Make sure those new wells are dug deep, Austin."

"Yes sir."

Randolph continued, "When I was a young boy, we had a drought that lasted over two years. We lost our cotton crop almost completely both years. That's why we must irrigate as much as we can."

Sally asked, "What did you do, Poppa?"

He answered, "We grew food by the river to feed us. All of us carried buckets of water from the river to the fields and orchard. We had enough food to eat and money saved to buy what we really needed to get us through the hard times."

Michael suggested, "So, the wells are for us and the livestock, because the pond might dry up."

Alice said, "That's right, son."

Sally reminded, "I have lots of chickens that lay lots of eggs!"

Alice replied, "You are doing a fine job, Sally."

She suggested, "I could handle more if you'd let Trudy help me."

Alice thought a moment and said, "Alright, but you two girls work together, and don't you dare make Trudy do all the work."

"I promise I won't, Mama."

When the meal was over, Michael got his father aside and asked him if they could talk in private away from Austin and Albert.

Randolph asked, "What's troubling you, Michael?"

"Poppa, if we go to war, Kramer, Gordon, and Matt will fight for the North. How can I kill my brother and cousins?"

"Follow your heart and soul, son. If you don't want to take their lives, then don't. Let's hope you don't meet on the battlefield. Taking a human life is serious."

"Have you killed a man?"

"No, son, and I pray I won't have to make that decision."

"Poppa, why are you letting the slaves build new quarters and a small church for themselves?"

"All over the South planters are losing slaves to the Underground Railroad. Just maybe, some of our slaves won't run if their lives are better here. I want them to have better clothes, quarters, and a place to go to worship and sing."

Harriet Tubman & the Underground Railroad

Austin thinks giving them Sundays to rest is stupid."

"I don't agree with his opinion."

"Albert thinks letting the slaves have picnics is stupid."

"Were the slaves smiling and laughing?"

"Yes sir."

"Then, they were happy."

"What happens if the South loses the war?"

"We're not at war yet. If war does come and we lose, plantation life will cease to exist as we know it."

"I just don't understand all this political uproar."

"Michael, I want you to live your life the best you can. Your mother and I have tried to raise you the best we could. We hope you've developed a set of values, and don't let Austin and Albert make you do anything you don't think is right. Kramer and Laura opened my eyes to a lot of things I needed to do for this plantation. I stopped the whippings, and I've tried to make life better for the slaves. If you look around, I think that has had a positive effect on their lives."

"I think so, too, because only seven slaves have run away since Kramer left."

"Do you love Kramer and Laura?"

"Of course, I do! Both of them have earned my respect. They just took a different path in life, and I'm proud of what they've done with their lives."

"Thanks, Poppa."

"Always remember, I love you very much, son."

"I love you, too, Poppa."

In Louisville around Eleanor's dinner table, the conversation was similar to that of her brother's dinner table.

Gordon commented, "If Lincoln is elected, the Lower South will secede from the Union, but I'm not sure about the other slave states."

Matt added, "The big question will be; what is Kentucky going to do?"

Edwin responded, "Kentucky might remain neutral since there's a strong pro-Union presence here."

Kramer remarked, "That means Kentucky might raise Union and Confederate regiments."

Edwin suggested, "That could happen in Missouri, Maryland, Delaware, and Virginia."

Gordon continued, "I bet the new president will rush federal troops into Maryland and northern Virginia to keep them in the Union. Washington, D. C. can't be surrounded by seceded states."

Matt asked, "Why would you say that about Virginia, Poppa?"

Edwin answered, "The mountainous parts of Virginia don't have much in common with the eastern part."

Laura commented, "Maybe, Virginia won't secede."

Edwin answered, "Not likely, because Virginia has the largest population and more industry in the southern states."

Sophie commented, "If there's a war, so many young men will be kilt and wounded. Kramer, are you goin' to be a doctor in the army?"

He replied, "I plan to, Sophie. The army will need every doctor they can get."

She remarked, "I'd be mighty worried about you boys."

Gordon chimed in, "Matt and I will keep an eye on him for ya."

Jupiter asked, "Can you and Ms. Laura teach me to help ya take care of the sick and wounded army boys?"

"I don't know, but I can sure find out. Do you really want to be my orderly?"

"Yes, sir, if Mr. Edwin will let me."

Edwin said, "If that's what you want to do, I won't stand in your way."

"Thank you, sir."

Laura added, "Dr. Mills and Kramer have found a perfect building to set up a small clinic. It only needs some minor repairs before we set it up with beds and supplies."

Eleanor responded, "That's wonderful! How many beds do you plan on?"

She answered, "We want to set up somewhere between 35 to 40 beds. Dr. Mills and Kramer believe Louisville's hospital won't be able to care for all the wounded coming from the front."

Kramer continued, "We plan to make the clinic available to the army. We know it's not much, but every bed will be important."

Eleanor commented, "I know some ladies who would help in the clinic. I'm sure Laura could teach them what they need to know."

"Of course, Aunt Eleanor."

Zeke added, "It sounds like the women folk will bes mighty important when the mens is off fighting."

Edwin remarked, "All our citizens will have to support our boys who are fighting."

Zeke asked, "Do you means like me, Mr. Edwin?"

"That's right. We'll have to help deliver supplies to the army and folks who live here."

Zeke went on, "Mr. Edwin, there's a young boy that hangs around de warehouse looking for a job."

"How old is he?"

"I'd say about fourteen or fifteen."

"Do you know anything about him?"

"He says he be an orphan and ran away from de orphanage."

"Where does he eat and sleep?"

"I don't knows, sir. I gives him some of my lunch."

Jupiter joined in, "I let him have some of mine, too."

"Is he trustworthy?"

Zeke answered, "I told de boy if he steals from us I'd take him back to de orphanage after I spanked his behind good!"

Edwin laughed and said, "Bring him by the office tomorrow, so I can talk to him. If I hire him, Zeke, he's your responsibility."

"Yes sir. I'll teach him good."

Eleanor suggested, "If he works out, we could feed him and find a place for him to stay."

Matt spoke up, "He can bunk with me if he's not a hoodlum."

Edwin responded, "Alright, we'll see what happens tomorrow."

The following day Zeke brought the young boy to Mr. Edwin's office.

"Zeke tells me you need a job."

"I needs a job bad, sir."

"What's your name?"

"It's Toby Wilder, sir."

"Where are your parents?"

"They be dead from typhoid, sir."

"Why did you run away from the orphanage?"

"Cause the older boys beat me up and kept stealing my clothes and food."

"How old are you?"

"I'm fourteen, sir."

"If I hire you, Zeke will train you to be a teamster and warehouse worker."

"I'll do anything you want me to do, sir."

"Where do you sleep?"

"I sleeps under the telegraph office steps."

"Where do you eat?"

"I eat the food the hotel throws away and what Zeke and Jupiter gives me, sir."

In a stern voice, Edwin said, "If you lie, steal, or don't give me an honest day's work, I'll drag you back to the orphanage myself!"

"I ain't going to do none of that, sir!"

Zeke spoke up and said, "He can stay with us and eat at Ms. Eleanor's table."

"Alright Toby Wilder, you're hired and you might as well start now."

"Thank you, sir! I'll be your best worker!"

"Where are your clothes?"

"This is all I have, sir."

Edwin took money out of his pocket and gave it to Zeke to buy the boy some clothes and a pair of shoes.

Over the next few months leading up to the presidential election, Toby Wilder learned quickly, worked hard, and became one of Edwin's best employees. Edwin's family had grown quite fond of the boy, especially Matt. The two were almost like brothers.

Jupiter was learning how to be a hospital steward and doing well. Kramer had decided to take Jupiter with him when he joined up. There was no doubt in Kramer's mind that war was on the horizon, and he needed Jupiter's help.

Abraham Lincoln & his running mate
Hannibal Hamlin

Abraham Lincoln
Stephen Douglas
John Bell
John Breckinridge

CHAPTER 4

The news that Abraham Lincoln had been elected President of the United States was the last nail in the peace coffin.

Austin rushed into the mansion, ran into his father's office, and shouted, "South Carolina seceded from the Union on December 20th! It's war!"

Randolph remarked, "Then, that means Alabama won't be far behind."

In an excited voice Austin shouted, "It won't be long before the Lower South secedes. It's time to raise an army and fight!"

His father replied, "Most households will send their sons to war with tears in their eyes."

Austin fired back, "Not in the South, because our boys are going to beat them Yankees in six months."

Randolph went on, "I hope you're right."

In Louisville, the Burdette family was not surprised South Carolina seceded, and they thought most southern states would follow soon afterwards.

January 1861 was a busy month for the Lower South. On January 9th, Mississippi seceded from the Union followed by Florida on January 10th and Alabama on January 11th. Both Georgia and Louisiana seceded on January 26th followed by Texas on February 1st.

Tensions ran high between Charleston, South Carolina and Washington, D. C. over Fort Sumter in Charleston harbor. South Carolina demanded federal troops withdraw from the fort, but when that didn't happen the Confederates fired on Fort Sumter on April 12, 1861. Shortly, President Lincoln called for 75,000 volunteers to put down the rebellion.

Attack on Fort Sumter

On April 17th, Virginia seceded from the Union which was very important to the South. The Confederacy needed Virginia, because of its population, the Norfolk Navy Yard, and the Tredegar Iron Works in Richmond. Arkansas captured Fort Smith and Little Rock and seceded on May 6th followed by North Carolina on May 20th. Tennessee became the eleventh state to join the Confederacy on June 8th.

Early in 1861, Kentucky declared its neutrality; however, both the Union and the Confederacy had other plans for the state. Major rivers and railroad hubs would determine Kentucky's fate, quickly.

Around the Burdette family table, Edwin looked at each face knowing that six months from now some of the faces would be absent, probably. Some Kentucky men were joining regiments being trained in Indiana, and he had lost some of his teamsters that worked for his freight hauling company.

Toby suggested, "Mr. Edwin, I know some fellers at the orphanage that would love to work for you. They aren't the bad ones that beat me up."

"Are they trustworthy?"

"Yes sir and they'll work hard for you and Zeke. All they want is someone who cares about them and will give them a chance at life."

"Alright Toby, give me their names, and I'll go talk to them."

Eleanor reminded, "Ms. Louise has offered some rooms at her boarding house to fellers working for you, and she'll feed them, too."

"That's great, honey! I'll stop by and see her."

Toby suggested, "Mr. Edwin, there's a few girls around my age that could help at the clinic with Ms. Laura."

Laura answered, "That's wonderful, Toby! We can house them above the clinic where I stay. All of us can eat here, because Aunt Eleanor and Sophie will insist."

Eleanor replied, "You are a smart girl. By the way, how is Myrtle coming along?"

Laura laughed until tears ran down her cheeks and answered, "General Myrtle is doing just fine!"

Kramer added, "She is one feisty, good-hearted woman that can turn a person inside out before they can count to three. Believe me; I don't want to get on her bad side."

Laura teased, "She thinks you are the handsomest man she has ever seen. If she was twenty years younger, she'd take you home with her."

Kramer laughed and responded, "I wouldn't be able to keep up with her."

Matt teased, "She'd probably kill you, lover boy."

Gordon teased, "She's one hunk of a woman, Kramer."

Kramer proposed, "What I need is a woman like her, only twenty years younger."

Edwin asked, "Do you know anyone like that, Eleanor?"

"Not that I know of, Honey."

Toby remarked, "Dr. Kramer, you have women buzzing around you like bees to honey. I wish I could attract women like that."

"Most of those women are silly and immature."

Matt teased, "Just wait until you put on a uniform. Then, we won't be able to peel all the women off of you."

Gordon asked, "Can we have the ones you don't want?"

"Help yourself, boys."

Laura suggested, "It ought to be against the law to be that handsome."

Matt fired back, "For Pete sakes, you're as beautiful as he is handsome. Both of you look just like your gorgeous mother."

Toby agreed, "Ms. Laura, men buzz around you, just to see you smile."

She fired back, "I don't have time for a man, right now, because getting the clinic going is more important."

Edwin suggested, "Don't give up on romance, Laura. Just ask all us ugly people."

The table roared with laughter, because Edwin had a great sense of humor. Lord knows, they needed to laugh every chance they could.

Eleanor teased, "Both of you will fall like bricks when the right one comes along."

Kramer shot back, "Ah, Aunt Eleanor, as long as that brick isn't Ms. Myrtle."

She fired back, "I ought to spank your behind, you rascal!"

Gordon teased, "Don't mess up his handsome behind."

Kramer shot back, "My behind is not handsome; it's just cute."

Matt teased, "It's not cute in the outhouse!"

Again, everyone roared with laughter. If only they could save these moments in a bottle, forever.

Myrtle received a telegram in May from her brother in Chattanooga, Tennessee informing her that his wife had passed away after a long illness. Arlene had suffered a stroke four months earlier and had never recovered. Their daughter, Madeline, had nursed her mother for those four months. Even though she was only seventeen, she had stayed by her mother's side to the very end.

Carl was very worried about recent events, so Myrtle

talked him into moving in with her, since both had lost their spouses. Myrtle thought Madeline needed to be near family while she grieved.

Carl knew he made the right decision when Tennessee seceded from the Union, because he was opposed to slavery just like his sister. He was confident Kentucky would remain in the Union, even though the state had declared its neutrality.

Carl sold his business in Chattanooga for a nice sum and managed to get a part time job in the telegraph office in Louisville. Once Madeline got settled into a routine, Myrtle would talk to her about the clinic. She believed the poor girl would be a good nurse for Dr. Mills and Laura.

Edwin made the trip to the orphanage and was pleased with the three boys and three girls Toby told him about. There was only one problem he didn't expect. One of the girls wouldn't leave her eleven year old brother behind, so he really didn't have a choice, but to bring him, too. Eleanor was probably going to box his ears good for being so soft-hearted. Between the two of them, they should be able to find something for the boy to do.

He took the seven youngsters to the mercantile and bought them clothes and shoes. It ripped his heart out to see how they reacted to their new things. One would think it was Christmas in heaven.

His next stop was at Ms. Louise's Boarding House to get the three boys settled in their rooms and fed.

His third stop was at the clinic to get the girls and Sammy settled in their rooms above the clinic and fed. Laura took charge of Sammy and made him her personal assistant which was fine with Edwin.

After leaving the girls, Edwin picked up the boys and took them to the freight company. He turned them over to Zeke to start their training. They all seemed very excited and eager to learn. The boys understood how important their jobs were, so the men could join the army. Zeke would have time to get the boys trained, because Gordon and Matt were waiting until the fall to enlist. Since Edwin was a good friend of John Harlan, they decided to enlist in the 10th Kentucky Infantry. At this time, Mr. Harlan planned to finish recruiting for his regiment in October in Louisville. The brothers knew Kramer needed time to get the clinic set up and train the women to help Laura before he joined up. The clinic would be very important in the care of the wounded and sick soldiers coming from the front.

The Union and Confederate armies eyed Kentucky like a rare diamond. One of the greatest blunders of the war was committed by the Confederate army. Gen Leonidas Polk ordered his 12,000 troops to occupy Columbus, Kentucky violating the state's neutrality. This resulted in Kentucky requesting federal troops to protect them from invasion.

On September 5th, Gen Ulysses Grant was ordered to seize Paducah, Kentucky, because it was a vital railroad junction and shipping center at the mouth of the Tennessee River.

Tennessee had built Fort Henry on the Tennessee River and Fort Donaldson on the Cumberland River in Middle Tennessee. The Confederacy realized how important these two rivers were to move supplies from one area to another. President Jefferson Davis knew the South had to control the Mississippi River for all the same reasons. Plus, if the Mississippi River and Valley fell into Union hands, Texas, Arkansas, and Louisiana would be cut off from the rest of the Confederacy.

The South built Island Number Ten near New Madrid, even though this area was in Missouri. This part of Missouri had a strong pro-Southern population. Fort Pillow was built about 40 miles north of Memphis on the Mississippi River and was armed with batteries to fire on enemy troops and shipping.

Events along these three rivers would shape the western theater fighting between Union and Confederate forces. Mother Nature would descend upon this region during the summer of 1862 with a vengeance. From 1862 into 1864, a drought would ravage the land and people affecting every part of their lives.

Eleanor, Myrtle, and the church ladies were busy getting ready for the church social to honor the men that were joining the army. Gordon, Matt, and Kramer looked dashing in their brand new uniforms. The men would have lots of food to eat and be able to dance the evening away with hordes of women. To round out the day, they planned to sing many of their favorite songs.

Eleanor asked, "Myrtle, how is Madeline doing at the clinic?"

"She's doing very well, but the poor child is so bashful and shy, because she was such a sheltered child growing up. She is so devastated over her mother's death, but I'm determined to get her out of her shell and enjoying life, again."

"If anyone can do it, it'll be you, honey."

Myrtle laughed and said, "That girl has a beautiful head of wavy hair, so I'm going to get rid of those pigtails, somehow."

Eleanor added, "She has the most mysterious dark blue eyes and long eyelashes I've ever seen."

"I'm hoping she'll grow into a shapely woman."

Eleanor agreed, "She sure looks like a teenage stick just like my Tess."

"Ain't that the truth!"

"Right now, my Tess and your Madeline are flat chested, so let's hope they'll blossom out soon."

"Lord honey, my watermelons exploded when I was sixteen, and I wish I could give some of mine away. My mama use to tell me my bosoms got to the dinner table five minutes before I did!"

Both women laughed like hyenas, because Eleanor couldn't picture Tess with a set of bosoms like that.

Laura walked up and asked, "What's so funny?"

Myrtle chimed in, "Bosoms on Tess and Madeline."

Laura giggled and commented, "If Tess had bosoms like yours, she wouldn't be able to walk!"

Myrtle fired back "I learned how to walk with mine!"

Laura shot back, "So that's why you look like you're walking uphill."

Myrtle fired back "Eleanor, you have my permission to slap Laura silly."

Now, all three women were laughing like hyenas invited to a fried chicken picnic.

Kramer came over and remarked, "You three ladies are sure enjoying the social before it gets started. Have you been sipping from a special bottle in the church?"

Myrtle put her hands on her hips and blabbed, "We were discussing bosoms. What is your opinion about bosoms?"

Kramer answered, "They are very necessary for a woman."

Myrtle blabbed, "I'm talking about size, you rascal!"

Kramer smiled and said, "All one needs is a handful!"

Laura laughed and asked, "What if the hand is empty?"

Kramer replied, "Bosoms are only a part of a woman's overall package. Don't worry, Tess will fill out soon. Laura looked like a string bean for quite a while, too."

Eleanor joined in, "I'm so glad you solved that problem Kramer. Maybe, Tess will end up with two pillows like Myrtle."

Myrtle fired back, "Mine are soft like pillows, for sure. You can't touch Kramer."

Kramer giggled and said, "That hurts my feelings, Myrtle!"

She shot back, "That won't be the only thing that hurts, you rascal."

Laura warned, "All the single women in the church want to dance with you, so you better eat plenty and no touching bosoms."

Kramer teased, "All the single men in the church want to dance with you, Sis, so eat hearty and no bosoms flying."

Myrtle blabbed, "Kramer save me a dance, Sweetie Pie!"

As he laughed and walked away, he stated "I will, Sweetie Pie!"

The social got under way as the congregation enjoyed all the food and desserts. Kramer grabbed a piece of apple pie and couldn't believe how delicious it was.

He asked, "Laura have you had a piece of this apple pie?"

"No."

"You better, because this is the most delicious pie I've ever had."

Laura took a bite and said, "It is delicious!"

He asked, "Do you know who made it?"

"Madeline."

"Do you mean Myrtle's niece?"

"Yes."

"I have to compliment her on this pie."

Before Kramer could find her, one woman after another grabbed him for a dance. He felt like bees were swarming around him, so he grabbed Myrtle for a dance.

Kramer blabbed, "Thanks, Sweetie Pie, these women are driving me crazy. You will not believe how many of them have offered their beds to me, and they're supposed to be Christian women!"

Myrtle laughed and answered, "You want a woman with class and no bed bugs. You'll find her one day. Just stay alive and come back to us."

He responded, "I'm a doctor, so that means I won't be carrying a musket."

"I'll pray that the Lord will protect you, Rascal!"

He asked, "Where is Madeline? I need to compliment her on her apple pie."

"She's reading a book under the big oak tree out back. Poor thing, she's so bashful and shy."

"Thanks, Sweetie Pie!"

Kramer walked over to the oak tree and spotted Madeline reading a book.

"Hello Madeline, what are you doing?"

In a startled voice, she replied, "I'm reading this book. Is there something wrong at the clinic?"

"Oh no, I wanted to compliment you on your apple pie, because it's the best I've ever tasted. I have to admit I was a pig and ate three pieces."

"I'm glad you liked it."

"Why aren't you dancing with the single men?"

"I'm not a good dancer, because I'm awkward. Besides, I'd only be a wall flower."

"I find that hard to believe."

"Why aren't you dancing with all those beautiful women at the social?"

"Those silly women are driving me crazy!"

"When you go off to war, they'll write you lots of letters."

"I won't read any of them. Would you write to me?"

"If you want me to, I will. All of us at the clinic will do our best for Dr. Mills, so you won't have to worry."

"That means a lot to me. Your Aunt Myrtle says you are bashful and shy. Why is that?"

"I'm not very good around crowds, because I'm skinny, awkward, and plain as an old shoe. It hurts when people make fun of me. If I stay to myself where cruel words won't hurt me."

"Can't you ignore the hurtful words, Maddie?"

"No. Dr. Waverly, you are a very handsome, self-confident man who can have any woman you want."

"I don't want that, Maddie. I want a special woman with heart and compassion."

"You'll find her one day."

"Maddie, sometimes you have to fight for what you want."

"I've been beaten down and made fun of too many times."

"Please don't hide in a shell, Maddie. It's time for the singing to start. Won't you come in to enjoy the music?"

"I'll be down, shortly."

As Kramer walked away, Madeline thought, "You will never know how much I love you. I would give anything to be your wife, but that will never happen. You would never fall in love with someone like me. I'll always be a plain old shoe that people make fun of."

CHAPTER 5

John Harlan collected his new regiment and went into camp in Lebanon, Kentucky in October, 1861. They would train for the next month and be mustered into Union service for three years on November 21, 1861. The 10th Kentucky Infantry was placed under the command of Gen George Thomas. They were assigned to the 2nd Brigade commanded by Col M. D. Manson.

Col John Harlan

Gordon, Matt, Jupiter, and Kramer spent Thanksgiving and Christmas away from home for the first time.

On December 31st, the 10th Kentucky left Lebanon and marched to Columbia, Kentucky, and then, on to Mill Springs.

On Sunday, January 19, 1862, Col Harlan ordered his regiment to march as quickly as possible to Mill Springs to help their fellow soldiers chase and catch Gen Leonidas Polk's Confederate forces.

Gordon commented, "We don't have any provisions, tents, or overcoats, so I hope we get some where we're going!"

Matt replied, "We don't have blankets or gloves, either. When we get to our boys, they'll fix us up."

Pvt Baker added, "It's darn cold, if you ask me."

Matt teased, "You'll be warm enough after an hour of this kind of marching."

Pvt Gleason complained, "My feet already hurt like the devil!"

The 10th Kentucky marched for six hours and covered 18 miles arriving just before dark. The regiment was ordered to occupy the woods in front of the Rebel fortifications and hold it if the Rebels attacked.

The men collapsed on the ground with nothing to eat but a cracker. There would be no tents, gloves, blankets, overcoats, or fire to warm them.

The following day the 10th Kentucky and the 14th Ohio entered the Rebel fortifications to find them empty. The men helped themselves to what supplies the Rebels left behind.

The regiment pulled duty at Mill Springs until February 11th.

Gordon complained, "All this heavy rain sure has made this area a mud hole."

Matt walked up and said, "Guess what I just heard?"

Pvt Lawson chimed back, "Don't tell us you're pregnant!"

He fired back, "No, you idiot! We captured Fort Henry on the Tennessee River. Can you believe most of the fort was underwater? Our navy gunboats bombarded them for less than two hours when they surrendered!"

Attack on Fort Henry

Pvt Cooley shot back, "Hot dang! Now, our navy has control of the Tennessee River south of the Alabama border!"

Gordon added, "Well, I'm getting some sleep, because we move out tomorrow for Louisville. Maybe, we can see our folks."

Matt shot back, "It would be wonderful to see them."

Pvt Monroe fired back, "Knowing our luck, the generals will have us marching our behinds off somewhere else. I still have blisters on my feet!"

Gordon went on, "So far, we've only lost Pvt William Vaughan who died from disease and Pvt Michael McMullin who was killed in action. I hope we won't lose too many men."

Pvt Ash added, "Don't forget our three deserters, so far."

Pvt Cox shot back, "Who wants a deserter next to him when the bullets are flying?"

Matt answered, "Not me! All of us soldiers have to pull together when our lives are at stake."

Gordon teased, "Little brother, you better be right by my side, or I'll bust your nose in half!"

Pvt Ash laughed and said, "You'll mess up his pretty face."

Pvt Monroe teased, "Neither one of you can hold a candle to your handsome cousin, Kramer."

Matt answered, "You have just devastated my manhood!"

Pvt Lavey commented, "You need to be ugly, so the women will feel sorry for you."

All the boys laughed and caught some sleep before the march the following day.

When the 10th Kentucky reached Louisville, they were ordered to board a steamboat that sailed down the Ohio River, sailed up the Cumberland River to Nashville, docked, and the regiment marched on to Pittsburg Landing.

The 10th Kentucky was ordered to board a transport at Pittsburg Landing and sail up the Tennessee River to

Chickasaw. They landed and marched east of Corinth near Iuka and destroyed a railroad bridge.

While the 10th Kentucky was near Nashville, the regiment received word that Fort Donelson on the Cumberland River surrendered to Gen Grant. Gen Simon Buckner's army suffered over 1,400 killed or wounded and over 12,000 troops were captured.

Confederate Gen Albert Johnston commanded all Rebel forces from Arkansas to the Cumberland Gap. With the surrender of Fort Donelson, Gen Johnston lost one third of his army. Also, the surrender opened Tennessee up to Union invasion, especially central and western Tennessee.

Charge at Fort Donelson

By February 28th, Union Gen Don Carlos Buell had captured Nashville.

Between February 28th and April 8, 1862, the Union set its sights on New Madrid, Missouri on the Mississippi River where the river makes a double turn. The Confederates had built a fortress on a large sandbar called Island Number Ten.

Union Gen John Pope unleashed his siege guns on the town being held by Confederate Gen John McCown. After one day of bombardment, Gen McCown pulled his troops out of the town to Island Number Ten. Admiral Andrew Foote's mortar rafts and gunboats bombarded the fortress for three weeks while Gen Pope's men dug a canal, so they could surround the Confederate forces. When Gen McGown knew his army was trapped, he surrendered.

This was the Union's first victory on the Mississippi River, and now, the river was open to the Union as far as Fort Pillow above Memphis. The Confederacy was losing control of the vital rivers they desperately needed to hold on to. To make matters worse, three weeks later, Admiral David Farragut captured New Orleans.

Union navy & Island Number Ten

The 10th Kentucky was spared involvement in the Battle of Shiloh on April 6-7, 1862. It resulted in a very costly victory for the Union army. Northern and southern newspapers blasted their armies' performance and the horrific casualty lists.

The South lost one of their best generals, Gen Albert S. Johnston. Gen Johnston was unable to stop Gen Grant's Army of the Tennessee and Gen Buell's Army of the Ohio from joining up in Tennessee. Union casualties numbered over 13,000 men while Confederate losses numbered over 12,500 men. Both sides had no idea the next three years would produce such horrible carnage in the western and eastern theaters of war.

Gen Albert Johnston   Gen Don Carlos Buell

The 10th Kentucky marched with the Union army towards Corinth, Mississippi. The town was a vital railroad junction for the Mobile-Ohio Railroad and the Memphis-Charleston Railroad.

The 10th Kentucky was part of Gen Speed Fry's 2nd Brigade, Gen George Thomas' Division, and Gen Don Carlos Buell's Army of the Ohio. The regiment's strength numbered 523 men.

Gen Speed Fry   Gen George Thomas

Union Gen Henry Halleck, overall commander of Union forces in the West, laid siege to the town from April 29, 1862-May 30, 1862.

Confederate morale was low, because typhoid and dysentery had killed almost as many men as the South had lost at the Battle of Shiloh. These diseases were caused by bad water which was only going to get worse from the drought through 1864. Confederate Gen Pierre Beauregard saved his army by moving his men, tons of supplies, and the sick on the Mobile-Ohio Railroad to Tupelo, Mississippi. When Union patrols entered Corinth on May 30th, the Confederate army was gone leaving behind campfires still burning and dummy Quaker guns (tree trunks as cannon barrels).

After an emotional goodbye at Evergreen Manor, the three Waverly sons made their way to Pensacola, Florida to join the 33rd Alabama Infantry in April 1862. While at Pensacola, Samuel Adams was elected colonel of the 33rd Alabama, Daniel Horn was elected lieutenant colonel, and Robert Crittenden was elected major.

Col Samuel Adams   Col Robert Crittenden

The Waverly sons would become part of Company B. The captain of Company B was Robert Ward, the 1st Lieutenant was Joseph Pelham, 2nd Lieutenant was John Simmons, and the brevet 2nd Lieutenant was Henry Smission.

The regiment drew gray woolen round jacket coats, pants, caps, and brogans. Each man got a leather cartridge box containing forty cartridges, a leather cap box containing percussion caps, a bayonet with scabbard, knapsacks, canteens, haversacks, and a smoothbore musket.

In early April 1862, the 33rd Alabama was ordered to Corinth, Mississippi. They arrived just after the Battle of Shiloh and heard all the bad news concerning the carnage during the battle. They were assigned to Col Alexander Hawthorn's Brigade and the Army's 3rd Corps.

As the days went by, several men became ill with the measles or dysentery from the bad water. They tried to get their water from any artesian wells, but that wasn't possible most of the time.

The regiment was issued wall tents, a covered ambulance, canvas covered wagons, and other items for cooking and cutting wood. They were issued new Enfield rifles with mini ball cartridges, new bayonets and scabbards.

After dark on May 29th, the 33rd Alabama was told to yell and make as much noise as they could when the empty trains arrived. Gen Beauregard evacuated his army from Corinth to Tupelo, Mississippi. The 33rd Alabama slept in a ploughed field several miles from Corinth. On the march, the men threw away all kinds of paraphernalia such as books, hammers, and pillows to lighten the weight they had to carry.

Next, the 33rd Alabama pulled picket duty on the banks of a creek near Booneville. The men enjoyed roasted fish and sweet potatoes wrapped in green leaves and cooked in the hot ashes of their campfires.

The regiment marched southward to Baldwyn and camped for a few days. Many of the men were sick from the brackish water and didn't want to eat.

While there Company B elected George Pelham brevet 2nd Lieutenant, because
2nd Lieutenant John Simmons was promoted to captain and became the regimental commissary quartermaster.

Then, the 33rd Alabama marched southward to Tupelo, Mississippi where the regiment received their new blue and white Bonnie Blue flag with a crescent moon near the center.

In June 1862, Gen Braxton Bragg replaced Gen Beauregard as Commanding Officer of the Confederate Army in the West.

Gen Braxton Bragg   Gen Pierre Beauregard

CHAPTER 6

After Randolph's sons left to enlist, he and Alice made the decision to change life at Evergreen Manor in order to survive the Civil War. He had to go further than just letting the slaves build new houses for their families and a church.

He asked Asa to bring four of the slaves he considered the respected leaders to the mansion to discuss his plans for the future. Asa and Leroy brought the men into the living room, and they all sat down.

Randolph walked in with Alice, and they all jumped to their feet.

Randolph suggested, "Please sit down and be comfortable, because we have a lot to talk about."

Oscar asked, "Have we done something wrong, Massas?"

He replied, "Oh no, everything is fine."

Jerome mentioned, "Massas, thank you for the banjoes, fiddles, and harmonicas. We taught ourselves how to play them."

Alice commented, "Music is a fine thing, and we are so pleased you're enjoying them."

Randolph remarked, "This war is not going to be short. The North is using its navy to blockade our coastline, so we can't get supplies in or ship goods out. Evergreen Manor must be able to feed itself in order to survive. We won't get any help from the outside, so if you will stay and help me work this plantation, I'll give each household 35 acres of my land."

Calvin asked, "Do you means de land will be ours, Massas?"

"Yes, and you can plant whatever you want on your land. If we all work together, we'll survive the hard times."

Sidney stated, "Massas, slaves can't own no land."

He replied, "I'll give all of you your freedman's papers, and you'll be sort of like a sharecropper. If you will help me work the plantation, we'll share what we produce. If there are any who want to leave, I'll give them their freedman's papers."

Oscar asked, "If the South wins de war, will you still do this?"

"Yes. I promise you I'll do this no matter who wins."

Jerome asked, "Can we raise chickens and other livestock, Massas?"

"Yes. When new chicks are born, we'll start dividing them up."

Randolph went on, "We must move our livestock around, so they aren't all bunched together. All of us will have to work together to protect this land. I expect bands of deserters or just plain outlaws trying to steal or harm us. I'm going to teach several of you how to use a pistol or rifle."

Calvin commented, "We'll help defend de plantation, because part of de land is ours. We'll roundup de best men for you to teach."

Alice remarked, "We'll need a warning system when trouble rears its ugly head."

Leroy stated, "We cans talk it over and come up with a system, Ms. Waverly. It's like you says, all of us have to work together to stay safe."

Randolph suggested, "Please call me Mr. Waverly or Mr. Randolph; however, when we have visitors go back to Massas. We need to act like nothing has changed."

Asa asked, "Do you want us to act real stupid like we be dumb slaves?"

Alice responded, "Exactly! Do anything that will give us an advantage."

Sidney added, "We understand what you mean, Ms. Waverly."

Oscar asked, "Did you stops planting cotton, because of deblockade, Mr. Waverly?"

"Yes. I planted more tobacco as our cash crop. The rest of the fields are planted with food for us and the livestock to eat."

Calvin asked, "Where are you going to sell de tobacco?"

He answered, "In the state, so the army can have it for the soldiers."

Jerome asked, "Is you going to sell corn meal to Eufaula, Mr. Waverly?"

"No, because we'll need all of it for ourselves."

Sidney mentioned, "Don't worry, sir. I'll run our trap lines, fish, and hunt. The woods are full of critters, and the pond has lots of frogs. A mess of frog legs is mighty good eating."

Alice answered, "That's the spirit! We'll feast on lots of different foods."

Sidney went on, "We respect you, sir. You has done a lot of good things for us. If there's some men who wants to leave, I says let them git on out of here, because we don't wants no troublemakers around."

Randolph suggested, "I agree with you. You men talk things over with everyone and get back with me in a few days with your decisions."

The men left in high spirits, because their dreams just might come true. They knew Kramer had a profound effect on Massas Waverly, because he was an entirely different person when it came to them. He had done a lot of things to make their lives better. Now, he was giving them part of his land and their freedom. They were sure if they worked together they could survive whatever the war had in store for them.

Beulah looked at Alice and said, "Ms. Waverly, don't you worry one little bit. If bad people tries to hurt us, we'll fights them good. It's a fine thing you folks have done. We laugh and cry just likes yous, and we have hopes and dreams, too. We just wants to be treated likes anybody else."

Alice replied, "We know that, honey. Just remember, not to shoot your foot off with your pistol."

She responded, "Honey child, I be shooting their feets plum off!"

Alice giggled and said, "I believe you would, Beulah."

Daisy was polishing a table next to a window when she suggested, "Come over here Ms. Waverly and look at this."

Alice looked and said, "Well, I'll be. Those baby chicks are following Sally and Trudy around like they are their mamas."

Daisy roared with laughter and chimed in, "Those two gals sure know their way around the chicken coops!"

Beulah piped in, "They even know where the chicken poop is!"

The three women laughed until they thought their sides would split wide open.

Beulah thought, "I'm glad Austin, Albert, Dora, and Little Thomas are gone. We have lots of fun when they're not around. Ms. Waverly is a fine woman. Massas Kramer sure changed his father in the best kind of way. Oh how, she wanted to see Kramer and Laura, again. Massas Michael was a lot like Kramer, but she wouldn't give two cents for the twins, because them boys were nothing but trash!"

A few days later, the colored men came back to Randolph with their decisions. Only three men and one family wanted to leave, because they didn't trust any white man. So, Randolph wrote their names down in order to finish their freedman's papers. When he gave them their papers, he warned them that the Confederate army was between them and the North. It would be a dangerous trip for them, because they had no idea what dangers faced them to get to the North.

Randolph tried to warn them of the dangers, but they were adamant about leaving. So, they left with a lot of food and water with high hopes.

Tragedy would strike the family when a farmer and his

son fired at them after they refused to stop. The boy's father yelled for him to run just as the father and mother were shot. The parent's son managed to get away and find his way back to Evergreen Manor.

Freddie crawled on the porch of the mansion too exhausted to speak. Sally came around the corner, saw Freddie, and ran to get her father.

Sally yelled, "Poppa, you got to help Freddie, because something is wrong with him!"

Randolph ran to the porch, leaned over Freddie, and took him in his arms.

He asked, "Freddie are you alright? Where are your parents?"

"They be both dead. Help me, Massas!"

Randolph asked, "What happened to them?"

"They was shot by some farmers."

Randolph replied, "Don't worry, Freddie, we'll take care of you."

The women in the house gathered around Freddie to take care of his needs. Randolph wanted to kick a wall, because he knew this would happen. The ladies got Freddie cleaned up, fed, and into some new clothes.

Beulah said, "Freddie, it looks like you be needing a new family. How about you coming to live with us?"

He replied, "I be willing to."

So, Beulah and her husband took nine year old Freddie into their family. They were proud of Freddie's determination to get back to the plantation. That showed them all the boy was brave and had spunk.

CHAPTER 7

In July 1862, the 33rd Alabama was ordered to watch the execution of two deserters who were handcuffed together sitting on their coffins in front of their graves.

Twenty-four soldiers loaded their rifles with eight ball cartridges and sixteen blanks and stacked those rifles in front of the deserters.

Another detail of twenty-four soldiers marched in front of the deserters. The detail was ordered, "Halt, front, take arms, right dress, make ready, take aim, and fire!" The deserters fell off their coffins dead with four rounds in their chests.

A few days later they were marched back to the same field to watch a deserter tied to a caisson wheel to receive 39 lashes on the bare back. The left side of his head and face was shaved, and he was made to run after the 39 lashes. This was called being drummed out of the service.

Michael commented, "I don't want to watch these events anymore. It was hard to watch, because they were so young."

Albert added, "I know how you feel, but I know deserters have to be punished, but it is hard to watch."

Austin blabbed, "In my opinion, the last deserter should have been shot, too!"

Albert fired back, "I'm not surprised you think that way."

Austin replied, "The two of you are too soft-hearted."

Albert shot back, "Well brother dear, I think you are too hard-hearted."

Austin fired back, "You're getting to be more like Kramer every day, so you better toughen up."

"Don't worry, I'll do my duty, Austin, and make sure you do yours."

During this time, LtCol Daniel Horn resigned and Maj

Robert Crittenden was promoted to lieutenant colonel. Captain James Dunklin was promoted to major of the regiment.

During the latter part of July, the 33rd Alabama was ordered to board box cars at Tupelo, Mississippi to begin a six day train ride through Meridian, Mississippi, Mobile and Montgomery, Alabama, and Atlanta and Dalton, Georgia. They camped at Tyner's Station not far from Chattanooga, Tennessee. Some of their sick who were in the hospitals were released and came back to the regiment.

In August, the 33rd Alabama marched to Chattanooga and crossed the Tennessee River on a ferry boat. The men were very happy to receive rations, two month's pay of $22.00, a $50.00 bounty, and some new clothing.

Sitting around the campfire, Austin blabbed, "I didn't join the army to ride on dirty box cars and get paid $11.00 a month!"

A tall soldier replied, "Well, listen to Mr. High and Mighty Planter. Did you expect the army to provide you with a personal carriage to ride in? You ain't no better than the rest of us to travel that way. You is dirty and sink like the rest of us, planter boy!"

Austin ordered, "You better shut your mouth, you backwoods cracker!"

Albert warned, "Calm down, Austin, because he's right!"

The tall soldier shot back, "Where I'm from, we settle arguments with our fists, because we ain't got fancy dueling pistols like you rich boys. Eleven dollars a month is big money in our parts."

Austin responded, "I told you to shut your mouth, you backwoods idiot!"

The tall soldier replied, "Well come on, planter boy, shut my mouth for me."

Austin jumped up and started for the tall soldier, and

suddenly, Austin was face down in the dirt.

Albert remarked, "Nice punch! Just what he deserved!"

2Sgt Galloway came over and demanded, "What's going on over here?"

Albert answered, "My brother tripped and fell flat on his face. The poor rascal knocked himself plum out."

2Sgt Galloway warned, "Just remember, no fighting! Save your fighting for the Yankees. I came by to tell you eight in our company have died since we left Tupelo, Mississippi. Privates Borden, Bartlett, Gandy, Herring, John Jackson, and Elvin Jackson have died from dysentery or dia-ree. Privates Chancy and Cumby have died from the measles."

Albert commented, "If this keeps up, disease will kill our regiment rather than bullets."

Michael responded, "The bad water has to be causing dysentery and dia-ree."

2Sgt Galloway ordered, "When your brother wakes up, take him to the hospital tent."

Albert replied, "Yes Sergeant! I imagine he has a broken nose and black eyes."

When Austin woke up, Albert escorted him to the hospital tent.

Albert commented, "Austin, you better control that temper of yours. You tripped going after that soldier and knocked yourself out."

Austin fired back, "That backwoods idiot hit me right in the face! I didn't trip, but that's alright! I'll get even one day."

Albert suggested, "Just let it go, Austin."

Gen Braxton Bragg ordered his army to march from Chattanooga, Tennessee into Kentucky during the latter part of August. He wanted to keep the Union army from trying to capture Chattanooga and Vicksburg, Mississippi.

A Union garrison commanded by Col John Wilder was behind elaborate fortifications at Munfordville, Kentucky. The town was an important station on the Louisville-Nashville Railroad and had a bridge that crossed the Green River.

Battle of Munfordville

On September 14th, Confederate Gen James Chalmers demanded Col Wilder surrender. When he refused, Rebel forces attacked, but were beaten back. The Rebels laid siege to the town on September 15th and 16th. Late on the evening of September 16th, the Rebels demanded Col Wilder surrender. Col Wilder entered Rebel lines under a flag of truce and was escorted around by Confederate Gen Simon Buckner. Col Wilder realized his three regiments couldn't hold back another attack, so he surrendered. Union Gen Don Carlos Buell didn't arrive in time to help Col Wilder's position.

Gen James Chalmers   Col John Wilder

The capture of Munfordville affected the transport of Union troops and supplies. Gen Buell would have to challenge Gen Bragg's Army in Kentucky. They couldn't afford to lose transportation centers in the state, or let the pro-southern population provide Bragg's Army with new recruits. If the Union army could run Bragg out of Kentucky, then they could concentrate on capturing Chattanooga and Vicksburg.

Cases	Diseases	Deaths
75,368	Typhoid	27,050
2,504	Typhus	850
11,898	Continual Fever	147
49,871	Typho-malarial Fever	4,059
1,155,266	Acute Diarrhea	2,923
170,488	Chronic Diarrhea	27,558
233,812	Acute Dysentery	4,084
25,670	Chronic Dysentery	3,229
73,382	Syphilis	123
95,833	Gonorrhea	6
30,714	Scurvy	383
3,744	Delirium Tremens	450
2,410	Insanity	80
2,837	Paralysis	231

Diseases & Deaths

CHAPTER 8

From February through May 1862, the 10th Kentucky suffered two more desertions and more deaths from diseases caused by the brackish water. Pvt John Johnson died in February, Pvt Henderson Baugh died in March, Surgeon William Atkisson and Assistant Surgeon Thomas Knott died in April, and Pvt Crow Scott died in May.

The 10th Kentucky marched with Gen Don Carlos Buell's Army to Tuscumbia, Alabama in June. In July, the regiment occupied the town of Eastport, Mississippi before marching to Florence, Alabama. Companies A and H were ordered to guard a railroad bridge in Courtland, Alabama. The two companies had 97 men, and the 1st Ohio Cavalry that went with them had around 40 men.

On July 25th, a Rebel force attacked and captured them. The two companies and cavalry had no other choice but to surrender when they were surrounded by 700 Rebels.

In August, Gen Buell's Army left Tennessee and followed Confederate Gen Braxton Bragg into Kentucky. The 10th Kentucky became part of the III Army Corps commanded by Gen Charles Gilbert, Gen Albin Schoepf's Division, and Gen Speed Fry's Brigade. The brigade was made up of the 4th Kentucky, 10th and 74th Indiana, 14th Ohio, and the 10th Kentucky.

Gen Charles Gilbert   Gen Albin Schoepf

On September 7th, Gen Buell's Army left Nashville and began chasing Gen Bragg's Confederate Army to Louisville.

Part of the Confederate army was commanded by Gen Kirby Smith who had captured Richmond and Lexington, Kentucky in the center of the state.

Gen Kirby Smith

Gen Buell's Army reached Louisville ahead of the Confederates, and Gen Buell had time to reorganize and reinforce his army with raw recruits.

Gen Buell sent 10,000 troops commanded by Gen Joshua Sill towards Frankfort, Kentucky to keep Gen Bragg and Gen Smith from joining forces.

Gen Joshua Sill

On October 1st, Gen Buell left Louisville with 55,000 troops, many of whom had had little training let alone combat experience. Two days before, Gen Buell was relieved of his command by Washington to be replaced by Gen George Thomas. However, Gen Thomas refused to take command while the army was in the process of moving to engage Gen Bragg's Army in Bardstown, Kentucky over three different roads.

The 10th Kentucky's III Corps of 22,000 men took the center road called Springfield Pike. Gen Charles Gilbert was promoted just a few weeks earlier, because Gen William Nelson was murdered during an argument with another officer named Gen Jefferson C. Davis.

On October 4th, the Confederate army of 16,800 men started concentrating around Harrodsburg and Perryville, Kentucky. The town of Perryville had six roads running through it. Secondly, a stand here would protect the Rebel supply depot at Bryantsville. Thirdly, both armies were desperate for possible drinking water, because the heat was hard on the men and the horses.

The drought had ravaged the area for months, and everywhere the men marched, the area would produce a cloud of choking dust. The dust coated their uniforms and hair, got in their nose and eyes, and fouled their weapons. When the wind blew, massive dust clouds blocked out the sun making it next to impossible to see where one was going.

When the soldiers made a campfire, they had to be very careful not to start fires turning the area into a blazing inferno.

Gen Buell had almost all his army at Perryville around 2:00 pm on October 8th. The 10th Kentucky didn't take part in the battle, because they were held in reserve.

Battle of Perryville

The 33rd Alabama got to Perryville on October 7th before noon. Gen Wood's Brigade was positioned north of town. On October 8th in the afternoon, Gen Bragg ordered an attack where the Benton Road crossed the Mackville Road called the Dixville Crossroads that was defended by the 75th Illinois, 22nd Indiana, 59th Illinois Infantry regiments, and the 19th Indiana Artillery. The three infantry regiments were made up of raw recruits with no combat experience, so this area of fighting would become known as the "Perryville Slaughter Pen."

Capt Samuel Harris's Artillery Battery was placed on a hill near Benton Road. Confederate Gen Wood's Brigade was ordered to attack around 5:00 pm. The 33rd Alabama entered the fighting with about 500 troops. The regiments formed into battle ranks and were ordered forward.

The Waverly brothers held their weapons tightly as their rank moved forward. Michael swallowed a knot in his throat as his heart pounded. Albert could feel his heart pound in his neck. His mouth was dry as the desert, and he kept telling himself to calm down. Austin was ready for the fight, because he wanted to kill him a lot of Yankees. It was time to teach the North a lesson for all the years they tried to tell the South what they ought to do.

The gray lines came within range of Capt Samuel Harris's Battery. Suddenly, the cannon fire erupted and rained death among the gray ranks. Pieces of shrapnel ripped holes in the battle ranks, and the men struggled to dress their lines. The soldier in front of Michael was thrown back into him, and both men went down. Michael could feel the man's blood on his face as he got to his feet.

Michael yelled, "Sweet Jesus, Pvt Spear is hit in the neck!"
Albert saw Pvt Aaron Ard hit in the left arm and quickly the sleeve turned crimson. To Albert's left, he saw Pvt David Brown drop wounded in both thighs. To Albert's right, Pvt David Keahey was hit in the right arm.
2Sgt Hopewell Wiggins yelled, "Hold the line and keep moving forward, boys!"
Exploding shells were joined by volley after volley of musket fire. The noise was deafening, and the smoke in the air hung like a curtain. Pvt John Miller was hit in the shoulder next to Austin and fell to the ground.
The gray ranks fired off volley after volley reloading as quickly as possible. Austin cussed as he tried to reload, because of his shaking hands. Pvt Daniel Phillips fell back into Austin wounded in the chest.
Austin struggled to get free, so he could reload. He thought, "There's no place to hide or shelter us!"
Michael fired off a shot and heard Pvt David Kelly scream in agony when he was hit in the right arm. Pvt Gabriel Smith dropped to his knees holding his bloody hand.
Austin stepped over Pvt Benjamin Stubbs seeing the man was dead. To Austin's right, Pvt Elisha Blankenship dropped holding his left hand.

Austin yelled, "Give me your musket, because mine is jammed!"

Suddenly, Albert thought he was in a different surreal world when he saw Capt Robert Ward riding towards the Yankee lines. Within seconds, one cannon erupted and sprayed grapeshot into the Rebel ranks. Capt Ward's horse was killed, instantly, and the captain fell mortally wounded in the hip. 1Lt Joseph Pelham was mortally wounded in the thigh. Pvt William Tiller's chest was torn open by grapeshot killing him on the field. 6Sgt Andrew Wiggins's right thigh was torn to pieces by grapeshot killing him, instantly. Pvt John Pearce dropped mortally wounded.

Michael threw up and prayed, "Please, stop this madness! I'm so afraid! I can't be a coward!"

4Sgt Hillary Galloway cussed as he tried to wrap his handkerchief around his wounded hand. Albert screamed when he was hit in the hand, and when he looked down, his little finger was gone. Michael helped him wrap it up the best he could. Another shell exploded nearby, and Pvt John Brown was mortally wounded in the jaw. He grabbed Michael and tried to tell him something, but all he could do was spit blood. Again, Michael gagged until he had the dry heaves.

2Sgt Hopewell Wiggins ordered, "Fall back men!"

The men could just make out Color Sgt Cornelius Godwin with the regiment's flag, and they rallied towards it.

Pvt Joseph Payne grabbed Austin's leg and begged him to help him, because he was wounded in the left leg, but Austin pulled away and kept moving.

While retreating, another shell exploded near Michael ripping his musket right out of his hand. He yelled, "God that was close!"

The soldiers gasped for air as they pulled back. Sweat ran down their faces and stung their eyes along with the smoke. The smell of gunpowder and death was strong.

Michael prayed, "Please, don't start a wild fire!"

Gen Wood's Brigade was replaced by Gen St. John Liddell's Brigade. The Rebels mounted another attack pushing the Union troops to Dixville Crossroads. Capt Harris's Battery was forced to withdraw when the battery almost ran out of ammunition. The Union troops withdrew and occupied a group of hills about 200 yards from the intersection. Four men from Company B were captured before they could get back to their lines.

Just before dark, the men in Company B that weren't injured helped carry their wounded brothers-in-arms to the field hospital. They carried the wounded water, dry straw to lie on, and covered them with blankets, because the October night was cold. Even though the men were exhausted, they checked the dead and removed their personal effects to send to their families.

Michael mentioned to Austin, "Lord, my shoulder hurts, and I feel like I just walked through Hades!"

Austin complained, "Those darn rifles kick like a mule. We'll be bruised up good for a while. I can barely raise my arm."

Michael stated, "I hope Albert's hand will heal up."

Austin replied, "He just got his little finger shot off! That's nothing serious!"

Michael fired back, "It is, if his wound gets infected!"

Austin shot back, "Stop whining!"

Michael went on, "Sometimes I wonder if you have any feelings at all!"

Austin responded, "Oh, I have feelings. Remember when Laura slapped me across the face? If our dear father hadn't grabbed my arm, I would have beaten her to a pulp and would have enjoyed every minute of it."

Michael asked, "Did you enjoy beating Kramer to a pulp?"

Austin answered, "I enjoyed every minute of it!"

Michael walked away shaking his head. He thought,

"Austin, you are a sick and dangerous person."

When Confederate Gen Bragg found out that the Union army had a corps on both the Lebanon Pike and Springfield Pike, he ordered his army to withdraw after midnight towards Harrodsburg to join up with Gen Kirby Smith's Army. The Confederate army had to leave 900 wounded men who couldn't travel behind.

Dr. Kramer Waverly would end up operating on and caring for some of the Rebel wounded. In the process, he found out the 33rd Alabama was involved in the Slaughter Pen fighting. He wasn't able to find out anything about his brothers, so he could only hope they were alright.

At the Battle of Perryville, Union casualties numbered over 4,200 men, and Confederate casualties numbered over 3,400 men.

The Confederate army marched through the Cumberland Gap to Knoxville, Tennessee. Union Gen Buell didn't pursue Gen Bragg's Army, aggressively, so he was relieved of field command by Gen William Rosecrans on October 24, 1862. This resulted in Gen Buell's career being ruined. Since he wasn't offered another command after the Battle of Perryville, he resigned in May 1864.

CHAPTER 9

Michael laughed and said, "Pvt Gabe Smith has a new nickname after he got stung by a bee eating honey."

Albert guessed, "Well, his neck swelled up like a cabbage, so I'd say Mumps."

"You're right!"

Albert added, "Since we got to Knoxville, we've gotten lots of food and things we needed. It's really good to have plenty of flour, rice, soap, fresh beef, bacon, and corn meal."

Michael remarked, "I got a new uniform, shirt, socks, drawers, and brogans, and we even got some money."

Austin commented, "At least, quite a few of our sick soldiers we left behind in hospitals have returned."

Michael asked, "Do your new brogans fit alright, Austin?"

He answered, "They're better than nothing. I miss my boots at home and decent clothes to wear. Army uniforms aren't comfortable."

Albert added, "I miss everything on the plantation, especially my wife and son."

Michael chimed in, "I know you do. At least, she's with her mother during the war, so she won't be alone."

Albert responded, "I still wish she was on the plantation where Poppa could protect her."

Austin piped in, "Stop whining, Albert. Your wife is fine where she is."

Albert shot back, "Shut up, Austin! You don't know how to love a woman!"

In November 1862, the 33rd Alabama cooked up three day's rations and boarded box cars by company to leave Knoxville. Company B ended up in the box car next to the tender which was full of wood.

Suddenly, near Cleveland, Tennessee, wood fell off the tender breaking an axle under Company B's car. The broken axle lodged under the second box car containing Company G, and those men riding on top of the cars were thrown off.

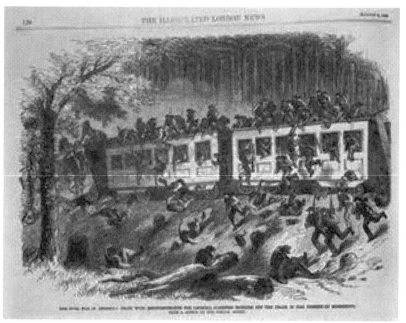
Train wreck near Cleveland, Tennessee

Michael yelled, "What's happening?"
Austin roared back, "How should I know?"
Then, the coupling gave way between the first and second box cars. The struggling engine dragged the first box car down the tracks several yards bouncing around with no wheels. Behind the first box car, the other cars piled on top of each other. When the engine stopped, Company B got out of the box car all banged up, but without any serious injuries.

Albert shouted, "Sweet Jesus, I was thrown all over the place!"
Michael shouted, "I have a bloody nose, and I feel like I've been beaten with a big stick!"
Albert saw what was behind them and shouted, "Sweet

Jesus, the cars are piled all over each other. We got to get the men out of those mangled cars!"

The troops went about rescuing the wounded, injured, and recovering the dead. Seventeen soldiers were killed in the train wreck and twenty were injured. The troops had to put the injured soldiers in box cars, so they could be sent back to the hospital in Cleveland, Tennessee. The dead were buried next to the railroad tracks in a mass grave.

Michael commented, "It doesn't seem right for a soldier to die in a train wreck, instead of on a battlefield fighting for the Confederacy."

Gen Bragg was low on supplies when he joined forces on October 10th with Gen Kirby Smith's Army. Both armies went through Knoxville and Chattanooga before turning towards Murfreesboro, Tennessee. Gen Bragg set up a defensive position along the west fork of the Stones River while Gen Kirby Smith's Army marched to East Tennessee.

Gen Bragg was frustrated with his senior generals; because they had requested President Jefferson Davis replace Bragg with Gen Joseph Johnston. President Davis chose not to relieve Gen Bragg or his unhappy generals, so the problem continued to fester. To make Gen Bragg even more frustrated, President Davis ordered him to send Gen Carter Stevenson's Division of 7,500 troops to Vicksburg, Mississippi to fight Gen Ulysses Grant.

Gen Bragg set about reorganizing his Army of Tennessee into two corps. One corps was commanded by Gen William Hardee containing three divisions commanded by Generals John Breckinridge, Patrick Cleburne, and John McCown. The other corps was assigned to Gen Leonidas Polk containing two infantry divisions commanded by Generals Benjamin Cheatham and Jones Withers. The cavalry command was under Gen Joseph Wheeler.

The 33rd Alabama became part of Gen Hardee's Corps, Gen Cleburne's Division, and Gen S. A. M. Wood's Brigade.

Gen William Hardee   Gen John Breckinridge

Gen Patrick Cleburne   Gen John McCown

Gen Leonidas Polk   Gen Benjamin Cheatham

Gen Jones Withers   Gen Joseph Wheeler

Company B lost its captain and 1Leutenant at the Battle of Perryville, but they were lucky enough to get back 2Lt Smission and brevet 2Lt George Pelham on a prisoner exchange. The company voted Henry Smission captain, George Pelham 1Lieutenant, Wade Hatton 2Lieutenant, and John Baldwin brevet 2Lieutenant. The rank of brevet meant it was not a commissioned rank.

The Union side made some changes, too. Gen William Rosecrans replaced Gen Buell, and President Lincoln made it clear he expected the Union army to go after Gen Bragg's Army, aggressively.

Gen William Rosecrans

Gen Rosecrans moved the Army of the Cumberland to Nashville, Tennessee and set about reorganizing, training, and resupplying his army. The Battle of Perryville proved raw recruits had to be trained properly before putting them into combat.

Gen Rosecrans divided his army into three wings. The Right Wing of 16,000 men was commanded by Gen Alexander McCook. The Left Wing of 14,500 men was commanded by Gen Thomas Crittenden. The Center Wing of 13,500 men was commanded by Gen George Thomas.

The 10th Kentucky came under the command of the Center Wing and Gen Speed Fry's Division.

Gen Alexander McCook   Gen Thomas Crittenden

In December 1862, Confederate Gen John Morgan made his second cavalry raid into Kentucky in order to get behind the Union lines and destroy as many supplies as he could.

Gen Rosecrans thought Morgan's Cavalry would do this, so he chose Col John Harlan's Brigade of 2,300-man infantry and a battery of artillery to chase Gen Morgan into Union troops waiting in southern Kentucky. The plan was to capture the Confederates before they could get back into Tennessee.

Gen Speed Fry suggested to Gen Rosecrans that cavalry should be sent after Morgan's Cavalry, but Gen Rosecrans wanted infantry to do it. Sending infantry to chase cavalry would prove Speed Fry right.

On December 27th, Col Harlan's command, including the 10th Kentucky, boarded a train in Gallatin, Tennessee to travel to Munfordville over clear tracks. At Munfordville, Col Harlan's command got off the train and started marching to catch Morgan's cavalry in Hardin County. The infantry and artillery marched for 24 hours in order to get to Elizabethtown 43 miles away, but they were too late to save the railroad trestles.

Col Harlan was told Gen Morgan was camped ten miles up the road by the Rolling Fork River. He pushed his exhausted, hungry troops another ten miles only to find Morgan's horsemen had crossed the river and were in Nelson County. There were a couple hundred men still on the west side of the river, so Col Harlan set up his artillery and started firing on their position.

Gen Morgan had sent five companies to destroy the Rolling Fork Bridge, but when they heard the cannonade they rushed back to Col Basil Duke's position at the river. Now, the Confederate force numbered 800 men. Col Harlan didn't realize that his cannons blocked the ford which the Confederates needed to use in order to escape.

Col Harlan sent his infantry in two lines with skirmishers out in front. Firing erupted from both sides, and Col Duke was sure his troopers would not escape, but Col Harlan pulled back. He did this because he thought the Confederates must outnumber him, because they weren't using artillery. He didn't know the Confederate artillery was already on the other side of the river with Gen Morgan. When the Union infantry halted, Col Duke sent three companies to capture a battery on a small hill that was keeping them from escaping. This gave Col Duke 15 precious minutes to get most of his men to safety.

One of the Union shells exploded near Col Duke, and he was hit in the head by a piece of shrapnel. His men put their unconscious colonel over Capt Tom Quirk's saddle that crossed the rain-swollen river to safety.

After the battle, Col Harlan marched his weary, hungry men to the Rolling Fork Bridge to set up a defensive position just in case Gen Morgan wanted to come back and destroy the bridge. Col Harlan refused to cross the rain-swollen river after Gen Morgan, because his men were exhausted and out of rations.

Col Harlan's command was ordered back to Nashville when Gen Rosecrans realized infantry couldn't chase after cavalry.

Gen John Morgan & wife   Gen Morgan's raid

On December 26, 1862, Gen Rosecrans marched his army of over 80,000 troops from Nashville to Murfreesboro to defeat Gen Bragg's Army. Of course, a third of the Union army was left along the way to protect the Union supply lines, depots, and railroad tracks. By December 30th, Gen Rosecrans had 41,000 troops in Murfreesboro compared to Gen Bragg's Army of 35,000 men.

Murfreesboro was located in the Stones River Valley in a

rich agricultural section. The area around the intersection of the Nashville Pike and the Chattanooga Railroad would become all too familiar to the fighting armies.

There were thick cedar forests in places that were thicker than the Wilderness of Spotsylvania in Virginia. Artillery and wagons had a difficult time moving over the cracked limestone outcroppings. Gen Bragg chose to defend this area northwest of the city, because it was fairly flat.

On December 30th, the Union army set up two miles northwest of Murfreesboro on the west side of Stones River.

The opposing armies set up in lines four miles long and about 700 yards from each other.

Confederate Gen Breckinridge's Corps was the only troops on the east side of the river.

That night, both side's bands started a battle of the bands playing songs like *Yankee Doodle* and *Dixie.* The soldiers sang as loudly as they could for their songs until one band started playing *Home Sweet Home.* Then, the soldiers joined together to sing this song they all loved.

Battle of Stones River

Gen Hardee's Corps was given the honor of attacking the Union right at 6:00 am. The Union forces under Gen Alexander McCook were eating breakfast when the divisions of Gen McCown and Gen Cleburne hit them like a tidal wave.

Michael commented, "This fog is so thick I can't see 50 feet in front of me."

Austin added, "I can smell coffee, so we can't be too far away."

Albert responded, "We're headed into a cedar thicket."

Lt Baldwin yelled, "Charge!"

Austin yelled, "There they are!"

Company B gave the Rebel yell and fired as they ran breaking the Union line. The Union soldiers were caught eating, and they had no other choice but to run through the cedar thickets the best they could or surrender. Many of the Union troops left their weapons and everything else behind them. A few pockets of soldiers with weapons would get behind trees, fire, and run until they could fire again.

The Yankees with weapons would cross a clearing and form up, but soon broke and fell back.

Michael yelled, "Look at those Yanks skedaddle. They're leaving their dead and wounded behind."

Just then, Michael saw Pvt Hardy Cain grab his hand and drop to the ground. On his left, Michael saw Pvt James Musselwhite go down wounded in the left leg.

Pvt James Thornton was hit in the right arm and fell up against Albert. "Hold on Thornton! Let me wrap your scarf around your arm."

Thornton pleaded, "Don't let them cut my arm off!"

Albert comforted, "It's not that serious. It's just a flesh wound; no shattered bones."

He replied, "Thank the Lord."

Pvt William Riley dropped in front of Austin wounded in

82

the right arm, but Austin kept going. The tall soldier that knocked Austin out by the campfire stopped and helped Riley.

Pvt Joel Ogborn fell wounded in the foot, and his wound would prove fatal.

When the 33rd Alabama started to run low on ammunition, they were called back to go to the ordinance trains to resupply.

By 10:00 am, the Confederates had captured 28 guns and over 3,000 Union prisoners. Any soldier in the 33rd Alabama that needed anything helped themselves to what the Union soldiers had left behind.

Michael teased, "Look Albert, I've got a Springfield rifle and 80 rounds, a Yankee blanket, gloves, drawers, a canteen, and an overcoat. The overcoat will keep me nice and warm."

Albert answered, "That's good! I found a Springfield rifle, brogans that fit, a blanket, canteen, canned milk, candy, canned peaches, coffee, and socks."

Albert asked, "Hey Austin, what did you find?"

He responded, "I grabbed a Springfield rifle, pocket knife, pocket watch, canned tomatoes, beef jerky, a blanket, socks, a shirt, and a shelter tent."

Michael remarked, "You did real good, so you and Albert can share the tent."

The tall soldier remarked, "I got a shelter tent, too, so you and I can share it."

Michael replied, "Thanks a lot. What else did you find?"

The tall soldier answered, "I found canned milk, peaches, applesauce, and stewed beef. We can feast tonight! I found brogans, ink, writing paper, a blanket, socks, and a Yankee newspaper from Michigan."

Michael suggested, "When you finish reading it, let me read it. We'll see what Michigan has to say about the war."

He replied, "Sure thing, and you can have some of the

paper to write a letter to your folks."

Michael said, "That would be wonderful! Lord knows if it'll ever reach home."

Austin thought bitter malice, "I'll get you one day, Mr. Tall Soldier! I'm going to get rid of my brother, too. I was the first born, so I should inherit Evergreen Manor. Lots of things happen on the battlefield. I just have to wait for the right time, so it looks like he was killed in action fighting for the Confederacy. Father and mother will have a son who fought bravely and is a hero of the South. I might even romance my brother's grieving widow, too. She'll be sleeping with the man who killed her husband, so isn't that a hoot? I don't know what to do with Michael just yet. There's no way he can inherit our plantation, because he's too stupid!"

Lt Baldwin mentioned, "Since we've been fighting since daybreak, we've been ordered to get a good meal and sleep on the battlefield. We've driven the Yankees back to the Nashville Pike, so let's bury the dead and move the wounded to our hospitals."

"Yes sir!"

The second Rebel wave to attack was made by Gen Leonidas Polk's Corps. Union Gen Philip Sheridan had his troops up and fed by 4:00 am that morning. His division beat back three different attacks while losing all of his brigade commanders killed in action. One third of his troops were casualties in a cedar thicket in just four hours.

Gen Rosecrans galloped around the battlefield trying to rally his troops even though his uniform was soaked in blood from his chief-of-staff who was beheaded by a cannonball while he was riding next to Gen Rosecrans.

Col William Hazen's Brigade held its line in a four acre heavily wooded area called the Round Forest which the soldiers renamed "Hell's Half-Acre."

Gen Bragg ordered Gen Breckinridge to cross Stones River and attack Col Hazen's Brigade. Slowly, Gen Breckinridge attacked the Union position twice, but both assaults failed.

On January 1, 1863, both armies took care of their wounded, rested, and observed New Years. Every soldier on the battlefield prayed the war would end this year.

On January 2, 1863, Gen Bragg ordered Gen Breckinridge to attack a hill on the east side of the river. Massed federal artillery ripped the attack to pieces. In less than an hour, the Confederates lost 1,800 casualties which was one third of Breckinridge's command.

On January 3rd, Gen Rosecrans received a large supply train and reinforcement. Gen Bragg only had about 20,000 men able to fight, and to make matters worse, a freezing rain started to fall that could raise the river and split his army.

Around 10:00 pm, Gen Bragg withdrew and began retreating to Tullahoma, Tennessee about 36 miles southward. Gen Rosecrans decided not to go after the Confederate army over muddy roads in the horrible weather.

The 33rd Alabama entered the Battle of Stones River with 320 combat ready men. They suffered 14 killed and 87 wounded. The Confederate army suffered over 11,700 casualties compared to Union casualties numbering almost 13,000 men. Four generals were killed in action.

After the Battle of Stones River, Nashville became an important Union supply depot, and the Confederates lost their influence in Kentucky and Middle Tennessee.

Gen Rosecrans would not go after Gen Bragg's Army for five and a half months until he started his Tullahoma Campaign.

Battle of Stones River

When Gen Bragg withdrew from Murfreesboro, he organized his army behind a high ridge called the Highland Rim in order to block the Union army from marching on Chattanooga, Tennessee. If Gen Rosecrans captured Chattanooga, he would control another vital railroad junction and be positioned to invade northern Georgia.

There were 1,100-foot ridges that separated the Duck and Stones Rivers. Four major passes went through the Highland Rim.

On Bragg's far left was Guy's Gap that led to Shelbyville. This was the easiest gap to get through, so he placed Gen Leonidas Polk's Corps at Shelbyville and had them put up fortified entrenchments.

To protect the major road to Chattanooga, he placed Gen William Hardee's Corps at Wartrace and had them fortify their position. Gen Hardee could reinforce Bell Buckle Gap and Liberty Gap, if needed.

A single cavalry regiment fortified Hoover's Gap, because it was so narrow two wagons couldn't travel side by side through it. At this point, Gen Bragg's front was almost 70 miles long.

The area Bragg's Army was occupying was poor farmland, so he had trouble feeding his army. So many of the agricultural supplies were moved through Chattanooga and sent east for Gen Robert E. Lee's Army. Sometimes, Bragg's men were close to starving while food went to the East.

Battle of Stones River

CHAPTER 10

In early February, Kramer, Gordon, Matt, and Jupiter were given 14-day furloughs to visit their home. They missed the Christmas seasons of 1861-62. All four were so excited they could barely sit still in their seats aboard the train. When the train stopped in Louisville, the three cousins and Jupiter rushed off the rail car and into the arms of their waiting loved ones. Their kisses were never so sweet or their hugs as comforting as they were that day.

With tears flowing down her cheeks, Eleanor said, "You boys have lost weight! I better put some meat on your bones!"

Gordon responded, "We plan to eat everything we can get our hands on!"

Edwin stated, "Eat all you want! All of us want you to know we are very proud of you."

Zeke added, "We prays for you every day."

Sophie went on, "Son, I gots to fatten you up, too!"

Kramer held Laura in his arms as she wept a river of tears. "We're all safe, honey. I think you have gotten more beautiful since we left for the army."

She replied, "Oh, you're just saying that to make me feel happy."

He chimed back, "Well, you certainly aren't uglier, you beautiful creature!"

Laura smacked his arm as the brother and sister laughed in each other's arms.

Matt jumped in, "Cousin, you are more beautiful, for sure!"

Laura fired back, "Oh, hush up, Matt!"

Edwin suggested, "Let's head home for a welcome home dinner fit for a king!"

When the four soldiers walked into the house, they were flabbergasted, because there was a huge Christmas tree in the living room decorated to perfection. The roaring fire in the fireplace crackled as the boys walked over to the Christmas tree and touched their favorite ornaments.

Tears streamed down their faces as their knees buckled under them in front of the tree.

Eleanor asked, "Is there something wrong?"

Matt wiped his tears and answered, "This is the most precious gift that all of you could have given us."

Gordon added, "Missing the last two Christmas holidays left a hole in our hearts."

Jupiter commented, "Everything be so beautiful. I'll never forget this special gift."

Kramer went on, "This is healing many of our emotional wounds. Aunt Eleanor, you are a remarkable woman. Sophie, I know you had a hand in this surprise, so you are a special woman, too."

Eleanor added, "Madeline suggested we do this for you, and we all thought it would be a wonderful thing to do for you boys."

Laura piped in, "Just wait until you have your Christmas dinner!"

Jupiter laughed and said, "I smells lots of good food!"

Sophie suggested, "Let's go into the dining room and see what Ms. Myrtle has on the table."

The table contained ham, roasted duck, sweet potatoes, corn, biscuits, bread pudding, and apple pie.

Myrtle ordered, "It's time for everybody to enjoy this special meal to honor our soldiers!"

Kramer remarked, "The meal looks wonderful! I'd marry you, if you weren't old enough to be my mama!"

She fired back, "You are such a terrible rascal!"

Kramer shot back, "But I'm your favorite rascal!"

She countered, "I ought to spank your behind good and wrap your tongue around your head!"

Matt laughed and added, "His tongue is always flapping in that mouth of his. If you need any help, I'll hold him down for you."

Myrtle blabbed, "I can tie him into knots all by myself, thank you!"

Kramer fired back, "I'll kiss you silly while you are tying the knots!"

Myrtle put her hands on her hips and shot back, "Shut up, you silly man, or I'll stuff it with this here sweet potato!"

Kramer put his hands up and said, "I surrender, because I want to enjoy that sweet potato one bite at a time."

Everybody had a good laugh, gathered around the table, blessed the meal, and filled their plates.

Gordon asked, "How is the freight company doing, Poppa?"

Edwin answered, "We have all the work we can handle, and the boys from the orphanage are a godsend. They work hard and earn every penny they make. In fact, everyone has gotten raises twice."

Zeke commented, "I wasn't sure about de boys at first, but theys very good."

Edwin continued, "We are concerned about the drought. If it continues into 1863, some river levels are going to drop a lot. If the Ohio River drops too low, supplies will have to be shipped by wagon train or by the railroad."

Matt mentioned, "We're praying for rain, because the water was bad and made a lot of our men sick or caused their deaths last year."

Edwin continued, "We read about how difficult it was to find good water."

Gordon replied, "Artesian wells were hard to find."

Laura asked, "How is army food?"

Kramer laughed and answered, "It's definitely not like this, but it's better than nothing."

The group finished the special meal, and everybody toasted in the New Year.

Kramer mentioned, "Myrtle, please thank Madeline for the wonderful thought and thank you for a special meal I'll always remember."

Eleanor stated, "The presents under the tree are for tomorrow evening after dinner, because we want to spread out the holiday for you. Saturday, the church is having a social for our soldiers."

Kramer asked, "Will there be music and dancing?"

Myrtle blabbed, "Of course, Sweetie Pie! Make sure you save me a dance!"

He shot back, "Alright, Sweetie Pie!"

Gordon ordered, "I want a dance with you, too!"

Myrtle fired back, "Alright, but don't you dare hug me too tight and crush my bosoms!"

He answered, "I'll be a perfect gentleman, Sweetie Pie!"

Sophie teased, "If you ain't, I'll spank your behind good!"

Jupiter teased, "The single woman at de church will be swarming all over you three. Dr. Kramer will have to beat them off with a stick!"

Kramer commented, "That's why Aunt Eleanor and Laura will have to help me get away from the bad ones."

Jupiter added, "Ms. Laura will have too many men buzzing around her to help you."

Matt commented, "Gordon and I will grab as many women as we can to help our dear cousin out."

Kramer added, "Hey, there are plenty of women to go around!"

Myrtle suggested, "Don't worry, Sweetie Pie, I'll come to your rescue if things get out of hand."

Sophie patted Laura on the shoulder and ordered, "Go on into the living room, because I know Kramer wants to know about the clinic. We'll take care of the kitchen and food."

She replied, "Thanks, you're a sweetheart."

Once everyone got settled in their chairs and admired the Christmas tree, Kramer asked, "How are things going at the clinic?"

Laura responded, "We are doing great! We have a steady flow of wounded and sick soldiers coming from the front. We handle a wide variety of wounds and mostly dysentery and diarrhea cases. The bad water you talked about has severely weakened these poor soldiers."

Kramer asked, "How many have died while at the clinic?"

"We have only lost eleven since we became a clinic for the army."

He commented, "That's incredible!"

"The girls, or should I say women, from the orphanage are wonderful. They are very good with the soldiers, and of course, Myrtle keeps them in line, because she's like a mother hen to them."

"How is Sammy doing?"

"Dr. Mills loves him. He does anything we ask him to do. You won't believe how funny he is around the patients, and he keeps them laughing and entertained."

"Do we get the supplies we need from the army?"

"So far, yes, but we don't know how the drought is going to affect the army's supply lines."

Kramer remarked, "Gen Rosecrans will not go after Gen Bragg's Army until he knows his supply lines are protected. The Confederates love sending their cavalry on raids to destroy depots, bridges, supply wagons, and railroad junctions."

Edwin asked, "What about our cavalry?"

Gordon responded, "We don't have as many cavalry units in the field, and they aren't as good, right now."

Edwin suggested, "They better learn quickly."

Matt added, "They will, because Gen Rosecrans knows infantry can't chase after cavalry. When we were sent after Gen Morgan's Cavalry, we were exhausted and hungry after marching over 24 hours just to get near him."

Edwin commented, "My Lord, you must have been dead on your feet!"

"Matt and I had blisters on top of blisters, and we both wore out our socks. I'll never forget how spent I was."

He responded, "I don't think I could have done that."

Matt went on, "We couldn't even will a surge of energy to kick in."

Laura commented, "I'm glad your regiment was called back."

Gordon answered, "We were happy to limp back to our camp."

Jupiter added, "We had to treat a lot of de soldier's feet with bad blisters. Army brogans ain't very comfortable shoes."

Edwin asked, "Do you like being a hospital steward (male nurse)?"

"Yes sir. I likes helping de soldiers."

Edwin inquired, "Have you had any problems with soldiers not wanting you to help them, because you're colored?"

"I only had a few of de soldiers tell me they didn't wants me touching them. They were from both armies, but Dr. Kramer tells them he has no patience for bigots."

Edwin mentioned, "I'm afraid there will always be prejudice everywhere you go."

Zeke remarked, "We runs into folks right here in Louisville that doesn't want us delivering supplies to them. It's like they don't wants us touching de boxes."

Kramer asked, "Have you heard anything from our family?"

"No, I'm sad to say. Mail between southern and northern states doesn't get delivered unless it's smuggled between the lines."

"The only thing we know is that my brothers are in the 33rd Alabama Infantry and were alive after the Battle of

Stones River."

Laura commented, "It's hard not knowing how they are."

Edwin mentioned, "You have very strong parents, and I'm confident they'll do whatever it takes to survive the war."

Kramer agreed, "I think so, too."

Matt commented, "I don't know about the rest of you, but I'm tired. I want to snuggle up in my bed and sleep like a log for a week."

Gordon agreed, "I'm having trouble keeping my eyes open, too."

Kramer went on, "I believe we're all coming down from the trip and all of the excitement."

The group headed for bed, crawled into their clean, comfortable beds with real pillows, and let their weary bodies relax. They didn't have to worry about bullets flying or shells exploding. Maybe, all the ugliness of war would let their minds rest for a short while.

The following day, the men slept in late and enjoyed a fantastic breakfast of eggs, bacon, potatoes, biscuits, and coffee. They ate until they thought their stomachs would explode, because eggs were like gold to them.

Gordon and Matt accompanied their father to the freight company, so they could see a lot of their friends.

Kramer and Laura went to the clinic, because Kramer was anxious to see how Dr. Mills and the patients were. When they got to the clinic, Dr. Mills was so excited to see Kramer. They hugged and shook hands like they hadn't seen each other for years. Sammy ran up to Kramer, saluted, and shook his hand. "Welcome home, Dr. Kramer!"

"I have heard good things about you, Sammy!"

"I work hard to help the soldiers get better."

"That's what we all want to do."

Dr. Mills and Kramer made rounds together, and Kramer talked to the patients one on one for several minutes. Of course, Sammy had to update the doctors on all the patients, too."

Dr. Mills commented, "We had some Confederate wounded come through here, and I recognized your work. They said the Confederate army retreated and left them behind."

"Yes, sir, I treat their wounded just like ours. I have to tell you, a lot of their soldiers are in poor physical shape due to their diet, so I know their rations are low."

Dr. Mills remarked, "I know, because we had to double their rations and care for them longer just to get them strong enough to leave."

"What bothers me the most is watching our sick dying from measles, dysentery, and diarrhea. The bad water killed more men than bullets. I watched two of our surgeons die from illness."

Dr. Mills replied, "I wish every minute that goes by that we had medicines to cure all these diseases. We're getting much better as surgeons, but we have a very long way to go in treating diseases."

"I came down hard on our hospitals insisting they be as clean as possible. I insisted on clean beds, patients, instruments, and doctors. You would not believe how filthy Union and Confederate soldiers are most of the time. They're infested with body lice, full of insect bites, and their feet are full of blisters."

Dr. Mills remarked, "The poor soldiers are marching all over the place in all kinds of weather, so personal hygiene is difficult to maintain."

"Many of our doctors are trying to impress upon our soldiers to stay as clean as possible, especially with their feet. Unfortunately, the more they march the more they wear out their socks and shoes. It seems like half our army is marching with brogans and no socks."

He asked, "Are the Confederate soldiers having the same problem?"

"Oh, they are much worse. You know it's bad when the Rebel soldiers steal clothes, shoes, and equipment from the dead from both sides."

He suggested, "That comes from an agricultural economy with very little industry."

"When I treat Confederate soldiers, I'm ashamed to be a rich planter's son."

He asked, "Why would you think that way?"

"Most of their soldiers don't own slaves. They scratch out a meager living on small farms hoping they'll have something to eat each day."

The doctor asked, "Why did they enlist?"

"They enlisted, because they wanted to fight for their home state, not against it. Some joined because their friends did. I talked to one rebel who joined, because he thought he could save his army money to buy a small parcel of land."

He went on, "Kramer, you stood up to your father, because you believed slavery was wrong, so don't be ashamed."

"I know Austin and Albert agree with slavery, but I don't know about Michael and Sally. When they came to visit, I got the impression they had questions about slavery and the status quo of a planter's life."

"Well, Kramer, let's hope they'll follow your example."

"I hope they will."

"Dr. Mills, our regiment has been very lucky when it comes to combat. We really haven't seen that much action, so far. I haven't had to operate on soldiers until I was exhausted and couldn't hold my instruments any longer."

"I pray the war will be over this year. By the way, are you going to the church social, tomorrow?"

"Oh yes, because I don't want to disappoint Aunt Eleanor and Uncle Edwin. I'm not looking forward to all the silly women buzzing around me like a hornet's nest."

"You are a very handsome man, so that's going to happen all the time. You might run across a woman that will steal your heart."

Kramer laughed and said, "I don't have time to romance a woman! I'll just dance with Laura, Tess, Aunt Eleanor, and Myrtle."

Dr. Mills laughed like a hyena and said, "Tell Myrtle to run off all the silly women, so they won't bother you!"

"That Myrtle is my kind of woman, if only she was twenty years younger I'd court her. She's full of fuss and feathers, but I like a woman who is feisty, full of spirit, and spunk."

"Boy, you might run across one or two at the social."

Kramer asked, "Do you know one like that?"

"Yes, I do, but I'm not going to tell you who she is. You'll have to find her yourself, you poor thing. It must be awful to have to fight off women all the time."

"Dr. Mills, you're playing dirty!"

"I want to see if you're up to the challenge, boy."

"So, you're challenging me to find her!"

"You're a smart rascal, so do you want to win the game?"

"Of course, I do! Is she ugly as a mule's behind?"

"I'm not going to tell you!"

"Is she a new member of the church?"

"In a manner of speaking, she is."

"What kind of answer is that? Now, you have me all confused."

"Good!"

"I might have to come back here and pull the rest of your hair out of your balding head. Why don't you grab ahold of Myrtle?"

He giggled and said, "Lord, boy, she's too much woman for me, because she'd kill me before I could court her."

"You sound like a chicken to me."

"You're right, and this chicken is going in the opposite direction far away from Ms. Myrtle, because I like living."

Kramer fired back, "I might tell Myrtle you would love to dance with her."

"Now, you're playing dirty, boy! If you do that, I'll pull all your hair out, and of course, that would take a long time to do."

Kramer asked, "Are we about even, now?"

"I believe so, so let the hunt begin."

The ladies of the church set out all the food, so the members, the soldiers, and the sailors could enjoy some home cooking. The military boys filled their plates high with all the goodies they missed so when they were away with the army and navy.

Kramer was hoping Madeline's apple pie would be among all the desserts. He was not disappointed, because he spied it on the table. He took a plate and filled it with three slices of pie. He looked around, but he didn't see Madeline anywhere; however, he did notice a very elegant, pretty woman with long, brown, wavy hair.

He thought, "I sure would like to run my hands through your gorgeous hair. I'm going to dance with you, because you intrigue me."

Gordon commented, "The folks sure put out a banquet of delicious food. There are lots of single women to dance with, and I plan on charming all the available women."

Kramer replied, "Make hay while you can, cousin."

Matt walked up and said, "Lord, this food is good! Just so you know, Kramer, I've picked out several ladies to dance with."

He suggested, "Don't forget to dance with Myrtle!"

"I won't, because I like her. She's like a mother hen making her chicks happy. Make sure you dance with her, too!"

Kramer answered, "You know I have to dance with my Sweetie Pie!"

"Cousin, you are one crazy bed bug!"

The cousins laughed and gobbled down as much food as they could hold. If they ate this much food while they were on furlough, they would gain back all the pounds they lost marching all over Kentucky, Tennessee, and Alabama.

Jupiter leaned back and patted his full stomach. "That was a meal fit for de heavens. I asked my mother about de woman helping her with de meal. Her name is Rosie, and I plan on dancing with her, because she be a mighty fine looking woman."

Gordon teased, "She ain't going to dance with you, because you're uglier than a cow! Besides, what happened to the girl you kissed goodbye when we joined up?"

Matt teased, "Don't listen to him, Jupiter, because women love men in uniform."

Kramer asked, "Is she new in the area, because I don't remember her at the last church social?"

He answered, "Yes. She fled Tennessee with her father, mother, and little brother. She's working at de clinic preparing meals for de patients, and she be a fine seamstress."

Matt asked, "Did they flee Tennessee when President Lincoln issued the Emancipation Proclamation?"

"Yes, and according to mother, de escape was very dangerous, and they was almost caught four times."

Gordon commented, "They must have been terrified!"

Kramer added, "Then, she's a mighty brave woman you need to charm."

Jupiter laughed and said, "I plans to do just that, because de other woman I kissed goodbye was just a friend."

Gordon teased, "Lord, Jupiter, you and Kramer are both crazy as bed bugs!"

The minister called the folks together and proceeded to thank the soldiers and sailors for their loyalty to the Union and all the sacrifices they had made. The men were introduced, and they received many handshakes, pats on the back, and hugs from a lot of women. A lot of women hugged on Kramer and asked him for a dance.

He thought, "Lord, I have to get away from all these crazy females!"

Myrtle grabbed ahold of Kramer and hugged the stuffing out of him. "Welcome home, Sweetie Pie! You look dashing in your uniform!"

He mentioned, "Sweetie Pie, you look wonderful! Have you been a good girl since I've been gone?"

"Of course, I have!"

"Haven't you found a man to kiss and love you silly?"

"Are you crazy? I don't want some old man worrying me to death, because I'm too old to be fooling around with some sex, crazy old coot!"

"Sweetie Pie, you are never too old for crazy loving."

"The music has started, so will you dance with me and shut your mouth, you rascal!"

"Can I whisper in your ears?"

"Not if you want to keep your ears, Rascal!"

"You wouldn't hurt a fly!"

"You better shut up before I smack your behind! I kill flies before they have a chance to hurt."

"Whatever you say is fine with me, Sweetie Pie."

So, Kramer laughed and guided Myrtle around the dance floor.

The dance floor filled up with couples, and Kramer saw his sister dancing with a good looking marine. Gordon and Matt had grabbed a lady, but he couldn't find the woman that had caught his eye, earlier.

Kramer asked, "I saw a pretty woman wearing a blue dress with long, wavy, brown hair. Do you know where she is?"

"She's over there dancing with the minister."

"Please, don't tell me she's married to the minister!"

Myrtle laughed until her sides hurt and answered, "No,

she isn't married."

"Why are you laughing at me, Sweetie Pie?"

"Don't you know who she is?"

"I've never seen her before."

"Oh yes, you have!"

"Sweetie Pie, I'm serious!"

"Go over there and ask her to dance when the music ends. The minister will let you butt in."

"Is she the minister's lady friend?"

"No! The music has stopped, so go over there and take her hand."

Kramer walked towards the woman as she turned his way, and his heart jumped when she smiled at him. He thought, "Who are you?"

Kramer spoke up, "Excuse me, Pastor, but I would like to dance with this pretty lady."

The pastor replied, "By all means, Captain Waverly."

Kramer took her hand and asked, "Ma'am, may I have the pleasure of this dance?"

"Of course you can, Kramer!"

"And what is your name, pretty lady?"

"I can't believe you don't know who I am!"

"Your eyes look familiar, but I can't place you."

"I'm Madeline."

Kramer's mouth dropped open in disbelief. "What happened to you while I was gone? You were a skinny, awkward girl who was very bashful."

"I grew up just like Tess."

"Let me tell you, you take my breath away, because you are so pretty and very elegant. I'm not letting anybody else dance with you. I'm your escort for the rest of the evening."

"You're mighty sure of yourself!"

"You wouldn't want to disappoint a brave Union soldier?"

"My aunt is right, you are a rascal."

"Good heavens, I call your aunt, Sweetie Pie! She's going

to kill me! She will probably roast me like a pig!"

"She loves getting your goat, because running you around in circles makes her happy."

"Why don't I call you Darling Sweetie Pie?"

"Maddie will be just fine. Darling is a bit early, don't you think?"

"Whatever you say is fine, Maddie."

While they were dancing, Kramer suggested, "You don't need to be bashful anymore, because you and Laura are more beautiful than anyone here. My mother and sister are very beautiful women, and you are just as gorgeous and elegant."

"You have a boat full of women running after you. Why did you pick me out?"

"Because you take my breath away, and you have a loving heart and soul. I want to court you, Maddie, because you are my destiny."

"What do you know about destiny?"

"I can see it in the stars!"

"Rascal, you are so full of nonsense!"

"You have to admit I'm interesting."

"Alright Rascal, but I want you to be sure I'm the woman you're interested in."

He asked, "Can you fall in love with me, Maddie?"

"Let's court and see what happens."

He responded, "That's fair enough. I can be very mysterious, and you might not be able to fight off my southern gentleman's charm."

"Then, we should have a good ole barn fight ahead of us!"

"You are a naughty woman, Maddie, but I'm ready for the challenge."

"So am I, Rascal. I can match your nonsense, intrigue, and bull with no problem."

Kramer laughed and suggested, "Let's get some apple

cider and go back by the tree you love to read under and visit. Tell me about your experiences at the clinic and what it feels like to be a grown up woman."

The couple settled under the tree and talked about the clinic, Kramer's life in Alabama, and Madeline's journey from awkward, skinny girl to an elegant, gorgeous woman.

Matt, Gordon, and Jupiter danced the evening away enjoying the time at home away from the horrors of war.

Laura and the marine only danced with each other. They were sort of courting, even though Laura kept saying they were only friends.

Jupiter and Rosie danced the evening away laughing, talking, and holding each other close.

Myrtle saw Madeline and Kramer go outside, and she roared with laughter. She knew her niece was just as feisty as she was. Kramer better hold on to his drawers, because Madeline could hold her own, now. She asked herself, "Would she end up with Kramer as a nephew-in-law?"

As the wonderful day drew to an end, Kramer and Maddie walked back towards the church.

He commented, "Thank you very much for a Christmas I'll never forget and cherish. Tears rolled down my cheeks when I saw the decorated tree. You'll never know how wonderful and healing that was to my soul." He wiped tears and took a deep breath.

"I thought that would be something special for you and the other soldiers."

"It was very special. Can I call on you tomorrow?"

"I'm finished at the clinic around 4:00 pm."

"That will be perfect! The rest of the family is going in different directions, so I'll have Aunt Eleanor make us up a picnic basket."

"It's too cold for a picnic, Rascal."

"It's not if it's in front of the fireplace by the Christmas tree."

"That's a wonderful idea!"

"You see, that's my dangerous, southern, gentleman's charm coming out to woo you."

"Don't worry; I'm keeping up my guard."

"May I kiss you, Maddie?"

"Yes, as long as you don't attack me like some crazy man!"

"I'll be real gentle-like, you pretty angel."

"You better be, or I'll bust your nose wide open."

Gently, Kramer kissed her cheek a few times, and then, kissed her lips several times. He thought, "So far, so good. I still have my nose." He took her in his arms and ran his hands through her hair. He knew right then Maddie loved him, because she returned his kisses and hugged him back. He thought, "You feisty devil, I'm going to marry you!"

Maddie thought, "I hope I did the right thing by kissing you back. I don't want to run you away. Will you love me as much as I love you?"

For the reminder of their furlough, the four soldiers courted their lady friends and enjoyed all the home cooking they could eat. All the men decided it wouldn't be fair to marry their lady friends, because they might not come back alive. They had to make sure they were really in love.

However, Kramer bought his beloved Maddie an engagement ring with the promise that they would marry the next time he came home. The other three decided their absence would be a good test to see if their feelings were the same upon their return. Kramer knew he didn't need a test to know how Maddie felt about him, and he sure wasn't going to let another man try to steal her away from him.

Laura and her marine were in the same predicament. They were very much in love, and she had agreed to marry him as soon as he returned. He had bought her an engagement ring and told her he wanted to see her walk down the aisle in her wedding gown. When his furlough was up, he was to report for duty on the *USS Lackawanna* which was a screw sloop-of-war. She was commissioned on January 8, 1863. The ship was being assigned to the West Gulf Blockading Squadron under the command of Capt John Marchand.

USS Lackawanna rams *CSS Tennessee*

She talked to Kramer about Warren, and her brother said he was a fine man. With Kramer's approval, Laura accepted the engagement ring and the promise to marry Warren on his next furlough. She missed talking to her mother and father and asking for their advice, so she just had to hope they would like Warren, too.

CHAPTER 11

In late January, a soldier in Company I of the 33rd Alabama reported to sick call and was diagnosed with smallpox. Company I was put under guard and the regiment was ordered to set up camp at the highest part of a creek swamp. The regiment was quarantined for almost a month. Those who died from smallpox were buried in the swamp with no military honors.

Not long after the regiment got off quarantine, they were formed up to watch a Union spy hanged. Michael thought Austin got far too much pleasure out of seeing the man swing lifeless as a ragdoll.

Shortly, the army marched to Wartrace to rest. Their new divisional commander, Gen Patrick Cleburne, raised the men's morale by holding competitions, rewarding the cleanest weapon, best appearance, and best hygiene. The troops were issued some new uniforms and shoes.

Several soldiers were granted furloughs in late February and March. Austin, Albert, and Michael were granted leave for ten days in March. They caught a train in Chattanooga to Montgomery, Alabama. From there they caught a boat down the Chattahoochee River to their plantation.

Freddie caught sight of them near the gristmill and broke out running for the Waverly mansion. He knew the former slaves would have to go into their slave acting mode. Everyone would have to be on their toes around the twins.

He ran up the steps, threw open the door, and found Randolph in the library with Sally.

"Mr. Waverly, your sons is coming up de road from de gristmill!"

Randolph ordered, "Sally find your mother and spread the word. Freddie let everybody know."

"I wills Massas Waverly. We'll go into our bested slave act."

Randolph thought, "It's been so long since our boys left to join the army, and I pray they are well. What are Austin and Albert going to be like? I'm not worried about Michael, because he's more like Kramer."

Alice rushed into her husband's loving arms with tears in her eyes. "I can't believe our sons are really coming home! I know they have suffered a lot marching hundreds of miles with their regiment. I pray combat hasn't turned them into hardened men."

He added, "I fear that, too. I'm most worried about the twins, and if they'll find out about our secret."

"What will you do if they confront you?"

He responded, "Remember when you reminded me that I was the master of Evergreen Manor and not Grady?"

"Sure, I do."

He commented, "I will remind them that I'm still the owner of Evergreen Manor, and you and I are running this plantation the way we want to."

"Good for you, Darling! We are a united front."

Daisy rushed up and said, "Don't you folks worry one bit, because we is going to pull off de best acting charade! We ain't going to let you down. Beulah and me will cook de boys up a fine meal."

Alice replied, "We trust all of you, and I'm looking forward to your special meal."

Freddie ran up and said, "Mr. Waverly, Oscar took a wagon to pick up your sons. Everybody knows what to do, and I'll make sure your boys get a good bath tonight before dinner!"

Randolph remarked, "Thank you, Freddie. You are a good young man I know I can count on."

The sons looked into the distance and saw a wagon headed towards them.

Michael commented, "It looks like Poppa sent one of the slaves to pick us up."

Austin complained, "It's about time, because I'm tired of walking!"

Albert suggested, "Can't you stop complaining for a few days?"

Michael added, "Ya Austin! You're a depressing person to be around, because nothing makes you happy!"

Austin fired back, "I'll be depressed and mad as long as I'm in the army. We should be officers making the decisions and giving orders!"

Albert suggested, "Men get promoted for bravery and following orders."

Austin shot back, "And they get killed when they follow stupid orders!"

Oscar pulled alongside of the boys and said, "Welcome home, Massas Austin, Massas Albert, and Massas Michael. We be glad ya'll is well."

The three climbed into the wagon, and Oscar headed for the mansion. Oscar suggested, "There are blankets for ya, because it's still chilly."

Michael remarked, "Thanks, Oscar, this blanket feels good. We steal Yankee blankets every chance we get."

Oscar asked, "Why you do that, Massas Michael?"

He replied, "Because theirs are better than ours, and you need plenty of blankets in the winter time."

When the wagon came in sight, Alice and Randolph ran to meet it. Michael jumped down and rushed into his mother's arms, and Alice held her son tightly while she cried. Albert hugged his father and told him how much he loved and missed him. Austin shook his father's hand and told him how much he missed Evergreen Manor. Michael wiped tears when he hugged his father. Albert gave his mother a big bear hug and kissed her cheek.

Albert commented, "Mother, you look wonderful, and I have missed Evergreen Manor every day I was away from here."

"We have a special dinner planned for you boys. All of you have lost weight, so we have to fatten you up."

Albert answered, "I'm ready for lots of home cooking!"

Austin took his mother's hands and kissed her cheek.

"Oh, Austin, you have lost a lot of weight."

He complained, "The army doesn't feed us the best food and many times we go without."

Randolph suggested, "Let's go inside where it's warmer. Oscar, I want to thank you very much for picking up our boys."

"Massas Waverly, it be my pleasure."

The family gathered near the fireplace in the living room.

Michael mentioned, "The sofa sure is softer than the ground we sleep on most of the time!"

Asa walked in and served each one a glass of apple cider and buttered biscuits with honey. He asked, "Massas Waverly, do you be a wanting wine at dinner, sir?"

"Yes, so bring up two bottles, Asa."

"Yes sir, Massas Waverly."

Albert continued, "I'm going to eat until I explode!"

Michael chimed in, "If I drink a glass of wine, I might fall asleep right there at the dinner table."

Austin blabbed, "Michael took a swallow of some moonshine once and gagged his head off. Wine will sure taste wonderful compared to all the bad water we have to deal with."

Randolph added, "We were worried about your situation, but the drought isn't as bad here. Our wells are doing fine, and we've been able to irrigate the fields near the river."

Albert asked, "Have you been able to ship your cotton

through the blockade?"

Randolph answered, "We didn't plant cotton last year. We planted tobacco as our cash crop, and the rest of our land was used to grow food for our plantation."

Michael replied, "That makes sense to me. Where did you sell the tobacco?"

He answered, "I sold it to the army."

Albert added, "The Yankees will trade just about anything for some tobacco."

Austin asked, "What about the gristmill?"

His father responded, "We grew extra corn, so we could stock up on cornmeal."

Albert asked, "How is the livestock?"

"The livestock is doing fine and growing, so far."

Sally rushed into the room and launched herself into Michael's arms.

Michael hugged her silly and said, "You sure have grown up a lot!"

"Mama says I'm growing up too fast!"

Albert hugged her and said, "You sure look mighty pretty. I think you favor mama a great deal."

Austin asked, "Are you still running around behind the chickens, girl?"

"Yes, I am! My chickens are very important, because they help feed us."

Randolph added, "Sally, Trudy, and Freddie do an excellent job with the chickens."

Albert chimed in, "You'll never know how much we miss fresh eggs. I can see a plate full of eggs and bacon in front of my eyes when we don't get breakfast, or we had a breakfast of hardtack and salt pork."

Sally piped in, "I'll get a basket full of eggs for you for breakfast!"

Michael added, "I'll be dreaming of them all night."

Austin blabbed, "Our sister is a regular chicken farmer!"

Sally fired back, "I'm proud of my chickens, so shut up, Austin!"

Alice suggested, "Austin, I do not want to hear that kind of ugly teasing while you're home. Do I make myself perfectly clear?"

He answered, "Yes, Mother."

Randolph warned, "Austin, I expect you to control your temper and be cheerful."

Austin shot back, "Fighting a war isn't cheerful, Father. We've been through hades!"

Randolph commented, "Your brothers have been cheerful and positive, and they've walked through hades just like you."

Alice ordered, "Relax, Austin, and enjoy your biscuits and cider. Before dinner, Freddie will have a warm bath ready for you. You'll be able to put on your clean clothes and sleep in your own bed."

Michael asked, "Will Leroy cut my hair?"

"Sure he will son."

Albert continued, "I'll go for a haircut and a shave, because I want to look good when I go to see my wife and son."

Randolph suggested, "Take a buggy, spend some time at her home, and bring her family back here for a visit. We haven't seen them since Christmas."

He responded, "That's a good idea, Poppa. I'll leave tomorrow."

Michael asked, "Have you heard anything from Kramer and Laura?"

Alice answered, "Not since December 1861. Kramer, Gordon, Matt, and Jupiter joined the army in November. They're in the 10th Kentucky Infantry. Laura is working at the clinic with Dr. Mills. Tess and Sophie are working as seamstresses with Eleanor. Zeke is working for Edwin at the freight company."

Austin blabbed, "Our army doesn't take kindly to colored men in the Union army. Right now, all of them are the enemy."

Randolph mentioned, "Kramer is a surgeon, and Jupiter is a hospital steward. Both of them are noncombatants."

Michael remarked, "I pray we don't meet on the battlefield, because I couldn't kill family eye to eye."

Albert added, "I couldn't either. Austin shut your mouth, because we already know what you'd do."

Daisy came in with more cider and biscuits. After empting the plate and pitcher, everyone agreed they didn't want to spoil dinner too much.

Randolph and Alice already noticed Austin was still a problem and an angry man. Both hoped there wouldn't be a nasty argument while he was home.

Sally got her mother aside and said, "Austin better not insult me again, or I'm going to smack him. He's still the same mean, ugly person he's always been."

"Be careful Sally, because he will lose his temper if you slap him."

"I have some tricks up my sleeve if he comes after me."

Between the family's snack and dinner, the sons took nice warm baths while Freddie helped them. Leroy cut their hair and massaged their heads. All three sons shaved for the first time in months.

It was so good to put on clean civilian clothes even though they were somewhat big now. The sons snuggled down in their beds and fell fast asleep. The brothers couldn't believe they slept until it was time for dinner, so maybe, they were starting to relax.

Asa called the brothers to let them know dinner was ready. Daisy and Beulah filled the lavish table with ham, wild turkey, sweet potatoes, green beans canned from the garden, cornbread, and for dessert apple pie made from their bumper crop of fruit.

Michael looked at the table and said, "I can't believe my eyes! We haven't had food like this since we joined the army. Thank you so very much Miss Daisy and Miss Beulah, because this is a royal feast!" He wiped tears from his eyes hoping nobody noticed.

"We wanted to welcome you boys home with a special meal, Massas Michael."

Albert commented, "I'm going to savor every bite, Daisy and Beulah. Thank you, ladies!"

Beulah commented, "We knows how much you love cornbread and apple pie, Massas Albert."

Daisy continued, "We fixed plenty, so eat all you can, Massas!"

Randolph told Asa, "The wine was an excellent choice, Asa."

"I knows you like that kind of red wine, Massas."

"Make sure you eat a plate full of good food!"

"Thank you, Massas."

The family filled their plates and enjoyed every bite; however, Michael just drank a very small glass of wine, because he didn't want to end up asleep.

Randolph asked, "So, Michael, you didn't like moonshine."

He replied, "That was some rot gut fire water, and I thought my mouth and throat would burn up. That soldier lied to me saying it was some smooth, southern whiskey."

Austin remarked, "You are so gullible."

Sally commented, "He's a lot younger than you, Austin, or does that mean you're an expert on moonshine?"

He answered, "I've had my share of moonshine over the years."

Albert laughed and said, "Sally, he was sick for two days and had a headache for four days after drinking half a bottle of moonshine one evening."

Michael giggled and suggested, "We should have mixed the moonshine with the bad water. Maybe, the water would have tasted better."

Alice said, "We worried about the sickness the bad water was causing and prayed you boys would be alright."

Randolph inquired, "We read about the train wreck your regiment was involved in. How were you affected?"

Albert responded, "Our Company B was thrown around the rail car a lot, but we only suffered a lot of bumps and bruises. Every time we get on a train we worry about something happening."

Alice mentioned, "I imagine a lot of the trains are in bad shape."

Randolph asked, "Do you think the Union army will attack you soon?"

Austin answered, "Oh ya! Gen Bragg will keep retreating towards Chattanooga. We have to hold, because Chattanooga is a vital railroad junction and leads to Georgia."

Alice commented, "The newspapers are very critical of Gen Bragg's operations against the Union army."

Austin fired back, "He's definitely not like Gen Robert E. Lee! I think he's an idiot!"

Albert continued, "Gen Bragg's subordinate generals want him removed from command."

Austin shot back, "Let's face it, they hate him!"

Michael added, "They want Gen Joseph Johnston to replace him."

Austin fired back, "If we lose Chattanooga, Gen Bragg will be removed from command. In my opinion, he isn't any better than Gen Beauregard."

Michael mentioned, "We have a great divisional commander named Gen Patrick Cleburne."

Randolph remarked, "The newspapers call him the

"Stonewall Jackson of the West."

Albert added, "He's a brave fighter that takes care of his men."

Sally inquired, "Is it true our army has lost more men from disease than in battle?"

Albert answered, "That's right!"

Sally asked, "What are they dying from?"

He replied, "The worst killers are typhoid, dysentery, diarrhea, measles, and smallpox."

Michael continued, "At least, the three of us didn't come down with smallpox when our regiment was quarantined for almost a month."

Alice commented, "We didn't know about that."

Randolph suggested, "It's probably a good thing we don't know about everything that happens in our army."

Michael replied, "That's right, Poppa. It would only make things worse on the families back home."

Albert asked, "How many slaves have we lost since Lincoln issued his Emancipation Proclamation?"

His father replied, "None."

Michael inquired, "Are you serious?"

Alice responded, "Your father and I are very pleased. Our slaves must not want to leave."

Beulah added, "We're happy here, and besides, it's too cold up north."

Albert inquired, "Have our neighboring plantations fared as well?"

Randolph responded, "No! In fact, they're having problems growing a cash crop let alone food to eat."

Austin wondered, "By the way, where is our overseer?"

Alice answered, "He joined the army, so your father is the overseer."

Albert asked, "How can you do all this by yourself?"

"I don't, because several of my trusted slaves help me run

Evergreen Manor."

Austin blabbed, "No slave is trustworthy!"

In an instant, Sally stood up and shouted, "Shut your mouth, Austin! You don't know what you're talking about! In my opinion, you are the one who isn't trustworthy!"

Alice requested, "Sit down, Sally. We all know Austin doesn't think like we do. Your brother probably wants to hit you about now, but he has to know his father will break his arm if he tries to do something as stupid as that."

Albert fired back, "Calm down, Austin, and for Pete sakes keep your opinions to yourself!"

Michael chimed in, "If Poppa has to break one of your arms, I'll break the other one!"

Austin stood up and said, "Father and Mother, I think it's best I leave tomorrow. I'll ride with Albert to Eufaula and head up river towards Montgomery. I'll go back and rejoin our regiment. Excuse me."

Austin walked upstairs, went into his bedroom, and closed the door. He thought, "I don't like what's going on around here. When we start fighting again, Albert has to go. Poor brother will be killed in action for the Confederacy. When the war is over, I'll have to do something with Poppa. I'm not sure what to do with Michael just yet. He's too stupid to run a plantation. That mouthy sister of mine will be sent packing, because she's turned into another abolitionist. She won't be living at Evergreen Manor when I come home and get rid of Father."

Michael commented, "The war has affected Austin, badly. He's so tense and angry. Most of the men in our company don't like him, so he's pretty much a loner."

Randolph remarked, "I think him leaving is for the best, because we want to enjoy you and Albert every moment. Sally doesn't deserve all his ugly teasing."

Albert chimed in, "We warned Austin to keep his mouth shut and just enjoy being home. He's already been knocked out cold by one soldier in our company, because Austin shot off his big mouth."

Randolph warned, "Be careful around him, because Austin's temper is out of control, and he's full of anger."

Michael agreed, "We will, Poppa. Sometimes, he scares me on the battlefield when he goes into his laughing fits."

Albert continued, "We slipped around and told the sergeant about it."

Alice inquired, "What did he do?"

"He talked to Austin, but it didn't do any good. Austin told us the sergeant needed to mind his own business."

Alice requested, "Please be careful around him, because Austin strikes me as a bomb ready to explode. Please Sally stay away from your brother as much as possible until he leaves."

"Yes Mama! I don't want to get near him anyway."

The tension at the dinner table eased, and everybody relaxed. Albert and Michael asked for another piece of apple pie that they inhaled.

Daisy asked, "What would you folks like for breakfast?"

Michael answered, "Scrambled eggs, bacon, buttered biscuits with honey, and lots of good coffee with sugar and cream in it."

Randolph and Alice laughed, because that was always the children's favorite breakfast.

She asked, "Would you like some canned peaches from our orchard, too?"

Albert fired back, "You bet we would! Oh how I've missed peaches and apples."

The family visited with each other for quite a while, and then, went to bed. Before going upstairs, Michael asked his father if he could accompany him around the plantation tomorrow, because he was anxious to see Evergreen Manor, again

After enjoying a wonderful breakfast, Albert and Austin left in the buggy for Eufaula for very different reasons. Albert just let Austin run his angry mouth, and he was quite thankful when they parted ways. What was he going to do with his crazy brother?

Freddie brought horses over to the mansion for Randolph and Michael, so they could make their rounds on the plantation. Michael already knew about the colored church and new slave quarters, but there was a lot he didn't know about, just yet.

Randolph looked at his youngest son and said, "My workers have stayed with me for several reasons. Austin will not agree with these reasons, because he's living in the past and a mean-natured person. The only way this plantation will survive this horrible war is by all of us working together to stay alive."

"I agree, Poppa!"

"I sat down one day with your wonderful mother, and we discussed our options. We had Asa and Leroy bring the men they thought were the most respected to the mansion, so we could talk over our plans. We answered a lot of questions and came up with a plan. Michael, promises aren't enough, sometimes, so my workers needed to know I was sincere. As we ride around, you will notice there are no rows of slave shacks. I brought in carpenters to teach my workers how to build homes, barns, pig pens, fences, chicken coops, repair the gristmill, and build an irrigation system."

"That's wonderful, Poppa! Have you built a lumber mill to take advantage of all our timber?"

"Yes! It was finished six months ago in a secure location."

"That was good thinking Poppa, because deserters don't care what they destroy."

"You will notice my workers have family homes with multiple rooms, nice fireplaces, windows, porches, and attics to hide supplies in. Some households raise chickens, others pigs, others goats, and others horses. All the households grow large gardens and have all the tools and utensils they need. Three of my workers were trained to be blacksmiths, and three learned to be wheelwrights."

"So, you gave them a choice if they wanted to be something other than a farmer?"

"Yes! Jerome, for example, can build a mighty fine wagon or buggy."

"Well, I'll be!"

"Freddie wants to be a cook, so Beulah and Daisy are teaching him."

"Doesn't he help Sally and Trudy with the chickens?"

"Yes. I have a group of workers who run trap lines to catch small game and fish in the pond."

"Let me guess; you have a group to go hunting with you, too."

"Yes I do!"

"Poppa, I'm proud of everything you have done, and it all makes sense to me. When Mama took Sally and me with her to visit Aunt Eleanor, I saw how different life was away from our plantation. We were so thankful to have spent that time with Kramer and Laura."

"Michael, you and Sally remind me of your brother and sister."

"Poppa, Evergreen Manor is yours, and you have to live in the present. Your land has to be a fortress that can survive on its own, because nobody else will feed you. Our army doesn't get half of what it needs from the government, so we steal as much as we can from the Yankees."

"I'm glad you understand!"

"I have a good idea what you have done, so don't worry, I'll keep your secret. I bet you don't have slaves anymore."

"That's right!"

"May I suggest you give each household some of our land?"

FAYE M. BENJAMIN

"It's already been done."

"They'll fight and work hard for their land."

"May I suggest you be very careful around Austin, because he's on the edge of insanity?"

"I know, and I play as dumb as possible around him. Even Albert gets tired of his mouth and opinions."

"As long as Albert and his family are around, the charade will have to continue."

Michael laughed and remarked, "Sally sure stood her ground with Austin, thank heavens."

"If he raised a hand to hit her, I would have broken his arm, too. As your mother says sometimes, life is full of surprises. I could see your mother punching Austin in his nose."

"Sally and I will never forget what the twins did to Kramer. We understood why Kramer and Laura went to live with Aunt Eleanor and Uncle Edwin, and why you sent Zeke's family with them. Austin was so stupid; he thought you got rid of the troublemaker abolitionists."

"As long as I live, I'll never understand Austin's brain."

"His brain is full of greed and hatred."

"By the way, son, this Sunday our workers have invited us to their church for a gospel sing, music, and a picnic indoors."

"I will be honored to attend, and I'll make sure I tell everybody that. I've learned to play the harmonica sitting around the campfire, too. Maybe, I can join them."

"Good for you!"

The family enjoyed Michael and Albert's family for the rest of their furlough. Little Thomas loved playing with his grandpa and uncle. When Michael and Albert headed towards Montgomery, they were rested, stuffed with food, and loaded down with socks, drawers, gloves, blankets, scarves, and shirts. Both men got money from their father to

120

buy new uniforms, overcoats, and brogans.

Both men wondered if 1863 would be a better year for the Confederacy. What would Austin be like this year? When was he going to enter the world of insanity?

Planter's life

Slaves use cotton gin

Cane Mill and Evaporator

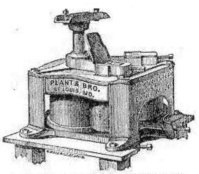
Sugar cane crusher

CHAPTER 12

Gen Bragg knew he had more cavalrymen than the Union, so he put his cavalry into action during the beginning of 1863. He ordered Gen Joseph Wheeler's Cavalry to attack and capture the Union garrison at Dover, Tennessee near Fort Donelson. Gen Wheeler's men were unsuccessful in their attempt to capture the Union garrison or play havoc with Union shipping on the Cumberland River.

In March, Gen Rosecrans's Cavalry detachment lost the Battle of Thompson's Station trying to cut Confederate communications. During the same month, Rebel Gen Nathan Forrest lost the Battle of Brentwood trying to cut Union communications at the station on the Nashville-Decatur Railroad. Confederate Gen John Morgan took his cavalry on raids into Pennsylvania and Ohio and ended up being captured.

In June 1863, Gen Rosecrans launched his Tullahoma Campaign much to the prodding of Gen Henry Halleck, Lincoln's general-in-chief. At this point, Gen Rosecrans had between 50,000-60,000 men compared to Gen Bragg's 45,000 effective troops.

Gen Rosecrans begged Washington to send him more cavalry units, but Washington turned him down. Instead, the general was given permission to mount and outfit an infantry brigade. Col John Wilder's Brigade of the 17th, 72nd, 98th, and 123rd Indiana regiments was chosen. The 1,500 Indiana boys found the horses and mules they needed from the countryside, made long handled hatchets for close combat, and were issued the seven-shot Spencer repeating rifle.

Little did Gen Rosecrans know that this unit and the 39th Indiana regiment from Gen McCook's Corps would be worth their weight in gold as mounted infantry.

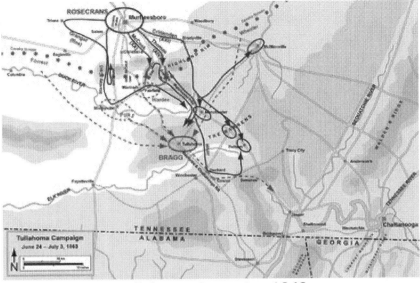

Tullahoma Campaign 1863

The 10th Kentucky was assigned to Gen George Thomas's XIV Corps, 2nd Brigade and the 3rd Division. Col John Harlan had to resign his commission, because of the sudden death of his father, so LtCol William Hays was promoted to lead the 10th Kentucky.

The 33rd Alabama was assigned to Gen William Hardee's Corps, Gen Patrick Cleburne's Division, and Gen S. A. M. Wood's Brigade.

This campaign would be Gen Rosecrans's finest military achievement. Unfortunately, his achievement would be overshadowed by the Union victories at Vicksburg and Gettysburg.

Col William Hays   Gen S. A. M. Woods

Gen Rosecrans's plan was to attack the Highland Rim by sending fake troop movements towards Shelbyville on Gen Bragg's left, and then, send Gen Thomas's Corps southeastward on the Manchester Pike against Hoover's Gap on the rebel right. The attack had to be done with quick precision in order to work.

On June 23rd, Gen Rosecrans sent part of his Reserve Corps and a division of cavalry west to Triune as the feint.

Before Hoover's Gap could be reinforced by the Confederates, Col John Wilder's Mounted Brigade, now nicknamed the Lightning Brigade, rushed to Hoover's Gap nine miles ahead of Gen Thomas's main body and captured the seven mile long gap the same day. His troops pushed through the gap and fought off charge after charge from Rebel forces cutting them to pieces. The Indiana boys laid in mud and the pouring rain delivering volley after volley into the Rebel ranks. The 20th Tennessee had very few men left after repeated charges against the Spencer repeating rifles. Rebel casualties totaled almost 150 men compared to Col Wilder's 61 casualties.

Wilder's Brigade held the gap until Gen Thomas arrived with the rest of the XIV Corps around 7:00 pm. The general was convinced Wilder's Brigade had saved thousands of men's lives, and, at least, three days of fierce fighting.

Gen Rosecrans sent Col Thomas Harrison and his mounted 39th Indiana Infantry to capture Liberty Gap. The Union brigade found two Confederate brigades commanded by Gen St. John Liddell and Gen Patrick Cleburne. When another Union brigade came up to support, the Union brigades attacked the rebel flank, because a frontal assault would mean suicide. At the end of the day, the rebels were pushed back a half mile from the southern entrance to the gap.

Mother Nature's weather would affect both armies for the next 17 days, because heavy rains would turn the roads into quagmires.

On June 25th, Rebel forces in Hoover's and Liberty Gaps tried to defeat Union troops, but they failed to recapture the two gaps. Bragg tried to put together a counteroffensive, but poor scouting and subordinate generals who considered Bragg an idiot doomed his plan. The situation left Gen Bragg no other choice, but to order Gen Polk and Gen Hardee to retreat to Tullahoma on June 27th.

By June 30th, Gen Bragg ordered a night withdrawal south of the Elk River to Cowan. By July 3rd, the Rebel army retreated to Chattanooga, and by July 7th the army was near Lookout Mountain.

The Union army faced an extremely difficult task in order to attack and hold the thirty mile long Cumberland Plateau made of rocky, barren, mountainous terrain, poor farmland, and a network of poor roads. Chattanooga was located between Missionary Ridge, Stringer's Ridge, Raccoon Mountain, Pigeon Mountain, and Lookout Mountain. Those names would become all too familiar to the soldiers who had to fight there.

Gen Rosecrans worried about his supply and communication lines once he crossed the Tennessee River. He knew Confederate cavalry would attack his rear, constantly, making it necessary to divert more soldiers to guard railroad tracks, wagons, telegraph lines, and supply depots.

By early August, Washington was demanding Gen Rosecrans attack the Confederate army as soon as possible. The general reminded Washington that the poor road conditions would slow his troop movements.

Gen Rosecrans's plan was to cross the Cumberland Plateau into the Tennessee River Valley. He wouldn't cross the river until he had collected plenty of supplies. Also, he planned to cross the river downstream while Bragg's forces were chasing after another deception of his.

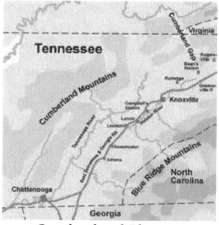

Cumberland Plateau

Col John Wilder's Lightning Brigade was sent north of Chattanooga to make the Confederates think Gen Rosecrans's army would cross the river there. His men made lots of noise, sawed boards, and threw them in the river to float downstream.

From Stringer's Ridge, the Union artillery commanded by Capt Eli Lilly was ordered to bombard Chattanooga for two weeks.

Gen Bragg fell for the feint and was certain the Union army would attack above Chattanooga.

On August 16th, the Union XXI Corps was ordered to attack Chattanooga from the west. Gen George Thomas's XIV Corps was ordered to march over Lookout Mountain south of the city along with the 10th Kentucky Infantry. The XX Corps and the Union cavalry were ordered to march southeast to attack the Confederate railroad supply line coming from Atlanta.

By August 31st, all the Union corps had crossed the river, and had built two bridges to move supplies.

Gen Rosecrans believed the Confederate army would end up trapped in Chattanooga or would have to evacuate the city.

By September 8th, one Union corps was near Valley Head, Alabama, the second Union corps was near Trenton, Georgia between Lookout Mountain and Raccoon Mountain, and the third Union corps was near Chattanooga.

Gen Bragg withdrew from Chattanooga and placed his four corps along Pigeon Mountain southeast of the city. The Rebel general knew the three Union corps were spread out over 40 miles in mountainous terrain. This meant they were too far apart to support each other if one were attacked. Gen Bragg had the opportunity to attack each corps separately and retake Chattanooga. Also, Gen Bragg was aware that Gen Thomas's lead division was 12 hours ahead of the main body near Dug Gap.

Bragg ordered Gen Thomas Hindman to attack Gen James Negley's Union troops at McLemore's Cove from the flank, and Gen Patrick Cleburne's Division to attack them head on through Dug Gap. Again, Gen Bragg's orders weren't followed by some of his subordinate generals. Gen Hindman followed his orders and had marched to within four miles of Gen Negley's lines on September 10th.

Gen Thomas Hindman   Gen James Negley

Gen D. H. Hill

Gen D. H. Hill claimed his orders arrived very late, and he couldn't advance, because Gen Cleburne was sick and Dug Gap was filled with chopped down trees.

Again, Gen Bragg ordered Gen Hindman to attack on September 11th. Gen Cleburne wasn't ill, so he had ordered his men to clear the chopped down trees from the entrance to Dug Gap. Now, he waited for the sounds of Gen Hindman's troops, but the Union divisions slipped back to Stevens Gap, safely. The Rebel opportunity was over.

Again, Gen Bragg ordered another attack on September 13th, but the Union XXI Corps slipped away and was able to concentrate around Lee and Gordon's Mill.

The armies on both sides maneuvered their troops knowing a major battle was brewing. The Confederate army was looking to recapture Chattanooga while the Union army wanted to crush Gen Bragg's Army. Then, Gen Rosecrans could push what was left of the Rebel army into Georgia and Alabama.

bacon, hardtack, & beans

Canned tomatoes & peaches

CHAPTER 13

Austin complained, "The generals are plain stupid! We should be defending Chattanooga, so the darn Yankees would have to attack us all dug in behind fortifications."

Albert chimed in, "Maybe, Gen Bragg doesn't want to be under siege like Vicksburg."

Austin blabbed, "We need to stop retreating and do some attacking."

The tall soldier suggested, "Make sure you tell Gen Bragg you have the answer to his problems."

He shot back, "I plan on it!"

Michael asked, "Ain't Gen Longstreet supposed to help us out?"

Austin commented, "Knowing our luck, he won't get here in time to help!"

Michael added, "We sure did break our backs clearing all the timber at the entrance to Dug Gap."

Albert fired back, "That's a fact, because my back still hurts!"

Austin shot back, "We did all that work, so we could attack the Yankees along with Gen Hindman. You see what happened! There was no attack by Gen Hindman's men or ours."

On September 19th, Gen Bragg's Army was positioned near Pigeon Mountain in a five mile long front. The 33rd Alabama was located on the left flank of the Confederate line. The Rebel army was in a heavily wooded area full of thickets which made rapid movements impossible.

The Union army was strung out for several miles on the east side of Missionary Ridge.

Gen Bragg was convinced he could attack Union forces on their left flank, turn the Union forces southward, and get between Chattanooga and Gen Rosecrans's Army.

Bragg ordered Gen Cleburne's Division, which contained

the 33rd Alabama, to march north to the Youngblood Farm near Gen Bragg's right flank. Gen Cleburne's men crossed Chickamauga Creek and arrived at the Youngblood Farm about 5:30 pm. When Gen Cleburne reported to Gen Polk's headquarters, he was shocked to receive orders to attack as soon as possible. By the time he could get his men positioned for the attack, it was sunset.

By 6:00 pm, Gen Cleburne had positioned his brigades in line with Gen James Deshler on the left, Gen Sterling Wood in the center, and Gen Lucius Polk on the right. The 33rd Alabama was set up with the 18th Alabama on its left and on its right were the 16th Alabama, the 45th, the 32nd, and the 15th Mississippi regiments.

Gen James Deshler   Gen Lucius Polk

Waiting behind a split rail fence in the tree line was the Union 5th Kentucky, 1st Ohio, and the 32nd Indiana.

As twilight descended on the small meadow called Winfrey Field, Gen Cleburne's men moved cautiously. Quickly, the fighting turned into chaos. Gen Deshler's Brigade missed their target, and Deshler was shot in the chest. Gen Preston Smith rushed forward to reinforce Deshler, but he rode into Union lines and was shot down.

Wood's Brigade pushed across Winfrey Field under heavy fire. Artillery shells screamed overhead landing among friend and foe alike. Gen John Jackson's troops helped drive the Yankees back, and the 33rd Alabama attacked over the Union breastworks firing at the retreating troops. Col Adams ordered his men to attack the 6th Indiana which was nearby.

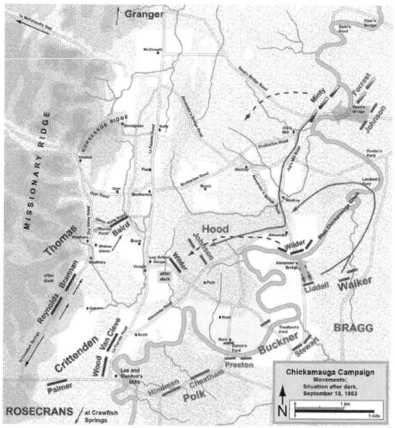

Battle of Chickamauga on September 18th

Michael thought, "I can't see a darn thing! Why are we fighting in the dark? My throat is so dry, my lips are cracked, and my head is pounding."

Austin shouts, "Why is the 16th Alabama retreating?"

Albert fires back, "How should I know?"

A shell explodes in front of them, and they can see the silhouette of the 6th Indiana troops. The 33rd Alabama hears the order to fix bayonets, so they obey, quickly. Albert trips over something and cusses. A shot rings out and hits the tree next to Michael's head.

He yells, "Sweet Jesus that was close!"

Austin yells, "I can't see a darn thing!"

Albert orders, "Shut up, the Yankees can hear you."

Suddenly, a Yankee rushes towards Michael and Michael fires at his chest. Michael tries to reload, but another Yankee jumps him, and the two soldiers wrestle in the pitch black woods. Michael manages to get his knife and stabs the Yank in the throat. The man went limp, so Michael knew he was dead.

Michael thought, "I didn't want to kill you. Forgive me. Where is everybody? I can hear soldiers in hand-to-hand combat, but who are they? What should I do? Where are my brothers?"

Austin saw a muzzle flash, headed for it, and he eased closer to the figure. The figure fired another shot, and Austin jumped him. Austin ran his bayonet through the Yankee pinning him to the tree.

Austin whispered in the Yankee's ear, "How does it feel to die, Yank? Too bad you're not my brother, Kramer."

"Sweet Jesus, help me!"

Austin blabbed, "Ain't nobody going to help you, Yank!"

Another shell exploded, and Albert was thrown up against a tree. He opened up his eyes just in time to see a bayonet aimed straight for him. He rolled away just in time for the bayonet to miss him. Albert grabbed the soldier's legs and pulled him down. They exchanged blow after blow until Albert knew he couldn't land another punch. The Yankee grabbed him around the neck trying to choke the life out of him. Out of nowhere, the tall soldier slammed the butt of his rifle across the Yankee's head.

Albert got to his knees and said, "Thank God, you came along. You saved my life!"

The tall soldier replied, "You saved my hide many a time. The artillery shells have started fires in the meadow, so we need to get out of here."

Albert asked, "Where is everybody?"

He answered, "Our regiment is in the woods by the 6th Indiana breastworks, because the Yankees have pulled back. Some of our boys are collecting the men, because we're running low on ammunition.

Albert remarked, "I'm thirsty and hungry enough to eat a bear!"

"So am I. Let's find our boys."

"Alright, then let's eat a bear."

By 9:00 pm, Gen Cleburne's Division controlled Winfrey Field, but the Union army still controlled the Lafayette Road. The 33rd Alabama grouped together in the woods that night in battle ranks. They received ammunition, drew rations, and slept the best they could after three hours of pure chaos. As the men tried to sleep, they could hear the Yankees building log breastworks.

September 20th would be a day of military blunders by both armies. Communications between commanding officers and their subordinate officers were poor.

Bragg decided to reorganize his army and assigned Gen Longstreet the left wing of his army when Longstreet arrived at Bragg's headquarters around 11:00 pm. The right wing of Bragg's Army would be commanded by Gen Leonidas Polk. His command would include Gen D. H. Hill's Corps, Gen William Walker's Division, and Gen Benjamin Cheatham's Division.

Gen D. H. Hill wasn't told he was demoted, nor did he receive orders concerning the September 20th battle plans from Gen Bragg. The attack was supposed to start at dawn, but Gen Hill didn't receive written orders until 6:00 am. Gen Bragg had to agree to another delay, so Gen Hill could get his men ready.

Gen John Jackson   Gen William Walker

By 9:30 am, the divisions of Gen John Breckinridge and Gen Patrick Cleburne were ordered to attack the Union line at Kelly Field. The two divisions had no idea they were charging into six Union divisions that had built log breastworks on Horseshoe Ridge.

The 33rd Alabama and the 16th Alabama started advancing around 10:00 am, and they were met with one murderous volley after another from the Union lines. The two regiments took cover in a small ravine for almost an hour. Gen Sterling Wood's Brigade got separated from the other units and found itself cut off and alone.

The 33rd Alabama and the 16th Alabama were ordered forward from the ravine. About 300 yards from the Union line, the two regiments were hit with horrendous rifle and artillery fire from the right flank.

Michael yelled, "Sweet Jesus, we're taking fire from the right. Where's the 16th Alabama?"

Albert shouted, "They're getting mauled like us!"

Suddenly, the man in front of Michael was shot in the head and fell back against him. Michael was covered in hair, tissue, and blood.

"Oh God! Oh God! He's dead!"

Albert grabbed his brother and yelled, "You're alright! Keep moving!"

The sergeant yelled, "Fix bayonets! Keep moving men!"

Austin was hit in the arm, but it was only a flesh wound. The man next to him grabbed his thigh and yelled, "I'm hit!" The ranks kept moving as men continued to drop. The regiment pushed across the Lafayette Road that was Gen Bragg's main objective.

However, the regiment had to retreat, because they had suffered 16 killed and 133 wounded out of the 219 men who were present for duty that morning.

Bullets kept hissing by the men as they moved back to safety. The men grabbed as many of the wounded as they could, because there were so many cries for help.

Michael gasped for air, licked his parched lips, and forced his legs to keep moving. Albert grabbed Austin to help him get back to safety. The tall soldier picked up a wounded corporal and worked his way through all the dead and wounded.

An artillery shell pierced the thick air and exploded nearby knocking some of the men down. The brothers got back up and kept running the gauntlet. Their lungs burned from the smoke, and their hearts pounded.

Michael thought, "I don't want to be shot in the back."

The men reached safety and collapsed on the ground. All of them gasped for air, drank from their canteens, and prayed their hearts wouldn't explode in their chests.

Albert thought, "This is madness! We didn't have any support!"

Austin got to the hospital tent and an orderly wrapped his arm. He thought, "I had the perfect opportunity to get rid of Albert, but I couldn't see in that black woods at Winfrey Field."

All the Confederate lines on the southern end of the battlefield kept pushing Union forces back. Union divisions and brigades fell back to McFarland's Gap along with Gen Rosecrans, Gen McCook, and Gen Crittenden.

Gen Rosecrans left for Chattanooga to organize his retreating men and set up the city's defenses. Gen Sheridan decided to take his 1,500 men to help Gen Thomas whose four divisions still held his position at Kelly Field and Horseshoe Ridge on the Union far left.

Union Gen Brannan arrived at Snodgrass Hill around noon and put his men to work throwing up breastworks. The 21st Ohio that was armed with five-shot Colt revolving rifles arrived and took up position next to Brannan's men.

Col Timothy Stanley's Brigade, which was part of Gen Negley's Division, arrived at Horseshoe Ridge, and he placed his men south of the Snodgrass house.

Gen John Brannan

Col Timothy Stanley

Col Charles Harker's Brigade, which was part of Gen Thomas Wood's Division, rushed to Horseshoe Ridge and set up next to Stanley's position south of the Snodgrass house. Both brigades worked feverishly putting up breastworks.

Gen Gordon Granger's Reserve Corps was waiting near McAfee's Church for orders to send reinforcements, but he never received any. Without orders, he sent two brigades from Gen James Steedman's Division and Col Daniel McCook's Brigade to march to the sound of the guns. Col McCook stayed near the McDonald house to guard the rear while Steedman's two brigades arrived in the rear of Horseshoe Ridge.

Gen Gordon Granger   Gen James Steedman

Just as Confederate Gen Bushrod Johnson started attacking, Gen Granger ordered Steedman's Brigades to block Gen Johnson's path.

When the 10th Kentucky marched towards the Battle of Chickamauga, they were assigned to Gen George Thomas's XIV Corps, Gen John Brannan's 3rd Division, Col John Croxton's 2nd Brigade, and Col William Hays, commanding the regiment. The 10th Kentucky entered the Battle of Chickamauga with 451 men fit for duty, and the 2nd Brigade entered with 2,164 men fit for action.

Col John Croxton

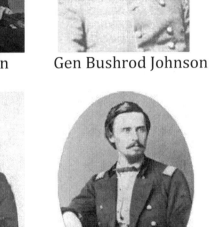

Gen Bushrod Johnson

Col Charles Harker

Col Daniel McCook

Battle of Chickamauga

Croxton's 2nd Brigade marched through the night of September 18th to get to their assigned position at McDonald farm. Around 7:00 am on the 19th, the brigade was cooking breakfast when they received orders to attack a Confederate brigade isolated on Reed's Bridge Road west of Chickamauga Creek.

It wasn't long before Col Croxton realized he wasn't moving against a brigade, but instead, he was facing two strong divisions. Gen Thomas could tell from the increased firing that there was serious action occurring, so he sent a brigade to assist Croxton's 2nd Brigade. The 10th Kentucky, at one point, charged Col Claudius Wilson's Brigade around 9:00 am, because they were hitting them on the right flank. The 10th Kentucky drove the enemy back some 200 yards, but they had to fall back suffering heavy casualties.

By 10:30 am, the 2nd Brigade had been pushed back about 400 yards by Col Claudius Wilson's Georgia boys after fighting almost constantly. Gen Baird's men reached Col Croxton and moved in beside his brigade, and Gen John King's U. S. Army Brigade arrived behind Croxton's men. More of Gen Baird's troops filed through Croxton's men, so they could fall back for ammunition and some rest. Croxton's Brigade drank as much water as they could and gobbled down hardtack and anything else they could eat from their haversacks, because they had been fighting for four straight hours. Company B had already lost 20 men in just an hour.

Col Claudius Wilson's Georgia boys were pushed back close to Jay's Mill Road before they were relieved by Col Daniel Govan's Arkansas Brigade and Gen Edward Walthall's Mississippi Brigade. The battle was so intense Croxton's Brigade was ordered back into action with six regiments. The 10th Kentucky was placed between the 10th Indiana and the 31st Ohio.

When Col Croxton's Brigade returned, they helped push

back the division of Gen St. John Liddell past the Winfrey field.

Gen Daniel Govan   Gen Edward Walthall

Gordon, Matt, and the men of the 10th Kentucky fired and reloaded as fast as they could.

Pvt Henry Ash asked, "Where are all these Johnny Rebs coming from?"

Gordon shouted, "They're like fire ants!"

Next to Gordon, Pvt Joseph Grant dropped wounded, and next to Matt, Pvt Samuel Smith fell wounded.

Matt fired and started to reload when Pvt William Tumey fell dead. Matt yelled, "Oh God, Willie, no!"

Lt Benjamin Smith went along the ranks shouting, "Get ready men, here come the Rebs!"

Rebel Gen Alexander Stewart's Brigades charged across Poe field at the Union divisions of Gen Brannan and Gen Reynolds. Matt and Gordon kept firing and became one with their weapon.

Matt tells himself, "Easy, aim, fire."

The air was thick with smoke, musket fire roared, and artillery shells screamed across the sky exploding with deadly accuracy. Gordon looked to his left just as a shell exploded in their ranks. Pvt Micajah Cox fell mortally wounded, Pvt William Kelly fell wounded in the thigh, and Pvt John Sweeney fell wounded in the hip and leg.

Gordon yelled, "Why did Gen Wood pull his men out of line. The darn Rebs are pouring through and trying to turn our flank!"

Pvt Henry Ash shouted, "We need reinforcements!"

Lt Benjamin Smith ordered, "Fix bayonets! Charge!"

Gordon and Matt ran towards the Arkansas boys believing they wouldn't survive this day.

Gordon thought, "Be strong and don't show the white feather."

The 10th Indiana and the 31st Ohio joined the 10th Kentucky as they raced towards the enemy. As if in slow motion, bayonets and muskets flashed in every direction as hand-to-hand combat enveloped the field.

Matt's musket was knocked out of his hands by a short Rebel. The two punched and wrestled until Matt found his knife and stabbed the Reb in the back. The Reb continued to fight, so Matt hit him in the neck. Slowly, the Reb lost his grip, shook some, and then, collapsed.

Gordon clubbed a Reb with his musket butt across the head. The soldier dropped, so Gordon turned his attention towards another Reb. He charged him with his bayonet, but before he could stab him the Reb fired his musket at close range. Gordon felt an intense, searing, hot pain in his stomach, and he dropped to his knees. He fell on his side holding his stomach in agony. Suddenly, he was very cold, and all he could see was fog. All the sounds of battle mixed together in one terrible roar.

He thought, "Why are my hands wet? What is happening to me?"

He saw Matt's face, but he couldn't seem to understand what his brother was saying. He felt Matt pick him up in the dense fog, but he didn't know where Matt was going. All he wanted to do was rest a spell and go back to fighting.

Gordon thought, "Matt can't carry me very far. Where is he going? Why do I feel so heavy? Why do you have tears in your eyes, Matt? I feel like I'm floating in a fog, and I'm so tired. Please let me sleep just a little while. What is that bright light? Whose hand is this? Do I take your hand?"

Matt yelled, "Please don't die, Gordon! Come back! No! No! Matt held his beloved brother in his arms and wept.

"We whipped the Rebs good, Gordon! They broke and took off running. You should have seen them skedaddle. How do I tell Poppa and Mama, because it will rip their hearts out?"

By 2:30 pm, Gen Brannan's Division was along Alexander Bridge Road to rest and get more ammunition. By 4:00 pm, Gen Brannan's Division was ordered to support the center of Gen Rosecrans's line.

Pvt Ben Estes said, "Matt, we're ordered to move to the center of our line."

Matt fired back, "I'm not leaving my brother here!"

Pvt Estes offered, "I'll help you carry him, because he was a good friend and soldier. Come nightfall we'll bury him real proper-like."

Matt tried to prepare himself for more combat, and how he was going to deal with Gordon's death. He wanted to find Kramer, but he had no idea where he was on this confounded battlefield. He wanted time to grieve and needed time to say goodbye to Gordon.

When the division reached its position, Matt placed Gordon's body several yards behind their camp. Later, Pvt Estes helped him bury Gordon. Matt wrapped his brother in a blanket and took his cap, pocket watch, haversack, and ammunition. Since Pvt Estes had his musket shot to pieces, Matt gave him Gordon's musket. His brother's shoes were almost new, so he gave them to Estes.

On September 20th, Col Croxton's 2nd Brigade would have

the terrible luck of being close to the Union sector where Gen Thomas Wood pulled his division out of the line on the right around 11:00 am. Just then, thousands of Confederate troops poured through the massive hole. Col Croxton was ordered to place his regiments around the 1st Ohio Light Artillery.

When the Confederates attacked Croxton's position, Croxton was shot in the leg and had to be removed from the field. Col William Hays took command of the 2nd Brigade.

Gen Brannan had his division fall back to Horseshoe Ridge to set up another line of defense. The 10th Kentucky, the 14th Ohio, and some 45 men of the 4th Kentucky started putting together breastworks to help them hold as quickly as possible. The men would spend the next five exhausting hours in a desperate struggle to hold Horseshoe Ridge at all costs.

The stand made by Gen Thomas's Corps, and the other units that went to his aid would earn Gen Thomas the nickname of the "Rock of Chickamauga." These troops refused to be beaten and didn't retreat until ordered to do so by Gen Thomas.

Gen Thomas's men and those who came to his aid were fighting for their very lives and dignity while Gen Rosecrans retreated to Rossville and sent a telegram to President Lincoln telling him of the Union disaster.

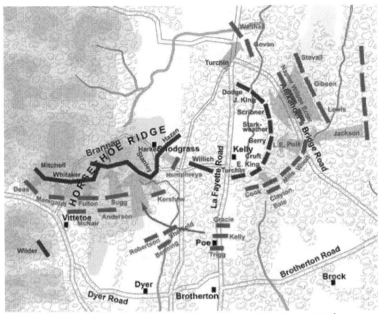

Battle of Chickamauga on September 20th

Gen Steedman's Division arrived around 3:00 pm and relieved Col Croxton's Brigade, so they could get more ammunition and rest for a short while. Steedman's man pitched into Confederate Gen Bushrod Johnson's attacking men, and the fighting was so intense that Col Croxton's Brigade was ordered back at the double quick after only 30 minutes of rest. The brigade, along with the 10th Kentucky, took up a position behind some rails and poured volley after volley into the enemy.

After three hours of intense battle, the Confederates withdrew. Col Croxton's Brigade had run out of ammunition and had been ordered to fix bayonets for the next onslaught. The officers of the brigade took guns and ammunition from the wounded and fired until it was all gone.

The men of the 21st Ohio Infantry fired 43,550 rounds during the desperate fighting on Horseshoe Ridge.

Kramer operated until his hands couldn't hold the instruments, and his eyes wouldn't focus. He was ordered to his tent to sleep, so Jupiter went with him to make sure Kramer followed orders.

"Jupiter, I'm so weary, but I need to eat before I sleep."

Jupiter took his boots off and said, "I'll gets you a big plate full and some coffee."

When Jupiter got back, Kramer ate everything on his plate and drank all his coffee. The doctor lay back on his cot and was sound asleep in less than a minute.

Jupiter said, "Sleep good, my friend. We have seen de worst battle ever. So many poor mens lost arms and legs, but you did your best. Jest remember, you cain't save all de mens."

Jupiter was relieved in a couple of hours and went back to Kramer and his tent just as weary. He took his shoes off, fell back on his cot, and smiled at his snoring friend before sleep overtook him.

By 6:00 pm, Gen Thomas received orders to fall back towards Rossville. As the Union forces withdrew, Gen Baird's Division lost quite a few men taken prisoners. Steedman, Wood and Brannan slipped away to the north. Three regiments were left behind to give the Union army on Horseshoe Ridge a chance to escape. The 22nd Michigan, the 21st Ohio, and the 89th Ohio held until they were surrounded and forced to surrender.

Gen Thomas collected the units around Rossville Gap knowing his magnificent soldiers were exhausted, hungry, thirsty, and very low on ammunition. However, no one could question their determination and courage.

Confederate Gen Bragg didn't pursue Gen Rosecrans's Army, because he didn't have pontoon bridges in order to cross the Tennessee River. Instead, he gathered Union equipment left behind, reorganized his men, and tended to his wounded.

The 10th Kentucky lost 166 men killed, wounded, captured, or missing during the three days of combat. This was about 40% of its force.

The Union casualties totaled close to 16,200 men compared to Confederate casualties of almost 18,500 men. The Battle of Chickamauga produced the second highest battle losses of the war behind the Battle of Gettysburg.

On September 21st, Gen Rosecrans's Army fell back to Chattanooga and set up strong fortifications. The Confederate army laid siege to Chattanooga by occupying the mountainous terrain around the city.

Matt finally found Kramer in Chattanooga where the hospital tents were set up. Kramer was changing bandages when Matt walked into the tent. Kramer looked up and smiled when he saw his cousin. Immediately, Kramer sensed something was wrong, and when he reached Matt, tears were running down his cheeks.

"Oh God, is it Gordon?"

"He was gut shot and died in my arms! I couldn't save him! It's not right!"

The cousins held each other and wept. The last time Kramer had wept was when his grandparents died. When the men composed themselves, Matt said, "I want you to keep Gordon's kepi, pocket watch, haversack, and his bible. I know his things will be safe with you, because I don't know what will happen to me."

He replied, "It will be my honor, Matt."

"Kramer, Gen Thomas was holding our left, and we fought like tigers to beat back the Rebs. Gen Rosecrans abandoned us and skedaddled with a lot of Union troops for Chattanooga."

"Many of my patients believe the army could have won the battle if Gen Rosecrans had stayed and organized his troops by Gen Thomas. Unfortunately, we'll never know and many a brave soldier perished in defeat. What worries me most is a possible siege of the city. If we don't keep our supply lines open, our army could starve to death."

He answered, "Ya, we could become the next Vicksburg, and I would rather die from a bullet than starve to death."

"Let's pray this situation won't befall us. I don't think President Lincoln will let us starve to death. He'll send troops to help us break a siege."

"I hope you know what you're talking about."

The 33rd Alabama had ten men placed on the Roll of Honor for bravery above and beyond the call of duty during the Battle of Chickamauga.

Cpl Alexander Bell	Co H	
3Sgt Richard Bush	Co G	killed in action
Capt W. E. Dodson	Co C	
Capt B. F. Hammett	Co B	
Pvt William Harris	Co K	
Pvt W. E. Hatten	Co I	
Pvt P. S. Lewis	Co E	killed in action
Pvt W. R. Mock	Co A	
Pvt J. D. Perry	Co C	
Sgt C. L. Sessions	Co D	killed in action

The 33rd Alabama lost their brigade commander, Gen Sterling Wood, who resigned, because he was threatened with a court-martial by Gen Patrick Cleburne for cowardice in the face of the enemy. Their new brigade commander was Gen Mark Lowrey.

At the Battle of Chickamauga, Capt Horace Porter from the Ordnance Department of the U. S. Army rallied enough retreating soldiers to hold their ground while under heavy fire to give the batteries and wagon trains time to escape capture.

Also, at the Battle of Chickamauga, Musician William Carson from the 15th U. S. Army saw the 18th U. S. Infantry waver, so he bugled to the colors to rally the men to hold their position. Shortly, he saw the 2nd Ohio Infantry waver, so he rushed to the colors bugle blaring. These actions made the Confederates believe reinforcements were arriving, so they delayed their attack.

These men were awarded the Medal of Honor for bravery above and beyond the call of duty.

Musician William Carson   Captain Horace Porter

CHAPTER 14

After Gen Rosecrans had his army in Chattanooga, he built strong fortifications in the old Confederate works which resulted in a three mile long semicircle around the city.

Gen Bragg had three options to choose from: outflank Rosecrans, assault his fortifications head on, or starve the Union army by siege. He chose to establish a siege line. So, the Confederate army occupied Missionary Ridge and Lookout Mountain, so he could observe the city, the Tennessee River, and the Union army's supply line.

Gen Bragg was very upset about the actions or lack of action by some of his subordinate general officers. On September 29th, he relieved Gen Thomas Hindman and Gen Leonidas Polk of their commands.

On October 4th, several general officers begged President Jefferson Davis to replace Gen Bragg, but their petition failed. Gen Bragg retaliated by relieving Gen Simon Buckner and Gen D. H. Hill of their commands.

The Union only had one supply line that wasn't controlled by the Rebels. It was a 60 mile long dangerous route over Walden's Bridge from Bridgeport, Alabama on mountainous roads. The heavy rains that fell at the end of September washed away a lot of the roads. In early October, Gen Joseph Wheeler's Cavalry attacked a Union supply train destroying 800 wagons and killing the mules and horses.

By late October, Union soldier's rations consisted of four cakes of hard bread and a quarter pound of pork every three days.

Gen Robert E. Lee sent Gen James Longstreet and his 15,000 men to Chattanooga from Virginia. Secretary Edwin

Stanton ordered Gen Ulysses Grant to go to Chattanooga and take Gen William Sherman's 20,000 men from Vicksburg with him.

Gen Grant was informed that he was now commander of all the Union forces from the Mississippi River to the Appalachian Mountains. He was, also, instructed to relieve Gen Rosecrans of his command.

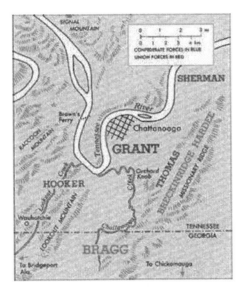

Gen Grant telegraphed Gen George Thomas, the Rock of Chickamauga, and told him to, "Hold Chattanooga at all hazards. I will be there as soon as possible." Gen Thomas replied, "We will hold the town till we starve."

After a treacherous journey, Gen Grant arrived in Chattanooga on October 23rd.

Gen Grant, Gen Thomas, and Gen Baldy Smith, the chief engineer of the Army of the Cumberland, set about breaking the siege. Gen Smith purposed that the Union army could seize Brown's Ferry that crossed the Tennessee River which would lead them to a road that turned south through Lookout Valley to the railroad station at Wauhatchie. The army could turn west to Kelly's Ferry on the Tennessee

River where Union supply boats could reach them. If the Union army could pull this off, the siege could be broken.

Gen Grant ordered Operation Cracker Line to get done in a hurry at all costs. By October 28th, Union forces took control of Brown's Ferry, Wauhatchie Station, and Kelly's Ferry. Now, the Union army could get supplies, weapons, ammunition, and reinforcements over the Cracker Line. Finally, Union soldiers and animals were delivered from starvation.

With the cracker line open, the Confederate army's situation was completely changed. Gen Bragg looked over his choices and decided his best option was to move around and attack Gen Grant's left flank.

In the Tennessee Valley, Lookout Mountain is a narrow plateau which rises to 1,700 feet and runs 85 miles southwest from the Tennessee River. Surrounded on the northern end of the mountain on three sides is an almost vertical 500 foot wall of rock. These vertical walls protected any forces that were positioned on top.

A weather anomaly occurs on Lookout Mountain about three to five times a year. The anomaly starts with fog surrounding the bottom of the mountain, and then, the fog rises and surrounds the entire mountain. The Battle of Lookout Mountain would be fought in this fog on November 24th. Some people would call the battle, the Battle Above the Clouds. Some soldiers would consider the fog a bad omen.

Lookout Mountain fog

Lookout Mountain & Tennessee Valley

Both armies maneuvered like chess pieces in November. On the 14th, Gen Bragg ordered Gen Stevenson's Division to defend Lookout Mountain, so he placed his brigades led by

Gen John Jackson, Gen Edward Walthall, and Gen John Moore on the bench of the mountain. The bench was a ledge that was 150-300 feet wide running along both sides of the mountain. The ledge was located about two thirds of the way to the summit.

Gen Stevenson put artillery on the crest of the mountain, but the cannons couldn't depress far enough to fire at the ledge.

Gen John Moore   Gen Carter Stevenson

In mid-November, Gen Grant, Gen Sherman, and Gen Thomas put their plans together to attack Bragg's Army. First, Gen Sherman would lead the main attack on Missionary Ridge's northern end. Second, Gen Joseph Hooker's men were ordered to capture Lookout Mountain. Once Lookout Mountain was captured, he was ordered to Rossville, Georgia to block any Confederate escape route. Third, Gen Thomas would support Gen Sherman.

Gen William Sherman   Gen Joseph Hooker

On November 23rd, the 10th Kentucky and its division

were ordered to the Rossville Road in front of some Confederate fortifications. They were to engage the enemy pickets, but told not to bring on a major attack. The enemy pickets were routed, and the division set up a line of defense between the Rossville and Moore Roads.

They camped at the position Monday night and held the area through Tuesday night. They were aware that Gen Joseph Hooker's men were attacking Lookout Mountain, and that Gen Sherman's men were setting up on the north end of Missionary Ridge.

However, Gen Sherman's men on November 24th didn't set up on the north end, but occupied Billy Goat Hill due to incorrect intelligence from his scouts. Across a deep ravine from Billy Goat Hill, the Rebels were fortified on Tunnel Hill which was the northern end of the ridge.

By November 23rd, Gen Thomas ordered 14,000 men to Orchard Knob, and they had no trouble running off the 600 Rebel troops that were defending it.

Gen Bragg had ordered Gen Cleburne's Division and another division to board trains headed for Knoxville to reinforce Gen Longstreet who was sent to attack a Union force commanded by Gen Ambrose Burnside. However, when Gen Thomas captured Orchard Knob, he ordered Gen Cleburne back.

Michael asked, "Where are we going, now?"

Sgt Wiggins answered, "We're ordered to Missionary Ridge to dig in on the west side behind some vineyard. We're to dig rifle pits and chop down trees, so they fall facing Chattanooga."

Albert suggested, "That tangled mess will take the Yanks forever to get through."

Austin agreed, "Ya, it will! We'll be able to shoot Yankees down in the mess all day."

Michael commented, "Don't the Yankees know they can't

take the mountain, because they won't be able to reach the top?"

Pvt Deason remarked, "If we run out of ammunition, we can roll rocks down on them!"

Pvt Burgess laughed and continued, "We won't run out of rocks, because this area and state are full of them!"

Gen Cleburne's men set about digging rifle pits and chopping down trees beginning on November 22nd. Also, they helped move a heavy siege gun to the top of Lookout Mountain, so it could fire on Union positions in the valley and Chattanooga. Occasionally, the siege gun fired on Union supply wagons moving towards the city.

On November 24th, the 33rd Alabama could hear the rattle of musket fire, but they couldn't see what was going on over at Lookout Mountain. The mountain and valley were covered in a fog by 8:00 am.

Michael commented, "I've never seen a thick, foggy mist like this before covering an entire mountain. That siege gun we busted our behinds dragging up the mountain won't help much in the fog."

Austin remarked, "I can't understand why Gen Bragg pulled Gen Walker's Division away from the bottom of Lookout Mountain."

Albert suggested, "Maybe, Gen Bragg thinks we need his help on our right."

Pvt Pete Brown asked, "What troops are defending the base of the mountain?"

1Sgt Martin Crawford answered, "Gen Walthall's 1,500 Mississippi boys are down there, now."

Pvt Dennis Lindsay asked, "How can you fight a battle in that confounded fog? You can't see nobody until they're right on you."

Michael added, "I'm glad we're not on Lookout Mountain."

The Rebel force on Lookout Mountain by November 24th numbered around 8,700 men. Union Gen Joseph Hooker would have about 10,000 troops when he ordered Gen John Geary to cross Lookout Creek and attack the mountain.

Around 8:30 am, Gen Geary's troops crossed a footbridge over Lookout Creek and pushed through the thick mist. The Mississippi boys retreated towards the Craven's house.

By noon, Union troops hit the Rebels on the east bank of Lookout Creek. At 2:30 pm, Gen Stevenson was ordered to retreat to the east of Chattanooga Creek. Throughout the afternoon and early night, six Alabama regiments stayed behind to cover the withdrawal of Gen Stevenson's and Gen Cheatham's Divisions. Around 2:00 am, the Confederates were ordered to leave the mountain, completely.

While the Rebels were withdrawing, the bright moon was covered by a complete lunar eclipse around midnight. All the soldiers couldn't believe they had witnessed two of nature's phenomenon. Many soldiers had no idea what was happening, so they considered it a bad omen or witchcraft.

One Reb next to Michael said, "That mountain covered in fog, and the moon disappearing be a bad omen. The whole place gives me the creeps."

Michael explained, "The earth is causing a shadow on the moon."

He replied, "I don't care what you say; it ain't natural! If I start seeing ghosts, I'm going to shoot them plum dead!"

Albert teased, "If you see ghosts, we'll shoot at them, too."

Austin blabbed, "You're nothing but a country cracker, boy!"

The Reb replied, "You ain't nothing but a spoiled planter's boy!"

Michael suggested, "Look, you can see part of the moon, now."

The Reb responded, "When all of de moon is back, I'll feel better, because this place is full of bad spirits!"

Battle of Lookout Mountain

At the Battle of Lookout Mountain, Pvt Peter Kappesser from the 149th New York Infantry rushed a Confederate camp and captured the flag of the 34th Mississippi Infantry, the color bearer, and the color guard. Later, he rescued a wounded comrade and carried him to safety. He was awarded the Medal of Honor.

Gen Bragg decided to fight it out on Missionary Ridge rather than retreat further into Georgia, so he sent Gen Stevenson to bolster his right flank.

The Union casualties at the Battle of Lookout Mountain totaled 408 men compared to Confederate casualties totaling a little over 1,000 men.

The Battle of Missionary Ridge would be fought on November 25th. Gen Grant decided on a plan calling for Gen Sherman and Gen Hooker to attack the flanks of Gen Bragg's Army, and then, roll them up towards the center of

Missionary Ridge. Gen Thomas was to support Gen
Sherman, but Thomas wanted support on his flank. So, Gen
Hooker moved across the valley to Rossville Gap around
10:00 am. His troops were delayed, because the bridge
across Chattanooga Creek had been burned. A footbridge
was put across by the 27th Missouri and a pioneer unit
rebuilt the bridge, so Gen Hooker's forces didn't arrive until
around 3:30 pm.

Gen Sherman commanded about 16,600 men as he got
ready to attack Tunnel Hill. On the other side, Gen Hardee
had 9,000 troops from Gen Cleburne's and Gen Walker's
Divisions. Gen Stevenson was arriving with another 4,000
men.

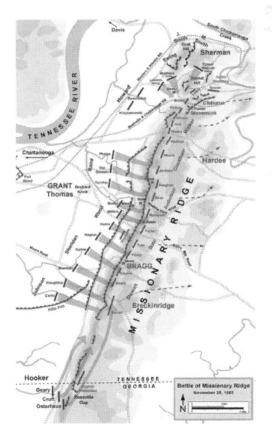

Tunnel Hill sat between two railroads, the Nashville-

Chattanooga Railroad and the Western-Atlantic Railroad. If his attack was successful, he would control both railroad lines. Sherman ordered a brigade to attack along the northern length of Tunnel Hill. He sent another brigade to attack from the northwest across open ground between the railroads. The third brigade was ordered to march through the valley and attack the east side of Tunnel Hill.

Waiting for the impending attack was Gen Cleburne's Division along with the 33rd Alabama. They had dug in south of the tunnel where the East Tennessee-Georgia Railroad passed through Missionary Ridge. The attack came between 10:00 and 10:30 am. Reinforcements moved to the ridge to Cleburne's left. Gen Cleburne sent Gen Lowrey's Brigade to man a hook of land projecting from Tunnel Hill that was north of the railroad tunnel.

1Sgt Crawford yelled, "Git ready, boys! Here they come!"

Michael thought, "Please protect me, Lord, and help me do my duty." His heart pounded as he aimed his musket at the oncoming blue line.

Austin thought, "Come closer Yanks and meet your maker!"

Albert thought, "I love you Dora and Thomas. I wish I was holding both of you in my arms, today."

1Sgt Crawford yelled, "Fire at will!"

The 33rd Alabama fired volley after volley at the Union troops that fell back when they were within 200 yards of the Rebel position.

Albert yelled, "The Texas Brigade is really catching it! Let them boys have it, Texas!"

Pvt Ben Buckner shouted, "The Arkansas boys are taking heavy fire, too! Hold your line Arkansas!"

Pvt John Hammock shouted, "Look at them Yankees skedaddle!"

The Union brigades attacked and fell back several times. When they came to within 80 yards of the Rebel lines, Gen Cleburne ordered a counterattack down the hill around 4:00 pm that forced the Union lines to retreat. Cleburne's men captured around 500 prisoners and eight enemy flags. Many of the Union troops were low on ammunition and too exhausted to fight on. Gen Sherman lost almost 2,000 men, because he only committed a few in his command. He had eight brigades in reserve he never ordered into battle.

Around 3:30 pm, Gen Grant was getting aggravated at the lack of progress on both flanks under Gen Sherman and Gen Hooker. He ordered Gen Thomas, the "Rock of Chickamauga," to take his 23,000 men and attack the enemy rifle pits at the base of Missionary Ridge. Gen Grant hoped this would cause Gen Bragg to pull troops away from the flanks to help Gen Sherman and Gen Hooker. Ahead of them were 14,000 Confederate soldiers defending the center of the ridge.

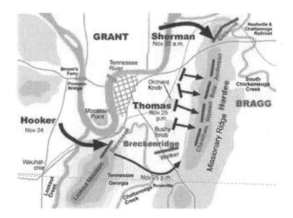

The 10th Kentucky was commanded by Col William Hays, assigned to the Third Brigade commanded by Col Edward Phelps, and the Third Division commanded by Gen Absalom Baird.

Col Phelps's Brigade would be the last brigade on the left.

1Sgt Edward Mittler gathered Company F around him and said, "I'm tired of Gen Sherman's and Gen Hooker's men blaming us for the defeat at Chickamauga. We are going to take that ridge no matter what. I'm not stopping until I get to the top!"

Pvt Henry Grant shouted, "We ain't stopping, neither! We'll show Gen Grant what we're made of!"

Pvt Squire Roberts yelled, "We're with you, Sergeant!"

1Sgt Mittler ordered, "Brigade form up in two lines with skirmishers out in front!"

Matt stood between his friends Pvt Ben Estes and Pvt Henry Grant. He drank from his canteen, licked his lips, and took a deep breath. He thought, "I don't care how hard the climb is to the top, because I'm doing it for you, Gordon. Protect me and give me the courage I need this day. Do you hear me Lord, because I'm not stopping until I get to the top?"

Around 3:40 pm, the signal guns fired, and the blue lines moved forward. Already, there was confusion among the officers on whether to stop at the rifle pits or swarm the top. The blue waves crashed into the 9,000 Rebels in the rifle pits at the base of the ridge. The shouting Union troops yelled, "Chickamauga! Chickamauga!" Those Rebels who weren't captured started climbing the 600 foot ridge to the top.

At the rifle pits, Rebel cannons and infantrymen poured fire down on the Union lines. Suddenly, Union units started climbing the cliffs as color bearers waved their flags for the men to follow them. Seeing the battle flags waving only propelled the men to climb the heights no matter what. Union Gen Turchin's Brigade charged up the mountain first without orders. There was no holding back, because the crazy Russian was going up.

The captain shouted, "Charge to the top! Rally around the colors, men!"

Both lines charged forward shouting, "Chickamauga!" Matt, Ben, Henry, and Squire started climbing the rocks helping pull one another higher and higher.

Some rocks gave way and Matt shouted, "Look out below! I'm going to get to the top if it's the last thing I do in this world. I'm coming Gordon! You hear me!"

Ben slipped on some rocks, but Squire grabbed him before he fell. To Matt's right he saw a soldier slip and fall several feet before someone could stop him. Matt stopped a short while to catch his breath, and then continued to scale the cliffs. His heart was pounding, and his head pounded from the musket and cannon fire. He grabbed hold of a tree growing out of the rocks just as the ledge he was standing on gave way.

"Sweet Jesus, hold tree, don't break on me!" His heart was racing as his hands strained to hold his grip. His feet were dangling unable to find solid ground. "Please Lord, help me! I'm going to the top!"

Ben yelled, "Hold on Matt, I'm almost there!"

It seemed like hours before Ben reached him and at that moment Matt's arms gave out.

Ben shouted, "I got ya, Matt. Let's rest a spell, because we need to catch our breath."

Matt responded, "My arms and hands are on fire!"

Ben answered, "Your hand is bleeding, so wrap it up with your scarf."

Henry yelled, "Look out, the Johnny Rebs are throwing rocks down on us."

Shortly, the friends started climbing as bullets hit the rocks and trees all around them with a thud or ping.

Gen Grant was furious that his orders to stop at the rifle pits weren't obeyed. Gen Granger looked at Grant and said,

"When those boys get started all hades can't stop them."

Another officer on Grant's staff suggested, "Gen Thomas's men held Missionary Ridge when most of Gen Rosecrans' Army retreated. They didn't pull out until they were ordered to, sir. Thomas's troops aren't going to stop until they run the Rebels off the mountain. You're watching your best soldiers showing you what true courage means."

Suddenly, a soldier higher up from Matt and his friends slipped, and his foot got caught in a crevice.

He shouted, "Help me! I can't move my foot!"

Squire worked towards the soldier and checked the situation. He said, "We have to move this boulder to free your foot."

The soldier remarked, "I think my foot is broken."

Matt, Ben, and Henry reached Squire and looked things over. The four men positioned themselves and pushed with all their power to move the boulder. It moved slightly, but not enough to free the foot. The men tried again, and the boulder moved a little more. On the third try, the boulder moved enough to free his foot. The soldier yelled in pain, and there was no doubt the ankle or foot was broken. Just then, Henry was hit in the head by a rock thrown from above, and Matt was showered by dirt and pebbles.

Henry cussed and said, "When I get to the top, I'm going to find that Reb and beat his head in!"

For some reason, the men started laughing, because they knew Henry wouldn't find out who the Reb was.

Matt teased, "Henry, your head is too hard to crack!"

Ben teased, "You might have a headache for a while, you poor thing."

Henry replied, "You boys shut up before I whip the lot of you!"

Ben commented, "Well, Corporal, you have to stay here while we head for the crest. We'll come back and get you off the cliff and down the mountain."

164

"Thank you for your help. You boys saved my life. Now, run the Rebels off Missionary Ridge for me."

The friends continued climbing to the top of the ridge trying not to slip and fall to their deaths. All the while they were peppered with dirt and loose stones, but that wasn't going to stop them.

Around 5:00 pm, three regiments were within 50 yards of the Rebel fortifications. The regiments moved closer and leaped over the Rebel breastworks yelling, "Chickamauga!" The officers moved the regiments to both sides and started rolling up the Rebel line. Many Rebel soldiers surrendered or fled for their lives. The Union brigades of Gen Turchin, Gen Van Derveer, and Col Phelps attacked the three Rebel brigades. During the fight, Col Phelps was killed trying to organize his men to attack.

The 1Sgt yelled, "Roll them Rebs up and run them off the mountain!"

Matt yelled, "Chickamauga, this is for you, my brother."

Henry shouted, "We got them boys on the run!"

Squire fired at a Reb running like the mountain was on fire, and he dropped. He said, "I hate shooting a man in the back."

Ben saw a young Reb turn and fire at him, but the shot missed. The Reb came at him with fixed bayonet, but Ben knocked it away and gave the soldier the bayonet before the Reb could get his knife. Ben remarked, "Please forgive me. Why didn't you surrender you dumb Johnny Reb? You can't be fifteen, darn't!"

Union units got mixed together, but they didn't care, because they weren't stopping until they had routed the enemy. They were like men possessed.

Around 4:30 pm, Gen Bragg's troops on Missionary Ridge were in a panic and retreating towards the east to South Chickamauga Creek. Gen Bragg was almost captured, but several of his staff officers were. Union forces had captured over 3,000 prisoners in the route.

The only Confederate divisions that didn't retreat in a panic belonged to Generals Cleburne, Cheatham, Gist, and Stevenson. They were ordered to withdraw and form Gen Bragg's rearguard.

Gen Bragg ordered his army to retreat towards Chickamauga Station during the night, and then, head towards Dalton, Georgia.

The Union army's casualties during its Chattanooga Campaign totaled a little over 5,800 men out of 56,000 men that took part in the battles. Confederate casualties were almost 6,700 men out of 44,000 men engaged.

The 10th Kentucky suffered two killed, ten wounded, and none captured or missing.

The 33rd Alabama suffered two casualties during the Chattanooga Campaign.

These men were awarded the Medal of Honor.

At the Battle of Missionary Ridge, Pvt Robert Brown from the 15th Ohio Infantry charged to the top of the ridge under heavy fire and captured the color bearer and flag of the 9th Mississippi Infantry.

Pvt Robert Brown

Also, eighteen year old 1Lt Arthur MacArthur, Jr. from the 24th Wisconsin Infantry seized his regimental flag, charged to the crest of Missionary Ridge, and planted the flag on the enemy works. His son, Gen Douglas MacArthur, was awarded the Medal of Honor during World War II.

1Lt Arthur MacArthur

Southern spirits were high after their victory at Chickamauga, but those spirits were smashed to pieces after the route on Missionary Ridge.

Missionary Ridge

CHAPTER 15

Now, the Union army had the monumental task of rescuing the wounded on the cliffs on Missionary Ridge.

Matt and Ben found the captain and asked, "Sir, can we get our wounded off those cliffs and boulders? I promised a corporal with a broken foot we'd come back and get him, and I'm a man of my word."

The captain responded, "Gather up as much rope as you can find from the Rebs to get started. Look and see if you can find any stretchers or anything to tie the wounded men on."

Matt asked, "Sir, do you think our stretcher-bearers below will start bringing down the wounded?"

"I should hope so!"

The four friends got busy finding ropes and anything they could use as a stretcher or back board.

Since one of Matt's hands had a nasty cut on the palm, he could only watch and use binoculars to guard the rescues.

Henry said, "Let's pull the closest men up, and the others we'll propel down to the bottom."

Squire added, "That makes sense to me."

Matt looked over the side and scanned the cliffs and boulders. There were several men less than 75 yards from them.

Several soldiers kept tying ropes together and nailing boards together to use as stretchers.

Ben propelled over the edge and worked his way to a soldier Matt had in sight. The man was wounded in the leg, so Ben tied rope around his chest and signaled the men to start pulling him up. The men pulled as a team straining with all their strength to get the soldier to the top.

Henry went over the side and worked his way over to another wounded soldier. He had been hit in the hip and side, so this required a stretcher. Squire went down to help Henry get the poor private tied to a stretcher. Matt yelled down that soldiers and stretcher-bearers were working at the bottom, as well.

Henry commented, "We'll start guiding him up, but we might not be able to go up."

Squire agreed, "If that is the case, then we guide him down as far as we can go and wait for the stretcher-bearers from the bottom."

Men in the company started pulling Henry and Squire in unison while they handled the stretcher.

Suddenly, Squire yelled, "Stop! We can't get him over this boulder! Slowly, move us over to our right! You move left! Everybody understand?"

Matt yelled down, "We got it, hardhead!"

Slowly, the rope gangs worked towards their left straining until sweat poured down their faces. When they were passed the boulder, the rope gangs started hauling them up.

Squire's feet were slipping, so he yelled, "Stop!"

Henry shouted, "There's a ledge about two feet up. Let the rope gangs pull you up to the ledge. Pull up about two feet and stop!"

Squire's feet found the ledge and yelled, "Stop! I need to catch my breath!"

Henry remarked, "We have to get these men off the cliffs before dark. We're running out of time!"

"I know, Henry! It'll be too cold for some of them to survive."

With a lot of hard work and luck, the rope gangs were bringing the wounded up as quickly as possible. After Henry, Ben, and Squire caught their breath and drank lots of water, they asked Matt had he found the injured corporal they left behind. Matt guided Ben to the spot; Ben studied the area, and blabbed, "Crap! He's about half way, and that boulder we moved isn't stable. In my opinion, it would be easier to take him down."

Matt suggested, "Take extra ropes with you, and we can drop your ropes down to you when you're secure for the next section to propel."

Henry responded, "That sounds good. There are plenty of trees and boulders we can tie our ropes to."

Ben asked, "What do you think you're doing?"

Matt answered, "I'll carry extra ropes with me, and I promise I won't get in the way."

Squire yelled, "Darn you, boy! I ought to blister your behind!"

Ben ordered, "We're losing daylight, so let's go!"

The rope gangs lowered the four men and a stretcher down until they reached the corporal.

Ben patted the corporal on the shoulder and said, "We ran them Rebs off the mountain for you!"

"That makes up for Chickamauga. I didn't think you'd come back for me."

Henry blabbed, "Shame on you, Corporal! When we say we're going to do something, we do it."

Squire added, "We're going to lower you down this ridge before it gets dark."

Matt asked, "Are you ready to get on the stretcher?"

"I'm ready."

They got to work getting the corporal secured on the stretcher, and Ben found a couple of sturdy trees and three boulders he thought would hold the weight.

The corporal commented, "I can hear men at the base working their way up rescuing the wounded."

Matt added, "We're hoping to meet up with them on the way down."

Ben suggested, "Matt and Squire, you watch the ropes and warn us if they don't hold. Henry and I will guide the stretcher."

Slowly, Ben, Henry, and the stretcher moved down the cliffs as loose stones peppered them here and there. Henry slipped and tore a hole in his britches, but was able to steady himself."

Ben teased, "I'm glad you have drawers on, so I don't have to look at your bare behind."

Henry blabbed, "I have you to know, I have the best looking behind in the company!"

Ben replied, "I wouldn't bet on it!"

When Ben and Henry went as far as they could go, Matt and Squire untied four of the ropes to be pulled down, and then Matt went down first and Squire followed on the fifth rope.

Again, they repeated the process and used one of Matt's extra ropes as the fifth rope. Ben and Henry started down with the stretcher, but they had to be real careful, because the rocks were very loose in this area.

Squire looked and yelled, "Matt, the tree is pulling up at the roots!"

Squire grabbed the rope and dug his heels into the rocks. Matt rushed over, grabbed him around the waist, and dug his heels into the rocks. The tree gave way and fell next to Matt and Squire. Both men held on for dear life straining every muscle in their bodies. They yelled down to warn Ben and Henry. Both men stopped and secured the stretcher and their position.

Henry asked, "What are we going to do? It's my rope that gave way."

Ben answered, "We'll see if they can find another place to secure it."

So, Ben yelled up and Matt assured him they could find another tree or boulder. Once the rope was anchored, Ben and Henry started down, again.

Squire commented, "I don't know if I can hold another rope if it gives way, because I'm exhausted!"

Matt added, "I think we'll make it. It can't be that much further."

Ben and Henry went down as far as they could go and secured the stretcher. Just then, Ben heard voices. He yelled, "Over here! We've brought down a stretcher! We need help!"

"What regiment you be with?"

Henry shouted, "The 10th Kentucky, and we have a corporal with a broken foot."

"Stay where you are Kentucky, we'll be right up."

Ben relayed the good news, so Matt told Squire to go down one rope, and he'd go down on another one. Squire made it down, and he promised himself he wasn't ever going mountain climbing ever again.

Matt made it half way down when his rope snapped into. He started sliding, and he fought to grab ahold of anything to stop his fall. Rocks and dirt were flying everywhere, and his shoes kept slipping in the loose ground. He grabbed a small tree, but it gave way. He grabbed a large rock sticking out, but it gave away, too. He saw a large boulder racing towards him, so he tried to grab it. As if in slow motion, his head hit the boulder, he saw stars, and everything went black.

Ben shouted, "Something is wrong, because this rope is slack! Sweet Jesus, the rope snapped!"

He called Matt's name several times, but there was no answer. He yelled, "Matt has to be in trouble, I'm going back up."

Just then, soldiers reached them, and Ben told them he was going back up to find his friend. The group put their heads together and came up with a plan.

Ben commented, "Dr. Waverly will kill me if I don't take care of his cousin!"

A stretcher-bearer remarked, "Sweet Jesus, you better get that boy off this mountain! Some of us will help you."

When they reached Matt, he was lying on a boulder unconscious. Shortly, Matt could feel someone holding him, but he couldn't seem to open his eyes or speak. He could hear voices all around him, and he wondered if he was still on the mountain. Then, he saw his beloved brother, Gordon, smile at him, and Gordon told him everything would be alright.

The stretcher-bearers rushed Matt to the hospital tent where Kramer was.

Ben yelled, "Jupiter get Dr. Waverly; it's Matt!"

Jupiter ran and got Kramer, and the two rushed to Matt's stretcher. Ben was telling them what happened, as Kramer examined his cousin. Jupiter followed orders from Kramer as the tandem worked together.

Kramer asked, "How long has Matt been unconscious?"

Ben answered, "When we got to him, he was out cold, but I have heard him moan a few times."

"That's good to know!"

Ben asked, "Is he going to be alright?"

Kramer smiled, winked, and said, "Matt is tough, and I'll work my magic."

Jupiter cleaned Matt's bloody head and hair. He said, "You might need to stitch this up, Doc."

"Oh yes, and I'll have to stitch his hand, too."

Kramer got Matt's jacket off and knew he had a broken arm, two fingers and a thumb to set.

Kramer looked at Ben and ordered, "You boys show me your hands."

Reluctantly, the men showed Kramer their hands which were seriously rope burned.

Kramer scolded, "Just what I thought. Sit down and let my hospital steward treat your hands and bandage them. I'll have meals brought in for you, because none of you are

going anywhere, so you might as well pick a cot for
yourself."

Ben replied, "Yes sir, Doc."

Jupiter asked, "How did you know de boy's hands looked
like that?"

"I caught a peek of Ben's hands. Rope burns can be nasty
wounds, and we don't want them to get infected. I admire
what those men did. They climbed those jagged cliffs to the
top and went back to rescue their wounded comrades in a
dangerous situation."

Jupiter added, "That be true devotion to de regiment and
caring about each other."

Kramer continued, "Alright Jupiter, let's take care of
Matt's injuries."

Jupiter added, "That poor boy be hurting plenty when he
wakes up. He's got lots of bruises and scrapes."

Matt thought, "Why do I hurt so badly? Where am I? I got
to get my eyes open. I remember, now, I'm on the mountain.
I got to get off this mountain, because it's cold, and I could
freeze to death! Help me!"

Jupiter jumped up and pushed Matt back on the pillow.
He comforted, "Mr. Matt, you is hurt. You be in the hospital
tent and Dr. Kramer fixed you up. Stay still and open your
eyes."

Matt blinked several times to get his eyes to focus, looked
at Jupiter, and declared, "You are a welcomed sight, good
friend. I hurt like the devil. What's wrong with me?"

Jupiter replied, "You gots a broken arm, thumb, and two
fingers. On top of that, you gots a nasty cut on your hand
and head."

"I feel like I fell down the whole mountain."

Jupiter giggled and replied, "Jest about!"

"I'm thirsty and starving."

Jupiter got up and responded, "I'll take care of that for
you! I'll be letting Dr. Kramer know you be awake."

"How are my friends and that corporal?"

"They have some rope burns, and de corporal has a broken ankle. They all goin' to be alright! Now, stays still and rest. I'll be back real quick!"

Matt sure didn't want to get up, because his head was pounding and even his behind hurt. When he sneezed, he thought he was going to die right there in the bed. He thought, "I ain't doing that again anytime soon. I don't want my tombstone to read, "He died sneezing!"

Kramer reached down and patted Matt on the shoulder and said, "You sure lost that fight with the mountain, but you didn't crack your head wide open."

"That's good to know! Boy am I glad to see you and Jupiter!"

Kramer answered, "We are more than glad to see you. You'll be here a few days, and then I'll move you to Chattanooga. If you continue to improve, I'll send you to my clinic on a 45-day medical furlough. Dr. Mills will send you home to finish recovering. Of course, that means you'll be home for Christmas."

"That's the best Christmas present you'll ever give me."

"I'm going to do my best to make it happen, because you need some female loving and attention."

"Listen to you! Cousin, you need to wrap your arms around Maddie until her corset pops!"

"I'm going to kiss her until her eyelashes catch fire!"

"We better shut up before we attack the first female we see!"

"You're right! I don't want some woman to kick my behind into the Tennessee River."

"I want to see that redheaded sweetheart I left behind. I might even ask her to marry me."

"I know one thing for sure. Maddie and I are going to get married as soon as I can get a furlough."

"Maybe, we could get furlough together."

"I'm going to work on that, for sure."

"Do you know where the Rebs are?"

"The last I heard they were retreating towards the northwest part of Georgia. I keep wondering if the 33rd Alabama is headed that way."

"Our division didn't fight Gen Cleburne's boys. They were around Tunnel Hill."

"You know, Matt, when the twins beat me to a pulp, they destroyed any love I had for them. However, I love Michael and Sally, dearly."

"I feel the same way. I guess the good book tells us to forgive the twins, but I'm having a hard time doing that."

"I guess I can forgive them, but I'll never respect or trust them, again. I don't plan on being around them."

"I hope I never see them on the battlefield, because I don't want to be around them, either."

Faces of the Civil War

CHAPTER 16

Gen Hooker was ordered to pursue the Rebel army, but a burned out bridge slowed his progress. By the night of November 26th and November 27th, Gen Hooker camped not too far from Ringgold Gap with his 12,000 troops.

The 10th Kentucky, along with its brigade, marched to Chickamauga Creek and waited for the bridge to be built over the creek. After about two hours, they arrived at Ringgold around midnight.

On November 28th, the brigade was ordered to destroy four bridges and track on the railroad three miles south of Ringgold. The following day the brigade was ordered back to Chattanooga.

Many of the men didn't have blankets, socks, shirts, and were low on rations, so, they were glad to get back to Chattanooga. The railroads were moving supplies to Gen Grant's Army, so the men were able to get the items they needed as well as food.

Gen Bragg ordered Gen Cleburne's 4,100 man division to hold Ringgold Gap at all costs until the Confederate artillery and wagon trains could get through the gap.

Around 3:00 am on November 27th, Gen Cleburne put Col Hiram Granbury's Brigade on the right side of the gap entrance. Opposite to Granbury was the 16th Alabama Infantry on the left side. Gen Cleburne placed the rest of his division inside the gap for support. His troops concealed themselves as best as they could and waited for Cleburne's signal to ambush the enemy troops.

The 33rd Alabama, part of the 45th Alabama, and some cavalry commanded by Gen Joseph Wheeler were left at Chickamauga Creek to skirmish with Union forces in order to slow them down. They were to fire a volley, withdraw a

short distance, fire another volley, and keep repeating the
process until they reached Ringgold Gap.

Albert asked, "Where is our brigade? Don't tell me they
skedaddled and left us with no support?"

A captain appeared at the mouth of the entrance and
ordered, "Join the rest of your brigade in the center on White
Oak Ridge."

Michael asked, "Where is everybody?"

He replied, "They're concealed in the rocks and trees, so
hurry before the Yankees enter the gap!"

The 33rd Alabama had just gotten into position when the
first Union troops entered the gap.

Austin licked his lips and thought, "Easy! Let them move
closer! We'll greet you with a curtain of fire!"

Around 8:00 am, the Yankees were within 50 yards when
Gen Cleburne gave the order to fire. The Yankees were
taken by surprise by the murderous musket and artillery
fire. The Yanks fell back, regrouped, and attacked trying to
turn Cleburne's right flank where the 33rd Alabama was
located.

The Rebel officers spurred their men on as Union
casualties piled one on top of the other face down. The
Union dead were piled from the bottom of the gap to the top
of the hill. Gen Hooker kept feeding one regiment after
another into the jaws of death. His army was four times
larger than Gen Cleburne's men, but he was unable to turn
either flank. Some Rebel regiments ran out of ammunition,
so they threw rocks down on the men in blue,

Around noon, Gen Cleburne received word from Gen
Bragg to withdraw, because the artillery and wagons were
safely through the gap. Slowly, Gen Cleburne fell back
leaving some skirmishers to conceal the withdrawal. Gen

Patrick Cleburne held the enemy at bay for five hours, so the army could escape.

Cleburne ordered his men to burn the bridge east of the gap. His command had suffered twenty killed and two hundred wounded. On the other side, Gen Hooker had lost 509 men killed or wounded. All those lives were lost when Gen Hooker could have waited for the Confederates to withdraw, or hit Gen Cleburne's position with a lot more men.

Gen Bragg took out his frustrations on Gen John Breckinridge claiming the general was drunk from November 23rd to November 27th. He relieved Breckinridge from command, and Bragg resigned on December 1st leaving Gen William Hardee in command until President Jefferson Davis could appoint a new commander of the Army of Tennessee.

Kramer walked over to Matt's bed where Jupiter was helping him bathe.

"I have good news to tell both of you."

Matt teased, "You just got busted to private!"

Kramer laughed and replied, "All three of us are going on furlough together starting tomorrow."

Jupiter shouted, "Praise de Lord! Miracles does happen!"

Matt's chin quivered, tears collected in his eyes, and he couldn't seem to speak. He was so weary, and he wanted his mother and father to just hold him in their arms. Here he was a grown man wanting something his parents had done for him when he was a young boy. He wanted his sister, Tess, to tease him about anything. Watching his family put up a Christmas tree would be a golden experience to him.

Kramer asked, "Are you in pain, Matt?"

He struggled to find the words, but he couldn't seem to answer. He gave up and burst into tears. Kramer took his cousin in his arms, told Matt to let his emotions go, because everybody needed to have a good cry, now and then.

Kramer comforted Matt and said, "You haven't had time to grieve for Gordon or relax since Chickamauga. You need to grieve, so your emotions and soul can heal. Don't be afraid to cry."

Jupiter added, "Mr. Matt, lots of de soldiers cry when we be taking care of them. They be privates all the way up to colonels. Fightin' be hard on all de soldiers!"

Kramer suggested, "Cry all you want to, cousin!"

Finally, Matt said, "I bet neither one of you cries like a baby."

Kramer responded, "That's not true. When you told me Gordon was gone, we fell apart and cried our eyes out. Later, I fell apart and cried in my tent that night. I cried when I lost a drummer boy, because I couldn't save him."

Matt asked, "What about you, Jupiter?"

"Dr. Kramer and me cried together when de drummer boy died. I got me a big stick and kept beating de devil out of a tree till de stick broke."

Matt responded, "That makes me feel better, but what are we going to do when we get home? I know I'll break down, again."

Kramer suggested, "Go ahead and cry. Both of us will bawl like babies, too."

The train carrying the wounded pulled into the Louisville station. There was a mob of people waiting to see their loved ones. Some soldiers were able to go home to recuperate, some were going to the Union hospital, and ten were headed to Dr. Mills's and Kramer's clinic.

Eleanor asked, "Do you see them, Edwin?"

"Not yet."

Madeline added, "I haven't seen them, either. Is this the right train?"

"It sure is."

Zeke commented, "I just want to see my boy!"

Sophie added, "I want to hold him in my arms for two days before I let go."

Edwin caught sight of them and yelled, "There they are coming out of the fourth rail car!"

Eleanor shouted her son's name and pushed through the crowd along with the others frantically trying to reach them.

Jupiter helped Matt down the steps, and Kramer scanned the crowd looking for the people who meant the most to him. When he saw Maddie, his heart jumped into his throat. She was even more beautiful, now. He thought, "How can that be?"

Eleanor and Edwin plowed through the waiting people like they were possessed. They broke through and nothing could stop them. All of them burst into tears when they got to their loved ones. Eleanor took Matt into her arms being careful not to hurt his broken arm. Matt buried his head in his mother's hair and wept.

Zeke and Sophie grabbed their son and all three burst into tears. Now, Jupiter felt safe and very much loved.

Maddie launched herself into Kramer's arms, he held her close, and planted a kiss on her lips Maddie would never forget.

"Don't ever stop kissing me like that, Rascal!"

"Your lips need to be kissed like that, Honey!"

"I pray every night that you'll come home to me."

"I do the same thing, my precious Maddie."

"I heard someone call you major. Have you been promoted?"

"Yes, I was promoted a few weeks ago."

"Congratulations!"

"I'd say that deserves another kiss from you, Honey!"

Maddie planted a lights out kiss on Kramer that turned his teeth upside down.

"Madeline Sawyer, you are a tiger in disguise!"

"And you, Kramer Waverly, are a rascal!"

"That's my middle name, woman."

Laura and Isabelle are covering for me, so I could meet you at the train."

"I'll make sure to do something special for them. I better hug Aunt Eleanor before she pulls my ear off."

Kramer and Maddie made their way over to Edwin, Eleanor, and Matt. With tears flowing down her cheeks, Eleanor hugged Kramer and said, "You'll never know how grateful I am that you and Jupiter took care of my boy. You three rascals will always have a special place in my heart."

Edwin continued, "We're mighty proud of you three fellers. Why don't we get into our carriages and go home where it's warm?"

Matt mentioned, "I hope there's some good food waiting for us, because we're all starved."

Sophie chimed in, "I think we can find a few crumbs to feed you boys!"

Kramer looked at Maddie and said, "Snuggle up close, Sweet Maddie, so we can stay warm."

She shot back, "Mind your manners, Rascal, or I'll have to beat you over the head."

"Ouch, but my head can take it!"

Eleanor chimed in, "That's a fact, Maddie, because Kramer has a very hard head!"

They all laughed and enjoyed the ride to Edwin's home. When they stepped inside, the house was warm, and the aroma of good food slapped the friends in the face like a tidal wave.

Jupiter blabbed, "That be food, so let me at it!"

Just then, Myrtle stepped through the door and ordered, "Nobody invades the dining room until all the food is set out. If you worthless scandals charge the room, I'll take this here skillet upside your heads!"

Kramer shouted, "Sweetie Pie is that you?"

"Of course it is, you fool!"

He shouted, "I'm coming over there and give you a big kiss."

Myrtle warned, "That's fine, but you ain't getting passed me, you ornery rascal!"

He replied, "I wouldn't dream of it!"

Kramer landed a big kiss on her cheek and decided to behave himself. Matt and Jupiter gave her a big kiss too and decided not to rush the dining room.

Myrtle fired back, "Don't think all these kisses are going to get you scandals any special favors! Rosie, Madeline, Eleanor, and I are going to set the table, so sit down and shut up until we're ready."

Maddie blabbed, "I don't know what's happened to those three varmints, but they better mind their manners if they want to eat."

Myrtle agreed, "Amen, brothers and sisters!"

Jupiter shouted, "We be real good!"

Rosie added, "Amen to that, too!"

Jupiter kissed Rosie's cheek, winked, and said, "It's so good to see ya'll!"

Rosie spun around, looked back, and said, "Don't try to sweet talk me, Jupiter!"

The four women marched back to the kitchen at the double-quick, so they could set out dinner.

Edwin commented, "I don't know what has happened to all those women. They act like they ate some loco weed."

The other men laughed until their sides were ready to burst.

Finally, Kramer was able to say, "Don't worry, Uncle Edwin, the weed should wear off soon."

Edwin chimed back, "I wish I knew where they are hiding it, so I can dump it in the fireplace."

Matt fired back, "Don't do that, Poppa, because I like the show!"

Edwin answered, "But I'm around it all the time!"

Matt went on, "Poppa, sometimes you have to make sacrifices, because of the war."

"Well, by the time the war is over, I'll be crazier than a bed bug eating that weed."

Zeke promised, "Don't worry, Mr. Edwin, I'll takes real good care of ya'll."

Kramer jumped in, "I think it's all Myrtle's fault, because she's a bad influence on the other women! It has to be a woman thing!"

Matt shot back, "Ya, cousin! Mama wasn't like this until Myrtle got her hooks into her. She's putting crazy ideas in Mama's head!"

Jupiter asked, "What air we goin' to do about it?"

Edwin answered, "Nothing, if we want to eat!"

Zeke shouted, "Amen, brothers and sisters!"

Shortly, Myrtle came out and said, "Alright, you pack of crazy squirrels, dinner is served! Remember to mind your manners, because I know the army hasn't taught you any."

Matt shouted, "I hope there's plenty to eat!"

Myrtle yelled, "You are already complaining, so you best be thankful for anything that's on the table!"

Matt replied, "I'm sorry, Myrtle. I wasn't thinking."

Myrtle fired back, "You don't have a brain to think with, rock head!"

Kramer shot back, "Matt has a brain, because I checked when I treated him."

Myrtle responded, "Neither one of you has a brain between you! Now shut up and sit down at the table."

It was all the boys could do to keep their hands off the food before it was blessed. They had gone hungry so many times over the last two years.

Myrtle ordered, "Alright, Edwin, bless this food good and proper before these boys go nuts looking at it. Fire away, man!"

Once the food was blessed, the feeding frenzy started. This was like old times during the Christmas holiday season.

The men leaned back in their chairs stuffed to the gills. They couldn't eat as much as they used to, because their stomachs were used to short rations or none at all.

Kramer apologized, "We're sorry, Aunt Eleanor, but we just can't eat a lot."

Eleanor mentioned, "All of you have lost weight, so I guess you'll have to eat more often. We have to put some weight back on you."

Kramer answered, "I believe that plan will work better."

Matt spoke up, "We want to thank all you ladies for a wonderful meal. The food is heaven compared to our rations."

Myrtle blabbed, "If you thought this food tasted like rations, I'd pull all your hair out!"

Kramer teased, "Sweetie Pie, you wouldn't do that to me!"

She fired back, "I'd pull half your hair out!"

Maddie suggested, "Rascal, she's going to win this boxing match with you!"

He conceded, "I surrender! You're right!"

Edwin asked, "Kramer, what are your plans for the clinic and Matt?"

"Matt will need to stay at the clinic as long as he needs medication, help to bathe, and help to dress himself. We have to be very careful with his broken arm and injured hand."

Sophie commented, "Mr. Matt needs to get well with de folks who love him."

Myrtle blabbed, "If he doesn't, I'll break one of his legs!"

Jupiter added, "Well Mr. Matt, you better gits well, because General Myrtle jest gave you de order."

He declared, "One thing for sure, Myrtle will court-martial me, if I don't."

Zeke chimed in, "Amen, brothers and sisters!"

Eleanor asked, "Are you staying here or at the clinic, Kramer?"

"I'll be at the clinic for a few days, because I have three cases that I need to watch closely."

She added, "I packed a box of your civilian clothes and some other items for you, if you need them."

"That will be just fine. Thank you very much."

Sophie asked, "De important question is, when is you and Miss Madeline going to get hitched?"

"We haven't had time to set a date, but we'll let you know tomorrow."

Myrtle blabbed, "Look at you, Madeline, you're blushing!"

She answered, "The question kind of caught me off guard."

Myrtle ordered, "Make up your mind, so we can get things organized. All of us are really excited about your wedding!"

Kramer teased, "Just think, Myrtle, I'll be part of your family!"

She fired back, "All families have a skunk in their closet, so we'll lock you up and throw away the key."

"Maddie will rescue me, Sweetie Pie!"

"Then, I'll lock both of you up in the closet!"

Maddie declared, "We can have some fun in the closet!"

Kramer stuck his tongue out and teased, "We won that boxing match, Sweetie Pie!"

Myrtle shot back, "The match was two against one. I'll get you the next time, Rascal! Alright ladies, let's clear the table, clean up, and I'll make up three plates the boys can take with you."

Jupiter replied, "Bless you, Ms. Myrtle, that be jest fine!"

Kramer suggested, "Make up a plate for Dr. Mills, if you can!"

Myrtle stomped into the kitchen fussing a mile a minute. All the boys knew what Kramer was trying to do. Every time Dr. Mills' name came up around Myrtle she went into a

186

fussing fit ready to do battle with the romance gods. Oh yes, Kramer got her all riled up, for sure!

Kramer looked at Matt and knew his cousin was getting tired and uncomfortable from the pain, so he asked, "Uncle Edwin, can you take us to the clinic, so I can get Matt settled down for the night?"

"Of course, I will."

When the group got to the clinic, Laura and Dr. Mills hugged and kissed their loved ones.

Laura declared, "I've been beside myself waiting for you to get here. I want to hug you and never let you go my dearest brother and cousin."

"Don't forget, Maddie has to hug on me, too!"

"Okay, we can take turns!"

"Help me get Matt settled, because he's hurting and worn out."

Dr. Mills said, "I'll get him something for pain."

Sammy ran up, saluted Kramer, and said, "Welcome home, sir!"

Kramer hugged the boy and remarked, "Thank you for doing such a good job at the clinic. I'm real proud of you."

Sammy stated, "I'll take real good care of Mr. Matt, so just tell me what I need to do. Mr. Matt, follow me, because I have a nice clean bed waiting for you."

Dr. Mills looked at Kramer and announced, "Sammy is the boss around here, and he even tells Myrtle what to do."

Matt fired back, "You must be joking!"

Laura continued, "It's no joke, because he even tells me what to do. That boy has been a godsend. He has such an uncanny way about him that demands respect. The soldiers love him, and they never give him any sass."

Dr. Mills commented, "Sometimes, I just watch him in disbelief, because he's like a guardian angel to our patients."

Kramer asked, "How old is Sammy?"

"He's thirteen."

"I hope he doesn't get it in his mind to run off and join the army."

Laura responded, "All of us tell him every day how important he is to us and the soldiers."

Kramer commented, "I'll make sure I tell him the same thing, because we can't afford to lose him."

Before Edwin and Madeline were ready to leave, Kramer got Maddie aside and said, "Whenever you want to get married, it's fine with me. I just want to savor every moment we have together during my furlough."

Maddie suggested, "Then, we'll have more time together if we get married before Christmas. We can spend our first Christmas together as an old married couple."

He smiled, winked, and agreed, "Then, I vote we become an old married couple."

Edwin remarked, "Kramer, I'll be by to pick you up tomorrow around 10:00 am, because we have some business we need to take care of as soon as possible."

He inquired, "What kind of business?"

Edwin smiled and replied, "It's kind of like a surprise. Alright Madeline, let me get you back home before Myrtle rips my head off and throws it in the outhouse!"

The following day Edwin picked Kramer up from the clinic and gave his nephew an envelope as they sat in the carriage. As Kramer read the letter, his mouth dropped open in disbelief, because the letter was from a lawyer representing John Avery, a member of their church.

Kramer inquired, "I don't understand this, Uncle Edwin. Why did he leave me his home? Didn't he have family to leave it to?"

"No, he didn't have any living relatives to leave it to. As you can see from the letter, he believed you could use a home like that for yourself or for the clinic."

"Where is the home?"

"It's a block over on the corner. The lawyer was kind enough to leave me a key, so Carl has been staying there to look after it until you decide what you want to do with the place."

"Now, you have my curiosity up, so let's take a look."

"As you know from the letter, everything in the home and on the grounds is yours, too."

"Uncle Edwin, I'm in shock! Does it need a lot of work to fix it up?"

"Let's find out, but it can't be that bad if Carl is staying there."

When Edwin stopped the carriage, Kramer's eyeballs just about fell in his lap, because it was so beautiful! The home had two stories with an L-shaped front porch. It even had a white picket fence around the grounds.

When Kramer opened the door, he was flabbergasted, again. The furniture was grand and almost like brand new. The first floor had a spacious living room, dining room, kitchen, coat-tub room, and two bedrooms. A spiral staircase led up to the second floor where there were four bedrooms.

Kramer commented, "I still don't understand this. Mr. Avery owned a lumber mill, his wife and youngest son died from typhoid fever, and his oldest son died from the measles before his regiment finished training in 1861. Didn't his wife have any family to leave the home to?"

"According to the lawyer, she had no living relatives, either."

Kramer pulled sheets off the furniture in the upstairs bedrooms. "My Lord, look how beautiful the furniture is! There are beds, dressers, chests, wash stands, and linens."

"Carl said he went around the house dusting, cleaning up the kitchen, and cleaning up the grounds."

"That was wonderful of him!"

"There's a carriage house in the back of the home complete with a carriage. Carl says Mr. Avery boards a couple of horses at the livery not far from here."

Kramer asked, "Does Maddie know about this?"

"No, because Carl and Myrtle believe this home will be a perfect wedding present."

"Maddie is going to faint when she sees this! Why did he leave it to me?"

"Because you were always good to him, and he admired your work at the clinic."

The men went back down stairs, and Kramer wandered over to the china cabinet. "Look at this! There are dishes, glasses, silverware, table linens, and beautiful candlesticks. Maddie isn't going to believe her eyes!"

Edwin inquired, "Do you want the house?"

"Of course, I do!"

"Then, let's go over to the lawyer's office and sign the paperwork, so the deal will be final and all legal."

Kramer was floating on air as he signed the papers and got the keys from Edwin. He would never forget this strange event in his life, and he couldn't wait until Maddie saw this wonderful gift from a very remarkable man. Destiny could sure hit you between the eyes when you least expected it.

Edwin dropped Kramer off at the clinic, he went to his office, closed the door, and wept. "I should be very happy, so why am I crying? Since the war has started, my tears were from sadness, death, and despair, so I'm just not used to tears of joy."

Laura knocked on Kramer's door, because he usually didn't close the door and stay in his office that long. She opened his door and caught Kramer wiping his eyes.

"What's wrong, Kramer?"

"Nothing is wrong, Laura. I just lost control of my emotions."

He told his sister the incredible story, and she was shocked, too. "That's wonderful! Mr. Avery was a kindhearted man. Both of you deserve something special, and I agree with Uncle Edwin, Myrtle, and Carl. The home will be your wedding present and honeymoon palace all in one!"

"I know Maddie will faint when she sees it!"

"Just make sure you catch her!"

Kramer inquired, "How are things going with your marine?"

"He's been assigned to the *USS Lackawanna* on duty along the Mississippi River. Recently, he was promoted to sergeant and misses me very much."

"I think Warren is a fine man, and I know you love him very much."

"I do, just like you love Madeline."

"I wish Poppa and Mama could come to our wedding and see how special Maddie is. I wish they could have met Warren, so they would know how happy you are."

"I hate not knowing how they are, and what's happening with the twins, Michael, and Sally. We don't even know if the boys are still alive."

Kramer mentioned, "I ask every wounded Confederate prisoner if they know our brothers, but I haven't had any luck. I wonder if the slaves have left Evergreen Manor leaving only Poppa, Mama, and Sally there to do all the work. I have no doubt that Poppa will do whatever it takes to survive the war, but I'm still worried about them."

"Well, the only thing we can do is pray they will be safe. Tell me about Matt's hand, because I've noticed he has a lot of trouble moving his fingers."

"I'm afraid he might lose movement in two or three of his fingers. I did everything I could to repair tendons. Matt is very lucky to be alive, because falling down Missionary Ridge unconscious almost killed him. His friends found him lying on top of a large boulder just a few inches from the edge. He was that close to falling to his death."

"Our army is in winter quarters, but where do you think they'll head in the spring?"

"Atlanta is a very important railroad center serving the Lower South. That's where we'll head."

"Do you think our army will attack Montgomery?"

"I don't know, but I'm sure Mobile will be under the gun."

"That means Warren could be involved since Mobile is a port."

"He could be, but let's enjoy my furlough and not discuss the war for a while."

"You're right!"

"I'm going to make my rounds and pick Maddie up. Should I take her over to the house?"

"If it were me, I'd love to see it as soon as possible. Aunt Eleanor and Sophie have made Maddie a gorgeous wedding gown as a present to her, and don't you dare tell her about it!"

"I'll keep it a secret. Today, we'll pick a date for the wedding, because I want to return to the regiment a married man."

"I have to admit I'm very excited about the wedding. Maddie is a wonderful woman full of love. Now, let's get your rounds over with."

When Kramer picked Maddie up, it was all he could do to keep the secret under wraps just a little longer.

Maddie commented, "You sure are mighty happy, Rascal! What's going on?"

He answered, "Maddie, my dear, you are in for a surprise of a lifetime."

"Let me see. You bought this carriage and horse we're riding in."

"Sorry, I'm using Dr. Mills' carriage today!"

He stopped the buggy in front of the home, helped Maddie get down, and opened the door to the house.

She asked, "Who lives here?"

"Well, your father is right now until we get married. This is our new home, Maddie!"

She screamed, grabbed ahold of Kramer like a grizzly bear, and kissed every inch of his face ten times. Maddie ran over to the sofa, ran her hand over it and said, "I've never seen such gorgeous furniture! The mantel on the fireplace has got to be marble! Oh Rascal, this is like a palace for a king and queen!" Suddenly, she stopped, put her hands on her hips, and declared, "I can't let you spend all your money to buy us a home as grand as this."

Kramer proceeded to tell her how they became owners of this wonderful home. She stood there with her hands on her cheeks in complete shock and amazement.

He asked, "Are you alright, Maddie?"

She burst into tears and launched herself into his arms. "I can't believe all this is ours!"

He suggested, "Look at the china cabinet, Honey."

She opened up the doors and shouted, "Everything is so elegant!"

He inquired, "Do you like the dishes and the other things?"

"How could one not love them?"

Maddie explored all the rooms in total amazement, and Kramer couldn't help but laugh at how excited she could get. While they were upstairs, he suggested, "Do you want to take a look in the attic?"

She nodded, so he pulled down the steps. He went up first and poked his head above the floor. He scanned around the good size attic and said, "There are a few trunks, a sewing machine, a desk, two baby cradles, and two chairs up here."

He crawled over to one trunk, opened it, and shouted, "Oh Maddie, these things look like they go on a Christmas tree. Another trunk has toys in it, and this trunk has baby clothes in it."

Kramer reached down and picked up a box and opened it. "Maddie look inside this box!"

She opened it and exclaimed, "It's a jewelry box, so these things must have belonged to Mrs. Avery. Can I keep this, Rascal?"

"Of course, you can! Everything in this house belongs to us, now! I think the two chairs go to the dining room table."

"I think you're right."

"It's getting cold, Honey. Let's head over to Aunt Eleanor's place to warm up and explore the jewelry box."

"I agree. Oh Rascal, a Christmas tree would be beautiful in front of the spiral staircase."

"Then, we'll put one up, Sweetheart! I'll ask your father to help me bring down the things in the attic, so we'll know what we can use."

"I hope the sewing machine works."

"If it doesn't, I'll buy you one for Christmas."

The couple stayed in excited conversation all the way to Eleanor's home. Once inside, the couple sat around the fireplace looking at the jewelry. The box contained several hair pins, three necklaces, five brooches, and four rings. Maddie could wear three of the rings, but the other one was too small, so she figured Tess could probably wear it.

Maddie's mind was spinning a mile a minute trying to soak everything in. How could anybody be this lucky? There was so much she and Kramer wanted to do while he was home.

The couple chose December 22nd to get married, so that gave the ladies enough time to organize the church service and party afterwards. Also, it gave Kramer and Carl time to empty the attic, stock the home, and put up a Christmas tree to surprise Maddie. The couple would decorate the tree on their honeymoon.

Kramer shopped around and started buying Christmas and wedding gifts. The sewing machine didn't work, so he bought one for Maddie. He remembered the necklaces from the jewelry box had red, green, and purple stones. He couldn't remember what the stones were called, but he found an angel necklace he liked that would be perfect for his soon to be wife.

Kramer was concerned about Maddie living in their home by herself once he left to go back to his regiment. Carl and Sammy agreed to stay with Madeline until he came home for good. Even Rosie said she'd stay with her as much as she could.

Finally, December 22nd arrived, and Kramer was standing at the altar with Matt and Jupiter. He was so nervous he wanted to scream. When his dear Maddie started down the aisle with her father, she took his breath away. Eleanor and Sophie had created a gorgeous wedding gown making his Maddie look like an angel. He kept fighting back tears as the couple exchanged their vows. Maddie prayed her knees wouldn't buckle, because, she would be a bawling mess. She would be so embarrassed she'd just die!

Suddenly, they were kissing as husband and wife! She couldn't believe how lucky she was. The couple greeted their family and friends at the banquet, opened gifts, and cut their wedding cake. It was such a magical time for them.

When it was time to leave, Jupiter and Matt brought the carriage around to drive them to their new home. Edwin and Carl had the fireplaces in the living room and master bedroom going strong. The couple was all set to spend their honeymoon together for several days. The Christmas tree was up for them to decorate whenever they wanted.

Kramer reached in his pocket and pulled out his wedding present for his wife. Tears ran down her cheeks as her finger touched the angel. He said, "This angel necklace is for my angel." He put the necklace around her neck and kissed her forehead.

She gave Kramer a pocket watch to replace the one he lost during the Battle of Chickamauga. He would always treasure the engraved words saying, "Come back to me, Rascal!"

As night surrounded the couple, they noticed an envelope on a pillow on their bed. Kramer read the outside that said, "If you need instructions, Sweetie Pie, open the envelope!"

Maddie said, "Let's open it anyway. I know my aunt did something silly."

Kramer looked inside and shouted, "It's empty!"

The couple burst out laughing and let Mother Nature take her course. It was more beautiful than either one expected it could be. As the couple held each other and drifted off to sleep, the war seemed very far away on that cold December night.

While the couple honeymooned locked away in their paradise, Jupiter and Matt were experiencing romance, too.

The redheaded Isabelle was a volunteer nurse at the clinic, so she learned what she needed to do to help Matt recover. Between Isabelle and Sammy, Matt was receiving the best of care. Both worked with Matt to move his fingers and walk to regain his strength. They made sure Matt ate more often, so he could gain some weight back. Isabelle cut his hair, and Sammy shaved his beard off. For some reason, it made him feel clean and very far from the front.

Jupiter and Rosie spent a lot of time together talking about everything. He really enjoyed helping her and her parents decorate their home for Christmas. Of course, the couple helped his parents do the same thing.

He dropped by the clinic just to visit Matt and the other soldiers, because he needed time away from the wounded and sick soldiers. He had looked upon the carnage at the Gates of Hades, and he wanted to erase as much horror from his mind as possible. Many times, he wondered how Kramer could stay so focused surrounded by insanity and blood.

Civil war coffee maker

CHAPTER 17

For the 33rd Alabama, they wouldn't be home for Christmas. After the Battle of Missionary Ridge, Gen Grant sent Gen Sherman's troops to capture the railroad junction at Meridan, Mississippi. The new commander of the Confederate Army of Tennessee ordered two divisions, including Gen Cleburne's Division, to march to Meridan. However, the Rebel troops were recalled when they reached West Point, Alabama, because Gen Joseph Johnston was concerned about the hit and run attacks Gen Thomas was launching along the Confederate lines.

When Gen Cleburne's men returned, they were ordered to set up their position along a creek east of the town of Dalton, Georgia. They were to dig trenches between their new location and their old camp.

Austin complained, "All we do is chase after the Yanks, and then get called back, so we did all that marching for nothing!"

Albert joined in, "Now, we dig trenches, build fortifications, and wait for spring."

Michael asked, "So, the Yanks are sending Gen Grant to the East. Who replaces him?"

Austin answered, "Rumors around camp say Gen Sherman gets it. The Yanks must think Grant can defeat Gen Robert E. Lee."

Albert suggested, "That's not going to happen."

Michael wondered, "I'm surprised they didn't pick Gen Thomas."

Austin commented, "It doesn't matter, because Gen Johnston will beat them."

Albert remarked, "It makes me mad we can't get a furlough to go home for Christmas!"

Austin blabbed, "Poor thing, you want to see your wife and son."

Albert fired back, "I love my wife and son. I want to see them and hold them in my arms."

Michael chimed in, "I miss Poppa, Mama, and Sally, plus I want some home cooking."

Austin responded, "I hope Sally keeps her big mouth shut!"

Michael commented, "Sally expresses her opinions like Mama, so there's nothing bad about that."

Austin fired back, "She'll end up an old maid with a big mouth!"

Albert ordered, "Shut up, Austin! If anyone has a big mouth, it's you!"

Michael jumped in, "Does anyone want some chitterlings? They taste real good!"

Albert replied, "Sure, I'll try some."

Austin fired back, "I can't believe you two would eat pig intestines, because that's slave food! Michael, you act like a slave most of the time, and you are so stupid!"

Albert jumped in, "Austin go somewhere else, so we can enjoy these chitterlings all fried up in flour."

Austin stomped off and thought, "I'm going to get rid of you soon, Albert. Maybe, the Yanks will kill Michael, because he's one stupid boy."

The time came for Kramer and Jupiter to return to their regiment. At the railroad station tears flowed, because the families of the men didn't want them to leave. Maddie held her husband tightly as she wept. Their honeymoon and Christmas had been so special, and she loved Kramer, dearly, with all her being. She was praying he would come back to her, because they had so many things they wanted to do which included starting a family.

It just about broke Kramer's heart to leave his crying wife behind. Their time together was so magical and more than he could ever imagine.

Jupiter and Rosie held each other, affectionately, as she wiped away tears. When he came home the next time, they planned on getting married. Jupiter gave her a necklace that represented his love for her, and he wanted Rosie to be very sure she loved him.

Both Kramer and Jupiter decided not to re-enlist when their three years were up in December 1864. Kramer wanted to return to the clinic to help Dr. Mills, because so many soldiers needed long term care, especially, the amputees.

Jupiter wanted to return to the freight company, because Mr. Edwin needed the help. He would need time to find a place to live with Rosie, because many white folks wouldn't accept a colored couple living next to them. Colored folk were fighting for their freedom and acceptance among the whites, but they would have to fight the prejudice that still remained.

As the train pulled out of the station, Maddie shouted, "Please come back to me, Rascal!"

He shouted through the window, "I will, Darling!"

Rosie shouted, "You comes back to me, Jupiter. You hear me!"

He replied, "I will, because we be gitting married when I gits back!"

Maddie held Eleanor and wept along with Tess and Laura. Sophie held Rosie as they both cried.

This scene would be repeated when Matt returned to his regiment after his medical furlough was over.

When Gen Grant left for the Eastern Theater, he ordered Gen Sherman to defeat Gen Johnston's Confederate Army, capture Atlanta, and drive through Georgia to the Atlantic coast. Gen Nathaniel Banks was ordered to capture Mobile, Alabama.

Gen Ulysses Grant   Gen Nathaniel Banks

Gen Grant gave Gen Sherman command of three Union armies in the Western Theater. The first was the Army of the Tennessee commanded by Gen James McPherson. The second was the Army of the Ohio commanded by Gen John Schofield. The third was the Army of the Cumberland commanded by Gen George Thomas.

Gen James McPherson   Gen John Schofield

By June 1864, Gen Sherman would have an army of 112,000 men to lead. He would stay near the railroads, so his army could receive supplies. He decided not to charge into the well-entrenched fortifications put up by Gen Johnston, but to strike and march around the enemy's flank moving closer and closer to Atlanta. He would use the same technique that Gen Grant would use in the East against Gen Robert E. Lee.

The 10th Kentucky's effective men were 16 officers and 420 enlisted men by May 1864. The regiment remained in the Army of the Cumberland commanded by Gen George Thomas. They were assigned to the XIV Corps commanded by Gen John Palmer. They still remained in the 3rd Brigade commanded by Col George Este who replaced Col Edward Phelps who was killed at Missionary Ridge, and the 3rd Division commanded by Gen Absalom Baird. The 10th Kentucky continued to serve with the 38th and 14th Ohio, the 10th Indiana and the 74th Indiana in the brigade.

Gen John Palmer   Gen Absalom Baird

Opposing Gen Sherman's Army would be Gen Joseph Johnston's Army made up of four corps. The three infantry corps were commanded by Gen William Hardee, Gen John Bell Hood, Gen Leonidas Polk, and a cavalry corps commanded by Gen Joseph Wheeler. After receiving reinforcements from Alabama, Johnston's army would total 65,000 men.

Gen John Bell Hood Gen Mark Lowrey

The 33rd Alabama would be under Gen Hardee's Corps, Gen Patrick Cleburne's Division, Gen Mark Lowrey's Brigade, and the regimental commander was Col William Hays. The regiment would number about 490 men fit for duty.

Gen Johnston had most of this army build entrenched fortifications on the crest of a rugged mountain going north and south called Rocky Face Ridge. The mountain had three passes that ran through it called Dug Gap, Snake Creek Gap, and Buzzards Roost Gap. Attacking these trenches head on would be suicide, and Gen Johnston was confident he could run Gen Sherman's Army around in the mountains for months causing him heavy casualties.

Dug Gap

Buzzard's Roost Gap

Johnston knew that his supply lines along the railroads would be much shorter than Gen Sherman's supply lines. The longer his supply lines got the more troops he would have to leave behind to protect the railroads. Let Sherman feed one brigade after another against his trenches while he maintained a defensive position, because he couldn't afford to lose men in foolish frontal attacks. Johnston could stop the Union army at Dalton, Georgia and keep them from striking the heart of the Confederacy. He had to protect the industry and railroad junctions at Atlanta, plus Johnston believed 1864 was critical for the South to win in both theaters, if they had any chance of winning the war.

CHAPTER 18

Gen Sherman was ready to move against the Rebel army in May 1864, because Chattanooga was well stocked with supplies for the army. Gen Sherman assigned Gen Thomas and the Army of the Cumberland the task of capturing Rocky Face Ridge. Maybe, they would be able to capture the crest after they captured Tunnel Hill on May 7th.

Two columns were to probe and attack Buzzards Roost and Dug Gap. Sherman's third column commanded by Gen James McPherson was to march through Snake Creek Gap and attack the railroad at Resaca, Georgia. The Confederates were well entrenched on the outskirts of the town, so Gen McPherson decided to withdraw to Snake Creek Gap and wait for reinforcements.

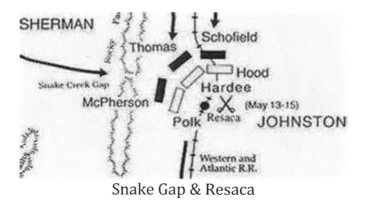

Snake Gap & Resaca

On May 7th, Gen Thomas ordered an attack in Dug Gap. Even though Thomas' men outnumbered the Rebels ten to one, his troops ran into murderous fire and boulders crashing down on them from above. Gen Thomas pulled back his army and decided to move further north to attack Buzzards Roost.

Gen John Schofield was moving southward from Red Clay while being harassed by the Rebel cavalry. He sent some

Union cavalry to get rid of Wheeler's Cavalry, because they were hitting him like a nest of yellow jackets. The unit got separated from Schofield's Army, and the Rebel cavalry rushed them at Prater's Mill causing the Union to lose 150 men in the defeat.

Gen Thomas ordered five all-out attacks at Buzzards Roost gaining no ground. On May 10th, Gen Sherman decided to join Gen McPherson and go after Resaca. Meanwhile, Gen Thomas was to keep up his firing at the enemy until the rest of the army moved out.

On May 11th, Union gunfire had stopped, so Gen Johnston sent his cavalry to find the Union army. When Johnston found out the enemy was heading towards Resaca, he couldn't let Sherman get behind him. Therefore, he withdrew from his strong fortifications heading south to Resaca as quickly as possible.

The 33rd Alabama and Gen Hardee's Corps were positioned along Camp Creek and started putting up earthworks. At this point, Company B had sixty men fit for duty. Gen Johnston entrenched his army on a ridge north of Resaca between the Conasauga and Oostanaula Rivers to protect the Western-Atlantic Railroad.

The only successful attack by Gen Sherman's Army on May 14th was on the Rebel's left flank. Union troops drove Gen Leonidas Polk's men off some high ground, so the Union boys dug in.

On May 15th, Union and Confederate forces battled each other with neither side gaining an advantage. Gen Sherman ordered pontoon bridges to be put across the Oostanaula River, and he sent a division across the river to attack Gen Johnston's supply line at the Western-Atlantic Railroad junction.

Gen Johnston met with his senior officers and told them he had no choice but to march southward towards Adairsville and Calhoun, Georgia. He couldn't be cut off from Atlanta, so by nightfall the Confederate army crossed the Oostanaula River and headed south.

In the early hours of May 16th, the Rebels set fire to a wagon bridge and a railroad span, so the Union couldn't use them.

As fate would have it, the Union troops repaired the bridges by the afternoon of May 16th.

Union troops that took part in the Battle of Resaca numbered 110,123 men. They suffered 4,000 casualties.

Confederate troops involved in the Battle of Resaca totaled 54, 500 men. They suffered 3,000 casualties. The first major battle of the Atlanta Campaign was over.

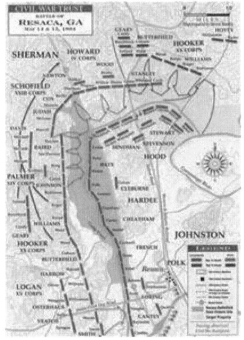

Battle of Resaca

The 10th Kentucky was involved in skirmishes at Armuchee Creek and Rome on May 15th. On May 16th, the regiment skirmished with the enemy at Floyd's Spring and near Calhoun. They saw general action at Parker's Crossroads where the regiment captured 60 Confederate prisoners without losing a man.

Gen Johnston couldn't find a good position to defend near Calhoun, so he continued marching to Adairsville. Gen Sherman divided his troops into three columns to follow the Confederate army.

Gen William Hardee established entrenched earthworks two miles north of Adairsville. The Union IV Corps, commanded by Gen Oliver Howard, ran into Hardee's entrenched men on May 17th. Two infantry regiments from the 24th Wisconsin and the 44th Illinois, commanded by Maj Arthur MacArthur, Jr., attacked the Rebel lines and were mauled, so Gen Thomas stopped any further attacks that day.

Gen Johnston saw that the terrain in this area wasn't good for defense, so he decided to withdraw further south and set a trap for the Union army. There were only two roads running south from Adairsville. One road went to Kingston and the second road led to Cassville. Gen Johnston figured the Union commander would split his army into giving Johnston an opportunity to attack one column and destroy it. Gen Johnston guessed Sherman would send the bulk of his army on the road to Kingston and the smaller forces to Cassville. The Confederate commander sent Gen Hardee to Kingston to hold off the Union army long enough for Gen Polk and Gen Hood to destroy the Union column headed towards Cassville.

Gen Johnston's plan didn't unfold like he had planned. On May 19th, Gen Hood started marching his troops along a country road east of the Adairsville-Cassville Road about a mile to set up his corps to attack while Gen Polk attacked the Union column head on. However, Gen Hood ran into a Union brigade commanded by Gen Daniel Butterfield, and after a short skirmish, Gen Hood withdrew to rejoin Gen Polk.

Gen Johnston figured his opportunity had passed, so he ordered Hood and Polk to move south of Cassville to set up a new line, and Gen Hardee would join them, later.

The Confederate corps commanders met with Gen Johnston that night, and what was said at the meeting was recalled differently by Johnston and Hood. No matter what was said at the council of war, Gen Johnston chose to abandon his position at Cassville.

During the night, the Rebel army withdrew over the Etowah River, and this decision caused many southern soldiers to question Johnston's ability as a commander. From May 19th to May 20th as the Confederate army withdrew to Allatoona Pass, southern morale dropped.

Gen Sherman decided not to attack Johnston at Allatoona Pass, so he marched his army towards Dallas, Georgia. Gen Johnston guessed Sherman would do that, so he placed the Rebel army at New Hope Church to block Sherman's path on May 25th.

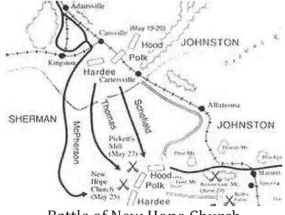

Battle of New Hope Church

The Union commander didn't believe Johnston had his main force at New Hope Church, so he ordered Gen Hooker's three divisions to attack. At first, the Rebels were pushed back about three miles, but then, Hooker's boys ran into the Rebel's main line. Because of the rugged terrain, Hooker couldn't form his corps to attack the Rebel lines in unison. His troops would pay a very high price, because Rebel artillery filled the air with canister and shrapnel from exploding shells.

The 33rd Alabama marched and took up their position on the right flank of the Rebel's main line of defense. The southern boys were ready to fire off a volley as soon as Hooker's troops were in range, and the artillery loaded canister and grapeshot to fire into the blue ranks.

2Sgt Wiggins shouted, "Easy boys! Make every shot count! Fire!"

Albert pulled the trigger, his aim was true, and the Yankee fell to the ground holding his stomach.

Austin fired and yelled, "I killed that Yankee stone dead!"

Michael fired and watched his target jerk, but the Yank kept walking with no weapon or cap.

Austin shouted, "Look at that stupid Yank! Part of his skull is gone!"

Michael saw the Yank jerk again and asked, "Why is he still walking?"

Austin fired at him, the Yank jerked, and just stood there. The Yank jerked again and crumbled to the ground. "It's about time you dropped!"

Michael thought, "You poor devil, you must have been shot six times. Why did you keep walking?"

Austin lined up a shot at a drummer boy, fired, and the boy fell to his knees over his drum. "You won't be banging on your drum anymore, you stupid kid."

Albert turned to his left just as 2Sgt Hopewell Wiggins fell to the ground shot in the right hip. Next to him, Pvt James Matthews fell to the ground holding his right arm.

Albert yelled, "Give me your ammunition!"

The Yankees made another charge at the 33rd Alabama firing off a volley, and the Alabama boys answered with one of their own. Soldiers in blue dropped from musket fire and canister shots ripping through their ranks.

Michael was next to Pvt John Deason when he was fatally shot. Blood and tissue sprayed Michael as he wiped his eyes, so he could see. He thought, "Oh God, Johnny, I'm glad you don't suffer?"

Next to Austin, Pvt William Pippin fell to the ground. Austin thought, "The Yanks sure killed you stone dead, you big mouth!"

Off to Albert's right, an artillery shell exploded sending deadly shrapnel in every direction. Pvt Acorn Brannon didn't have a chance as pieces of metal ripped through his body. Pvt James Barefoot fell to the ground screaming in agony after shrapnel ripped part of his arm away. 3Sgt Ridic Wiggins fell grabbing his knee as he yelled and shook from the stabbing pain.

The lieutenant yelled, "Here they come again boys!"

The brothers aimed and fired as their company sent another deadly volley into the blue ranks. The smell of gunpowder was heavy in the air. Their ears roared from the musket fire, screams of the wounded, and the cannonade. Each man had to enter his own little world to concentrate, reload, and fire.

The blue ranks fell back, and the brothers reloaded.

Michael gasped for air, fumbled for his canteen, and drank as quickly as he could. Sweat was running down his face as he looked out in front of him to see a gruesome scene of dead and wounded covering the ground like fall leaves. He turned his face away wishing he was home fishing with his father.

Stretcher-bearers were moving the wounded to the rear as quickly as they could, and more ammunition was passed out among the men as they waited for the next blue wave to hit them.

The brothers grabbed some cornbread out of their haversacks and gobbled it down. A wild turkey charged out in front of the 33rd Alabama, and a shot rang out. A soldier grabbed it and sprinted back to the Rebel lines. Albert thought, "I can eat that whole turkey, right now."

In about fifteen minutes, the lieutenant yelled, "Ready boys, here they come again! Steady! Steady! Fire!"

Another deadly volley tore through the blue ranks, and the Yankees answered with their own volley. Albert's musket was shot out of his hands, so he grabbed Pvt Matthews' musket. He saw 1Sgt Martin Crawford drop in the torn up grass and underbrush wounded in the side.

The brothers heard the familiar hissing, screaming sound of an artillery shell. They curled up in a ball covering their heads with their hands. The ground shook as dirt, leaves, limbs, and rocks showered down on them. As if in slow motion, Pvt William Burgess was lifted off the ground and propelled several feet behind the line. He landed and screamed in agony, because his left sleeve was torn and blood was running down his hand. His head and side were on fire, and he wondered how badly he was hurt as he drifted in and out of consciousness.

Michael looked around, but couldn't find Pvt James Johns. Suddenly, Michael realized he had a bloody nose. He felt himself, but couldn't find any wounds.

Austin yelled, "That was too close!"

The brothers brushed themselves off and got ready for the next round. Both sides kept at each other until the

Yankees fell back. Now, it was a waiting game. Would the Yanks charge at them, again?

Albert yelled, "Where is Pvt Johns? He was right next to Burgess!"

Austin shouted, "Burgess is back there with part of Johns!"

Albert fired back, "Sweet Jesus, he didn't have a chance!"

Austin blabbed, "That's war for you, brother dear. Some live and some die. It's simple at that."

Michael shouted, "Austin, you sure have turned into a coldhearted monster!" Michael crawled back to Pvt Burgess to help him until the stretcher-bearers could pick him up.

Another attack didn't come, so both sides dug in for the next day and tended to their wounded.

Union losses at the Battle of New Hope Church totaled 1,665 soldiers. For the Confederates, their losses were only 350 soldiers. Clearly, the Union forces suffered a mauling defeat they weren't prepared for.

Battle of Pickett's Mill & New Hope Church

CHAPTER 19

On May 27th, Gen Sherman ordered Gen Oliver Howard, who had fought in the Eastern Theater, to outflank the Confederates. Gen Howard's IV Corps of 14,000 men marched along Pumpkinvine Creek for five hours and arrived at Pickett's farm and gristmill.

Gen Sherman wanted to march around Allatoona Pass and cut off Gen Johnston's escape route. Gen Howard's men would run up against the best Confederate commander in the Western Theater named Gen Patrick Cleburne, the Stonewall Jackson of the West.

The 33rd Alabama, part of Lowrey's Brigade, had about 493 soldiers fit for duty. Gen Cleburne's Division was located on the far right flank of Gen Johnston's Army. In front of him were three Union divisions commanded by Gen Milo Hascall, Gen Jacob Cox, and Gen Thomas Wood.

Gen Milo Hascall   Gen Jacob Cox

This area was a densely wooded, rugged terrain the troops would find extremely difficult to maneuver in. Cleburne ordered his pioneers to cut trails through the thick underbrush and woods, so he could move troops and supplies between his brigades, quickly.

Cleburne sent one of his brigades to scout the Union left flank, and they ran into troops commanded by Gen Oliver Howard. The Union soldiers tried to turn the Confederate line and get behind the Rebel position. Gen Cleburne extended his lines on the right into a wheat field.

Gen Oliver Howard

For some unknown reason, Gen Howard only ordered one brigade to attack Cleburne's position, even though he had six brigades he could have used. The Union brigade got lost in the tangled terrain and suffered heavy losses. Then, Gen Cleburne sent Lowrey's Brigade, including the 33rd Alabama, to assist his brigade that was attacked earlier. Gen Lowrey's men arrived around 5:30 pm with the 33rd Alabama leading.

Union Gen Thomas Wood ordered another attack around 6:00 pm. Confederate Gen John Kelly placed two of his Arkansas regiments to the left of the 33rd Alabama, and the three regiments decided to charge together. The 33rd Alabama plowed into the Union troops in a cornfield, but fell back to the safety of the woods, so they could blaze away at the enemy.

Gen Lowrey appeared on the battlefield and rode up and down the 33rd Alabama's position inspiring his men to fill the air and cornfield with bullets. The Union forces retreated, but regrouped at the edge of the cornfield. The two sides continued to fire at each other as night was rapidly approaching. The corn stalks were ripped to pieces as twilight descended on the battleground.

About 10:00 pm, Gen Hiram Granbury's Texas boys charged the Union troops in front of them and sent the Yankees running. Soon, all the Union forces withdrew leaving the field to the Rebels.

Gen Hiram Granbury

At the Battle of Pickett's Mill, Union casualties numbered 1,600 soldiers compared to Confederate losses totaling 500 soldiers.

Gen Sherman was worried about his supply lines, because his men were running low on rations. He decided to side step Gen Johnston's Army and head to Marietta, Georgia.

Sherman was elated when he found out Union Gen Stoneman's Cavalry had captured Allatoona Pass on June 1st. This was very important, because it had a railroad, so Sherman could get supplies for his army. Sherman couldn't help the week long delay to his Atlanta Campaign, because his army needed food and supplies.

Between June 5th and June 15th, the Confederate army fortified and entrenched on Pine Mountain setting up an artillery position. At this point, the Rebel line ran from Lost Mountain to Brushy Mountain. On June 10th, some Union artillery was moved in order to cover the summit of Pine Mountain.

On June 14th on the summit of Pine Mountain, Confederate generals Johnston, Hardee, and Polk were observing enemy positions when Gen Sherman noticed the officers clustered together. He ordered his artillery to open fire on the officers, and Gen Leonidas Polk was almost cut in half by an artillery shell killing him instantly. That evening with a heavy heart, Gen Johnston withdrew his troops on Pine Mountain.

Pine Mountain where Gen Polk was killed

Gen Sherman ordered his army to advance on June 15th. Gen Schofield bypassed Lost Mountain and headed towards some high ground on a knoll realizing he could set up artillery batteries that could fire on Confederate Gen Cleburne's position from the flank. The Rebel army was fortified on a ridge west of Pine Mountain and Pine Knob.

Gen Cleburne ordered his troops to dismantle Gilgal Church, so they could use the wood to make their trenches stronger.

Union Gen Daniel Butterfield's Division was facing three Confederate brigades under the command of Gen Cleburne. Butterfield knew what had happened to Union troops that charged head-on into Gen Cleburne's men at Missionary Ridge and Ringgold Gap. However, he still ordered a head-on charge at the well-fortified position. Butterfield believed if Gen John Geary and he hit Cleburne's position on the right at the same time they could overrun the Rebel trenches.

Neither general was able to break the Rebel line, so they withdrew after battling for only 45 minutes.

Gen Daniel Butterfield   Gen John Geary

Michael drank from his canteen and wiped the sweat running down his face. He asked, "When are the Yankees going to learn our trenches are the best in the world?"

Albert answered, "I guess never."

Austin remarked, "They should keep it up, so we can have lots of target practice. I just don't like burying their dead behinds."

Albert shot back, "At least, we can help ourselves to their clothes and supplies. I got Yankee pants and shoes on, right now."

Michael added, "I got Yankee drawers, pants, and socks on!"

Austin thought, "I tried to kill you, Albert, three times when we were fighting in that cornfield and thick woods. Each time you moved just as I pulled the trigger. How can you be so darn lucky? Don't worry, brother dear, because I'll get you yet."

More ammunition was passed out, so the brothers and the rest of Gen Cleburne's men could settle down and wait for the Yankees next move.

Late in the evening, Gen Cleburne's Division was ordered to withdraw and fortify a ridge east of Mud Creek.

The Union army lost 650 men at the Battle of Gilgal Church. Gen Cleburne only suffered 250 casualties.

Gen Johnston moved his army towards Kennesaw Mountain on June 18th and June 19th. The men put up fortifications in the shape of an arc west of Marietta, so Johnston could protect his supply line on the Western-Atlantic Railroad.

Gen Joseph Johnston

Gen Johnston knew Sherman's tactics, so for him to charge head-on into Sherman's men meant he would suffer heavy casualties he couldn't afford to lose. Johnston believed he had to entrench, delay, and only attack if he knew he could win. He would have an adversary in Gen John Bell Hood who believed by constantly attacking an army one could win no matter what the casualties were.

When the Atlanta Campaign started and to this point, Gen Johnston had lost 10,000 men. During this same period, Gen Robert E. Lee had lost 40,000 men in the Eastern Theater.

By June 18th, the constant rain had turned the roads into a muddy quagmire, so for Gen Sherman to try a flanking movement would be almost impossible. His cavalry informed Gen Johnston that Sherman's three corps were trying to turn the Confederate left towards the railroad. Union Gen James McPherson set up in front of the Confederate fortifications. Gen Sherman's line ran from Noonday Creek on the left to Nose's Creek on his right. Even though the area had soaking rains for 19 days, Gen Sherman decided to follow his objectives.

Gen Johnston moved Gen Hood's Corps to his left on June 20th, because the enemy was moving more men in that direction.

Gen Hood found out on June 22nd that Union troops were pushing back the Confederate cavalry, so Gen Hood decided on his own to attack. He didn't inform Gen Johnston he was attacking, nor did he know the Union position or numbers. By not conducting reconnaissance, Gen Hood had no idea what was in front of him.

Gen Hood ordered Gen Hindman and Gen Stevenson to attack. In front of them was Gen Schofield's Army of the Ohio and Gen Hooker's XX Corps that were well entrenched. The Confederates marched towards Peter Kolb's farm. Two Rebel brigades reached the farmhouse and ran into the 14th Kentucky and the 123rd New York regiments. The Rebel brigades were pushed back in heavy fighting, but Gen Hood ordered them to attack, again. The two Rebel brigades charged again and suffered heavy losses before they retreated.

For the third time, the two brigades were ordered to attack. As the men marched over the muddy quagmire trying to keep their footing, the Union line fired volley after volley at the Rebel brigades causing them to retreat with heavy losses.

When the fighting ended because of darkness, Confederate losses were over 1,000 soldiers compared to Union losses of just 350 men. Gen Johnston commented that Gen Hood lost soldiers the Confederacy couldn't afford to lose just for his moment of glory and to boost his reputation.

Gen Sherman was stopped from outflanking Gen Johnston's Army by a group of small mountains. Sherman had to capture the rail center at Marietta, so he could feed and supply his 100,000 men. He couldn't use the rail center as long as Rebel artillery was entrenched on Kennesaw Mountain at the northern end of the mountain. Gen Johnston was entrenched on the east side of Kennesaw while Gen Sherman was positioned on the west side.

Meanwhile, the 10th Kentucky and its brigade moved in front of Pine Knob on June 10th. They spent four days digging trenches and fortifying their breastworks. Rebel pickets sniped at the brigade's skirmishers causing no casualties.

From June 14th to June 17th, the Rebels fired on the brigade's skirmish lines constantly until they pulled out of their position.

The brigade lost 27 men during this period, but the 10th Kentucky only suffered one wounded.

On June 19th, the 3rd Division commanded by Gen Absalom Baird, including the 10th Kentucky, was ordered to take up a position at the base of Kennesaw Mountain.

Between June 20th and June 26th, the brigade endured severe artillery fire from the Rebel batteries as well as constant sniping from Confederate sharpshooters.

During the period, the brigade suffered 28 casualties, and the 10th Kentucky was fortunate to only suffer two wounded.

On June 25th, Gen Sherman informed his subordinate generals they had no choice but to attack the Confederates in a series of head-on assaults to start on June 27th. The Union army had fought for two months over 70 miles of difficult terrain that the Rebels had turned into connecting trenches that were well-fortified with anti-personnel devices and artillery positions. The 691 foot Kennesaw Mountain with its 1,808 foot long ridge stood in Gen Sherman's path to capture Marietta and drive the 15 miles to Atlanta. The mountain controlled the entire area, so he had to capture it.

Kennesaw Mountain

Gen James McPherson's Army of the Tennessee was positioned on the northern end of Sherman's Army west of Kennesaw Mountain. Gen George Thomas' Army of the Cumberland was positioned to anchor the center of

Sherman's line. Gen John Schofield's Army of the Ohio was placed at the southern end of Sherman's line.

In front of Gen McPherson was Confederate Gen William Loring who replaced Gen Leonidas Polk who was killed on June 14th. In front of Gen Thomas was Confederate Gen William Hardee. Gen Schofield and Gen Hooker would be going up against the unpredictable Gen John Bell Hood.

Gen Thomas and Gen Howard inspected their lines looking for the best area to attack, and they chose Cheatham Hill. Gen Howard met with Gen Jefferson C. Davis and told him to storm the enemy position on Cheatham Hill. Gen Davis sent two brigades a mile to the rear to camp and strike the Rebel lines on the evening of June 26th.

Gen John Palmer ordered a brigade commanded by Gen Charles Harker to support the left flank of Col Daniel McCook, Jr.

Gen William Loring   Gen Jefferson C. Davis

Gen Thomas believed Rebel Gen Benjamin Cheatham didn't have well-fortified trenches. However, a thousand of Cheatham's Tennessee boys were well-entrenched at the top of the hill. In front of them was a field of felled trees with sharpened branches facing the enemy called an abatis and entangled underbrush, boulders, and thick trees. Gen Cheatham had concealed batteries that could cover this area with canister and grapeshot. Also, the general had Gen Patrick Cleburne's men on his right flank.

On the morning of June 27th, Union artillery of over 200 guns along a five-mile front opened fire on Kennesaw Mountain. To many Union soldiers, Kennesaw blazed with fire almost like a volcano.

For 15 minutes they launched shell after shell on the mountain. When the artillery barrage fell silent, 5,500 Union soldiers charged into a small area along Noyes Creek. The boys in blue overran the 63rd Georgia Regiment and the reserves sent to support them. The fighting was hand-to-hand as the Yankees charged the main Rebel line.

However, the boys in blue entered a murderous crossfire that stopped them, and their commanding officer ordered his men to retreat after 10 minutes, so they wouldn't be cut to pieces.

North of this action, Union soldiers tried to capture a spur of land called Pigeon Hill, but ran into tangled woods, large boulders, a stone palisade, and steep, rocky slopes. There was no way they could get near the Rebel lines. Another group of Union soldiers tried to capture Rebel lines running between Pigeon Hill and Little Kennesaw. The Union troops were caught in a tangled, wooded gap they couldn't maneuver in, so it would become a death trap if they didn't retreat.

Another brigade marched into a knee-deep swamp on the southern end of Pigeon Hill and was unable to break through the main Rebel line. They came under murderous crossfire and had to retreat or be mauled by Confederate fire.

Gen Thomas' troops didn't start their attack until 9:00 am, because they were behind schedule. Two divisions from Gen Thomas' Army of the Cumberland of 9,000 men advanced commanded by Gen John Newton and Gen Jefferson C. Davis. They didn't march in a broad line, but in a column formation for a heavier punch.

Battle of Kennesaw Mountain

Three Union brigades formed at the bottom of Cheatham Hill commanded by Gen Charles Harker, Col Daniel McCook, Jr., and Col John Mitchell.

Col John Mitchell   Gen John Newton

The Rebels looked down on the green valley as it turned blue from thousands of Union soldiers. They crossed a part of John Ward Creek and entered an open space.
Col McCook's men crossed a wheat field and started to climb Cheatham Hill. The soldiers ran into tangled woods, thick underbrush, steep, jagged slopes, dangerous boulders, and felled trees. Col McCook's men were subjected to murderous musket and cannon fire. Col McCook and some of his men reached the Confederate trenches, and the colonel jumped upon the parapet (a wall or elevation of earth or stone to protect soldiers) waving his sword only to be mortally wounded. Col Oscar Harmon assumed command, but he was also killed. Col McCook's brigade lost almost all its field officers and almost a third of its men.

Col John Mitchell's Brigade which was to the right of Col McCook ended up in fierce hand-to-hand combat suffering similar casualties before they were ordered to withdraw about 25 yards from the Confederate lines into a small dip, because they were protected from the enemy's fire. The soldiers kept firing at the Rebel position, so their trapped comrades could escape. Col McCook's and Mitchell's Brigades suffered 824 casualties. Of that total, 131 soldiers were killed in action.

Gen Cleburne's Division was ordered to position itself on the right side of Cheatham Hill. This would be the center of the Confederate line. The 33rd Alabama along with Lowrey's Brigade faced Gen John Newton's Division. Cleburne's trenches were well-fortified in a densely wooded area full of tangled underbrush, and Cleburne had his men chop down trees and drive sharp stakes into the ground.

Gen Charles Harker and his men clawed their way towards Cleburne's line manned by a Tennessee brigade. Harker was shot in the chest and arm and dropped dead 15 feet short of the Confederate line.

The 33rd Alabama fired volley after volley into the Union soldiers climbing the steep deadly slopes.

Austin laughed and yelled, "I killed you stone dead Yank! Sorry you fell on that stake!"

Albert yelled, "Chickamauga, boys!"

Michael aimed and fired over and over again until his hands and face were black from gunpowder. His heart pounded, his mouth was bone dry, his ears roared, and his trigger finger was cramping. He looked at the surreal scene in front of him in horror, because dead soldiers were laying everywhere, and the wounded cried in agony. Their cries tortured his heart and soul.

The Union soldiers fell back after their colonel was killed leaving their dead and wounded behind.

Austin yelled, "Chickamauga, boys!"

Michael asked, "Do you think they'll charge us, again?"

Albert answered, "I don't know, but I hope not."

Austin said, "Watch this!" He fired at a wounded Union soldier laying on his back across a boulder begging for help, and Austin laughed when the young soldier stopped begging.

That was the last straw for Albert. He grabbed Austin by

the jacket, punched him in the face, and slammed him to the ground sitting on his chest.

Albert yelled, "Don't you ever do that again, or I'll beat you to a pulp! That was murder in my book!"

Austin shouted, "I put the Yankee out of his misery like you would a horse!" Austin tried to punch Albert, but Michael stepped on his arm.

Michael warned, "I wouldn't do that, Austin, because that was murder. That Yankee soldier was a human being not an animal, and it seems to me you like killing too much."

About that time, the lieutenant came over and asked, "What the hades is going on?"

Michael replied, "The three of us just had a disagreement, but it's been settled."

The lieutenant ordered, "Get back on the line! Save your fighting for the Yankees!"

Austin got up, wiped his bloody nose, and went down the line away from his brothers.

Albert commented, "I think Austin has gone crazy."

Michael suggested, "I think so, too. We better keep a close eye on him from now on."

Albert responded, "I agree. By the way, thanks for helping me out."

Michael replied, "You were doing the right thing, because something is wrong with Austin."

Albert replied, "He's a mean person, and he has too much of the devil in him."

The only Union success came from Gen Schofield's Army on the Confederate left. Two of his brigades along with Gen Stoneman's Cavalry were able to cross Olley's Creek putting them within five miles of the Chattahoochee River. The river was the last one protecting Atlanta, and the Union was closer to it than the Rebel army was.

A patch of woods north of Cheatham Hill caught fire burning several wounded Union soldiers to death that were left behind during their retreat. A colonel from an Arkansas regiment took a white flag and started waving it on top of their entrenchments. He yelled to the Union troops to come and rescue their wounded.

Unarmed Yankees started removing the men when many Confederate soldiers left their trenches to help rescue the wounded and remove the dead. Less than fifteen minutes earlier both sides were killing each other in a frenzy.

The next day under a flag of truce Union officers gave the Arkansas colonel a pair of ivory-handled Colt .45 pistols. Strange events did happen during the Civil War like this one.

When the day was over, the Union losses stood at 3,000 men compared to the Confederate losses of only 1,000 men.

The 10th Kentucky was fortunate during the Battle of Kennesaw Mountain, because their brigade was held in reserve and was never ordered to attack.

The 33rd Alabama suffered two killed and one wounded.

For the next five days, both sides remained in their trenches unwilling to attack.

On July 2nd, Gen Sherman's Army moved around the Confederate left flank and headed towards Atlanta. Gen Johnston was forced to withdraw from the mountain and set up positions at Smyrna.

Faces of the Civil War

CHAPTER 20

Freddie ran like the wind when he saw two riders heading up the road that led to Evergreen Manor. One rider was Judge Canby Anderson from Montgomery, and the other rider was a neighbor named John Baker.

Freddie ran into the mansion and told Ms. Alice who was headed up the lane.

Alice said, "Freddie tell our workers about the riders, and I'll tell Mr. Randolph."

"Yes'um, Ms. Waverly!"

Alice knocked on Randolph's office door and walked in. Randolph was going over some plans with Calvin concerning timber and firewood.

Randolph smiled and asked, "How is my beautiful wife?"

"I'm fine, Darling. We have visitors coming. Judge Anderson and John Baker are headed this way."

"It looks like we have to become actors, Calvin!"

"Yes'sa! I'll spread de word, Mr. Randolph!"

Alice added, "Freddie is spreading the word, too."

Randolph wondered out loud, "Why would Judge Anderson be coming here?"

"I was thinking the same thing."

"Let's go out and greet our guests. Maybe, they have some news!"

Suddenly, Alice realized, "They could be bringing casualty lists! Oh Lord, Randolph, they could be bringing us bad news!"

Randolph warned, "Honey, we don't know that. Whatever the news is, we'll make it through together."

Sally came around to the porch and joined her parents. She commented, "I hope it's not bad news!"

Her father responded, "Let's wait, ladies, before we fall apart."

"You're right, Poppa."

Calvin added, "I'll take real good care of de horses, Mr. Randolph."

"I know you will, Calvin. I'm anxious to see how nosy they are. This should be a real good show we'll remember for a long time."

Calvin laughed and slipped back around the side of the mansion.

Shortly, their visitors rode up, and Calvin appeared to take away the horses.

Randolph ordered, "Make sure you feed and water their horses, boy!"

Calvin answered, "Yes'sa, Massas Waverly, I be a doin' that, rights now!" Calvin wanted to laugh, but he saved it until he got inside the barn.

Randolph shook Judge Anderson's hand, patted him on the shoulder, and asked, "What brings you here from Montgomery?"

The judge responded, "There's lots of news to pass on to you. Don't be worried, because your sons aren't on the casualty lists from the battles, at Lookout Mountain, Missionary Ridge, Pickett's Mill, New Hope Church, and Resaca. We don't know about our losses at Kennesaw Mountain, yet."

John Baker added, "The Yankees are marching towards the Chattahoochee River, Randolph!"

Alice inquired, "Where is our army, John?"

"They're setting up near Smyrna."

Sally asked very concerned, "Are the Yankees going to invade Montgomery and us?"

"We don't know, Miss Sally."

The judge commented, "Randolph, you need to know that the state government will evacuate Montgomery and relocate in Eufaula, if the Yankees head into Alabama."

"I'm glad to know that."

Alice suggested, "Let's all go inside and enjoy some food and drink, gentlemen."

John Baker remarked, "That sounds wonderful, Ms. Alice!"

Daisy and Beulah smiled and giggled, because it was time to have fun messing with the minds of two members of the southern aristocracy who were not true southern gentlemen. Their secret was important to keep, so Mr. Waverly and his family could be protected from bigots.

Asa stepped up to Judge Anderson and suggested, "Massas Judge, let me take your hat and gloves."

Leroy took John Baker's hat and gloves and commented, "Massas Baker, you is looking mighty fine today!"

"Well, thank you, boy!"

Freddie came up and said, "Massas Judge, here's a cool cloth to wipe your face, because it's right smart hot today. Massas Baker, here's one for you, too, sir."

The judge commented, "That does feel good, boy!"

Randolph suggested, "Let's go into the parlor, so we can visit."

Leroy asked, "Massas Waverly, what kind of wine do you wants me to bring up?"

"If I remember right, both the judge and Mr. Baker like red wine."

Baker replied, "That's right, Randolph!"

Leroy remarked, "I'll brings up de best wine for de gentlemens!"

Alice thought, "So far, so good. Asa, Leroy, and Freddie were doing just fine."

Randolph asked, "John, how is your son doing?"

"He's doing fine and still at Fort Morgan. I'm worried about Mobile, because it's our last port on the Gulf of Mexico that we control. Thank the Lord, our blockade runners are still getting through from Havana and the other Caribbean islands carrying supplies."

Randolph added, "I'm sure the Yankees will attack Mobile to complete their blockade. If they capture Mobile and Atlanta, I fear for the Confederacy."

Judge Anderson commented, "I agree! My son is serving on the ironclad ram *CSS Tennessee* that's stationed in Mobile Bay. Our boys will beat back anything the Yankees throw at them!"

Leroy came into the parlor with apple cider for the ladies and red wine for the gentlemen. Beulah came in with fresh ham biscuits and apple pie. She went into her charade and said, "I remember de gentlemens like this here food, so I says to myself, I has to serve ya'll this here tray after your long, hot ride to Evergreen Manor."

Alice chimed in, "That was mighty nice of you, Beulah. Make sure you eat some, too."

"Yes'um, Ms. Waverly. I'll check back to see if de gentlemens would like more."

John Baker commented, "Most of my slaves have run away, and I don't have enough slaves to plant all my land. I only have two house slaves left, and I don't understand why your slaves haven't run away. How are you keeping them here?"

Alice answered, "We treat them like human beings, because they laugh and cry just like we do."

Judge Anderson blabbed, "Darkies aren't equal to us! They are property!"

Randolph shot back, "All of us are working together, so we can eat and survive this war."

Baker asked, "Do you mean to tell me you work in the fields!"

Alice chimed in, "All of us work in the fields when it's necessary."

Baker shot back, "A planter and his family doesn't work in the fields!"

Randolph reasoned, "John, we're at war, so we must do whatever it takes to survive. Sometimes, we have to change."

Sally wanted to bust the judge and Mr. Baker in the nose, but she knew at this moment she needed to control her temper. She said, "I think you gentlemen need another slice of pie, because those apples came from our orchard."

The judge replied, "Miss Sally, I'd love another slice, because your orchard produces the best fruit in Alabama."

After the judge and Mr. Baker gobbled down another slice of pie, they poured another glass of wine down their throats.

The judge warned, "Randolph, you need to keep a good lookout for bands of deserters roaming around, because three plantations up north have been hit. They took horses, money, jewelry, and food. They even killed five people, so the deserters are very dangerous."

Randolph asked, "How large are the bands?"

"The Confederate bands run from three to eight. They even burned one planter's mansion to the ground."

The judge suggested, "The militia hasn't been able to catch them. They disappear in the woods to their camps I guess. You need to keep a watch out for them."

Randolph asked, "When do they hit?"

"So far, they show up during the day to do their dirty work."

Alice mentioned, "Thank you for the warning. Would you like to have dinner with us and spend the night?"

The judge answered, "No, we have to get back to John's place, but thank you very much for the delicious food and refreshing wine."

Daisy appeared with a basket and said, "Here are some ham biscuits for yous to eat on de ride back, Massas Baker and Massas Judge."

"Well, thank you, girl!"

Calvin brought their horses around, they saddled up, and the two visitors rode down the lane. Everyone breathed a sigh of relief, because the charade worked to perfection.

Asa commented, "Deserters can be real bad, Mr. Randolph."

Randolph answered, "I know, Asa. I think all the men need to get together and set up a 24-hour watch, because we can't afford a run in with deserters who are nothing but hoodlums and trash."

Alice commented, "Don't forget about the women around here, Darling. We can handle a pistol just fine."

Randolph laughed and said, "I knew you were going to say that. Of course, you ladies will be involved in our plan to protect Evergreen Manor."

Randolph met with his male workers, and they came up with a plan to cover the mansion, gristmill, lumber mill, barns, and horse corrals. The ladies in the mansion, including Sally, would carry a pistol in their petticoats. If the deserters hit Evergreen Manor, they would walk into a hornet's nest full of angry human bees with lots of fire power.

Jerome told Randolph the freedmen would fight for their land and homes like bears. They would fight for everything that made up Evergreen Manor.

After the visitors left, the next day was very hot and quite humid.

Sally complained, "I wish we didn't have to wear so many clothes in the summer, because it makes me feel like a human torch!"

Daisy teased, "Miss Sally, I don't see no smoke coming from your petticoat."

"That's because I'm already fried to a crisp. My legs look like fried bacon!"

Daisy teased, "Is them legs hairy, Miss Sally?"

"Shame on you, Daisy, you have a twisted mind! The hair was burned off a long time ago!"

Daisy blabbed, "You know, some men likes bacon legs. They likes that wood burned smell."

"Daisy, you're crazy as a bed bug!"

Daisy shot back, "I'd rather be a bed bug than a chigger!"

"Well, right now, I feel like a fire ant in hades!"

Alice breezed in and asked, "Who feels like a fire ant?"

Sally fired back, "Me! I wish I could jump into the Chattahoochee River and cool off!"

Alice laughed and said, "At least, you'd drown the fire ants!"

The ladies laughed like hyenas at a wedding banquet.

Alice commented, "I'd love some cornbread with honey, Daisy."

Daisy replied, "I'll get you some, but is you pregnant, Ms. Alice? Every time you be pregnant before you craved honey cornbread!"

"I assure you I'm not pregnant!"

Beulah walked in, and Sally knew right away something was wrong.

She asked, "What's wrong, because you don't look good?"

"My head be about to blow plum up! My brains be on the ceiling soon."

"You always seem to get a headache when the weather is bad."

"I knows, Ms. Alice, but the sun is shining hot as ever! Ain't a cloud in the sky!"

Alice ordered, "You rest and if it doesn't go away soon you can have some laudanum or wine."

Sally teased, "Just don't get drunk on the wine!"

"I ain't getting drunk on no wines after what happened to you, girl!"

Sally fired back, "I only had three swallows!"

Alice teased, "After three swallows, you threw up for

236

hours and was so dizzy you couldn't walk!"

Sally went on, "I wanted to die, because I was so sick. No wine is going in my mouth, again!"

Daisy blabbed, "Sometimes, when it be real hots like today, I gits the dia-ree. By the time I finds a bucket, pot, or outhouse and gits all my confounded clothes out of the way, the dia-ree be running down my legs!"

Sally chimed in, "When the men get dia-ree, all they have to do is pull their drawers and pants down, so it just ain't fair!"

Alice shot back, "Amen, brothers and sisters!"

Asa walked in and asked, "What you ladies be laughing about?"

Daisy blabbed, "Dia-ree running down people's legs, nosy!"

Asa turned and said, "Oh Lord, let me gits out of here!"

Sally yelled, "Chicken!"

The ladies laughed until tears ran down their faces.

Around 4:00 pm, Freddie felt like something was wrong, and he wondered if some deserters were close by. He looked around, but he didn't see any strange folks lurking about. He thought, "Lord, it's mighty hot, and the sun is just beating down on me. I gots to git in the shade for a while and cool down."

He sat under a tree, but that feeling kept nagging at him. Shortly, he got up and headed for the lane. He looked off to the west, and something told him it was going to be real bad.

He sprinted to the gristmill where Randolph and some of the men were.

He yelled and pointed, "Mr. Randolph, please believe me, because it's going to be bad! We gots to take shelter and gits the livestock, now!"

Randolph looked to the west, and the sky was black. He ordered, "Oscar shut down the gristmill, head to your home, secure everything you can, and get in your cellar! Freddie run and warn the folks in the house and get the chickens in their house!"

"Where is you going, Mr. Randolph?"

"I'm heading to the fields, so the men can help me round up the livestock!"

Randolph jumped on his horse and rode to alert Calvin and the other men. As the black clouds moved closer, Freddie sprinted to the mansion. He raced up the steps, threw open the door, and ran towards the laughing. He slid into the kitchen and yelled, "A bad storm is coming this way, and we gots to git the chickens in the chicken house and take shelter!"

Daisy commented, "The sun is shining, boy."

Freddie grabbed Ms. Alice's hand and pulled her to the window. "Please, Ms. Alice, look at the sky out that way!"

When Alice saw the black angry clouds, she turned and ordered, "Daisy and Beulah, close all the shutters and get the cellar and wine cellar ready for us!"

"Yes'um!"

Alice shouted, "Come on Freddie and Sally, we have to get the chickens inside!"

The three worked feverishly to get the chickens collected and into the chicken house.

After Asa and Leroy closed the shutters on the outside of the house, they ran up and said, "We'll get de horses in de barn, Ms. Waverly."

She yelled, "We'll put the porch furniture in the barn!"

Randolph got to the plantation horse barn, alerted Calvin, and they galloped towards the worker's homes. They warned each house, and the women and children rushed to close shutters and round up their chickens, goats, or any other livestock.

Calvin and Randolph galloped towards the cow pasture, and much to their relief, the men were already bringing in the cattle. Together, they got all the cows in the barn and things secured.

Sidney ran up and told Randolph the lumber mill was shut down and closed up. The men looked at the sky and saw a long, huge cloud spinning around and around almost touching the ground. The wind picked up, the lightning flashed and cracked, and the rain started to pound the earth.

Randolph yelled, "Sidney get home and get in your cellar!"

Calvin shouted, "We gots to git to the barn!"

The two men pushed their horses as fast as they could gallop. The wind was blowing harder, and the rain was getting heavier. As the men approached the barn, leaves and sticks were blowing everywhere. They heard a loud boom, and a tree fell across the road in front of them. The horses panicked, bucked, and Randolph was thrown into the fallen tree. Calvin managed to get off his horse and run towards Randolph. His beloved former owner had blood running down his head and face, and he was unconscious and tangled up in the tree.

Calvin grabbed him under his arms and started pulling him out of the tree. He didn't care about the horses, because the two of them needed to get to safety. The wind blew rain into Calvin's face making it hard to see, but he struggled with all his strength to pull Randolph out of the tangled mess. Finally, he broke free, so Calvin started pulling him towards the barn, because it had a cellar. Leaves and limbs kept hitting them as Calvin got closer and closer to the barn. Both men were soaked to the skin when Calvin reached the barn door. He threw it open, pulled Randolph inside, and closed the door. He got to the cellar door, lifted it open, and slid Randolph down the steps as best as he could. Calvin crawled inside and closed the trap door. He gasped for air as his body burned from the exertion. It was pitch black in the cellar, but he didn't care. All he could hear was a roaring in his ears.

Everyone ran towards the mansion from the barn as they

were being pelted with leaves, limbs, and heavy rain. By the time they got inside the mansion, they were all soaked to the skin. The ladies went into the root cellar, and the men went into the wine cellar. Thanks to Daisy and Beulah, candles lit up the cellars, towels were there to wipe off with, and food was there to eat.

"Please Lord keep my husband safe and all the people on Evergreen Manor," Alice prayed.

Sally asked, "Why isn't Poppa back here?"

Her mother answered, "He probably took refuge somewhere else. Don't worry, Sally, your father is a very smart man."

Daisy commented, "The men will make sure Mr. Randolph stays safe."

"Daisy don't you dare have a case of the dia-ree in this cellar," Sally teased.

Everybody laughed and Daisy shot back, "If I do, I'll sit next to you!"

Everyone couldn't help but howl with laughter, because Daisy could always match Sally's teasing with plenty of her own.

Beulah started passing honey cornbread and other food around, because it was dinner time. Everybody ate as the thunder boomed and the lightning crackled across the sky. The rain slammed against the shutters and the sides of the buildings, and the roar from the wind was deafening.

Leroy commented, "This storm be really bad, and I hope nobody gits hurt."

"We'll have lots of damage to clean up," Asa remarked.

Freddie asked, "Have you seen a long, spinning cloud like that one before?"

"Nope, and I hope we doesn't see anything like that ever again. It scared de bejesus out of me. I think it be de devil's work!"

"Me, too," Freddie responded.

Randolph moaned, opened his eyes, and shouted, "I can't see!"

"Calm down, Mr. Randolph, we be in the barn cellar. You has a nasty cut on your head, and as soon as de storm is over, we'll git out of here."

"The last thing I remember was flying through the air!"

"Your horse bucked you off and throwed you into de tree. I almost couldn't git you out!"

"My head sure does hurt!"

"Does you hurt bad anywhere else?"

"No, not really, but I'm real sore like Ms. Alice beat on me!"

"Sweet Jesus, don't let Ms. Alice hear you say that!"

The men laughed and Randolph remarked, "She really would spank my behind!"

"That's de honest truth!"

"Calvin, I want you to know I consider you a close friend. You saved my life!"

"Thank you, sir that means a lot to me."

It wasn't long before the wind, rain, and lightning stopped. The horrible roar was gone, so the folks in the mansion climbed out of the cellars and ventured out.

Leroy commented, "Things look good in de house, Ms. Alice."

"I don't see any broken glass, so far."

As the group went from room to room opening shutters, they didn't find any damage from the storm. When they stepped outside, they were so thankful that the chicken house and barn were fine. For as bad as the storm was, there were only a few trees down in the yard.

"There be leaves, branches, and limbs all over de place," Freddie remarked.

Suddenly, Alice saw Randolph's horse and she screamed, "Oh God, where is Randolph?"

Beulah saw Calvin's horse and shouted, "That's Calvin's horse!"

"We have to find them!"

Freddie reminded, "Mr. Randolph was headed to git Calvin at the horse barn!"

The entire group rushed towards the road that led to the horse barn with Freddie in the lead.

When all was quiet, Calvin pushed on the trap door, but he couldn't get it open more than a few inches. Randolph and Calvin tried to lift it together, but it still wouldn't budge more than a few inches.

"Something must be on top of the trap door, Calvin."

"How is we going to git out of here?"

"We're going to have to wait for help. Freddie knows I was headed here to get you."

"We don't have no other choice but to waits and hopes de folks come looking for us."

"Just think Calvin, the cellar is cooler than the outside."

"Thank the Lord for that."

When the group got to the horse barn, Asa slowly cracked the door open and slipped inside. The horses were mighty nervous, so Asa didn't want to spook them into a frenzy. He made his way to the door that led to the corral and opened it, so he could lead the horses out one by one.

Calvin heard someone talking and shouted for help. Asa knelt down by the trap door and said, "Hold on a bit, so I can get de horses in the corral. Part of de roof fell in, so we're going to have to move all de boards out of the way."

"We sure are happy to hear your voice, Asa!"

"Is you alright, Mr. Randolph?"

"I will be as soon as we get out of here!"

"Is you alright, Calvin?"

"I'm fine!"

Asa, Leroy, and Freddie moved the horses outside and

opened the door, so the ladies could get inside. Together, everybody got the roof debris moved, so they could open the trap door. Randolph sure was glad to see daylight and his wife's face.

"Be careful Alice, because I'm banged up some and really sore."

"Sweet Jesus, Honey, you're a bloody mess! We've got to get you home, so I can patch you up!"

Sally shouted, "Please don't die, Poppa!"

Freddie pleaded, "You gots to be alright, Mr. Waverly!"

"Sweet Sally and Freddie, I'm alright for the most part."

Daisy mentioned, "Mr. Randolph, the house, barn, and chicken house be fine!"

"There be a few trees down, but they didn't hit nothing," Beulah added.

Shortly, Jerome, Trudy, and Sidney rushed into the barn and were relieved to see everybody alive.

Jerome asked, "Mr. Randolph is you going to be alright?"

"I'm just banged up a little. I want to know how everybody is and what damage we have!"

Sidney went on, "All our homes be safe, de cattle barn be good, de lumber mill be good, and de crops looks alright."

Trudy continued, "Poppa says there be a big area where we was going to cut trees that be tore up. It goes all de way to Mr. Baker's land."

"The trees are down and all twisted up," Sidney added.

Alice suggested, "Let's get you home, so I can clean you up."

"Calvin and I are hungry, too!"

Daisy fired back, "We'll feed both of you full of good food!"

Asa and Leroy grabbed ahold of Randolph and slowly helped him walk to the mansion. He had to admit he was a little woozy.

Alice ordered, "Calvin, let me take a look at your arm

when we reach the house."

Calvin looked at his left sleeve and couldn't believe his sleeve was red with blood, because he couldn't remember being hurt. "Maybe, I gots de nasty cut pulling Mr. Randolph out of de tree."

When the concerned group got back to the mansion, Oscar and some of the other men were waiting to report the damage in their areas.

"Sweet Jesus, Mr. Randolph, is you alright?"

"I will be soon, so talk to me while Ms. Alice fixes me up."

Freddie teased, "You gots a black eye already, sir!"

Alice took off his bloody shirt and cleaned up all the cuts and scrapes. He sure didn't like his vinegar bath, because it burned like fire. Cleaning up his head, face, and hair was a different story. Alice knew she would have to sew up the nasty cut on his head. Randolph moaned and groaned, but he managed to make it through the ordeal.

Alice cleaned up Calvin's arm and bandaged it.

Beulah teased, "Calvin, you acted like a baby!"

"No, I did not!"

Randolph suggested, "Oscar tell me about your area."

"The gristmill be fine, and we didn't lose any fruit trees only some limbs."

"That's good to hear! Tomorrow, I want to see the damage, so we know how much repair work is necessary."

Both Randolph and Calvin gobbled down their dinner enjoying every bite.

Sally asked, "Do you think Mr. Baker has any damage?"

"I don't know, but tomorrow we'll check on his family."

Everyone headed in different directions to get some badly needed rest and sleep after a difficult day. They all considered themselves very lucky and blessed.

Poor Freddie had fallen asleep on the sofa after running

all over the plantation spreading the alarm. Alice said to leave him there, because he earned every minute of sleep he could get.

When Randolph put his head on his pillow, he fell asleep in a few minutes thanks to some wine. Alice shook her head, because her husband looked like he'd been on the losing end of a free for all fist fight. She thanked the Almighty he was sleeping by her side and everybody was safe. So far, they had trees to cut up and a barn roof to repair. Thank heavens; their crops had escaped damage, because they needed all of them to survive.

After breakfast the next day, Randolph, Sally, and some of the workers went over to check on John Baker and his family.

As Sally and Randolph sat on their wagon seat going down John Baker's lane, Sally shouted, "Poppa, part of their home is almost gone. Look at all the trees that are down and twisted all up!"

Randolph suggested, "Be very careful walking around, Sally."

She asked, "Did the storm do all this damage?"

Her father replied, "I heard my father talk about a tornado that happened south of us. I think a tornado went through part of our land and hit here. I pray they had time to get to their cellar."

The closer they got to John Baker's home the more convinced Randolph was that a tornado had touched down here.

Oscar rode up and said, "Mr. Randolph, this be bad! We'll help you go through what's left of de house."

Randolph suggested, "Right now, the most important thing is finding the Baker family."

Everyone slowly picked their way through the rubble

looking for signs of life.

Oscar saw an arm, so he started digging through the rubble. He shouted, "Mr. Randolph, it is Mr. Baker's mother!"

Carefully, Randolph went over to see, and he knew she was dead.

Sidney saw clothing, so he started digging through the bricks and furniture. He shouted, "I've found Mr. Baker, but he's dead!"

Randolph looked at him and said, "Sweet Jesus, John, may you rest in peace!"

Asa called out, "Mr. Randolph, Mrs. Baker is over here! I think she's dead, too."

Randolph went over and knew she was gone, too.

Sally yelled, "Help me! Someone is under this sofa!"

The group helped move the sofa and bricks only to find the two house servants dead.

Sally commented, "They didn't have a chance!"

Oscar found the cellar door and opened it. No one was inside, so he knew they still had to find Mr. Baker's sixteen year old daughter.

Sidney asked, "Was Judge Anderson staying with Mr. Baker?"

"Yes, but he was heading back to Montgomery this morning."

Sally suggested, "Maybe, he left before the storm hit."

"I sure hopes so," Oscar mentioned.

Asa called out, "Over here! I need help moving de china cabinet, but be careful, because there be broken glass everywhere."

Under the china cabinet was Mr. Baker's daughter. The group knew the heavy cabinet had fallen and killed her.

Sally cried and said, "The whole family is gone! It just ain't fair!"

The group moved the bodies outside and continued to look for Judge Anderson.

Randolph thought, "We have to look for John's other slaves and find the livestock, too."

The group was unable to find the judge, so they turned their attention to the livestock and field hands. They searched for quite a while, but they didn't find Baker's slaves. The men found three horses, six cows, and several chickens still alive. Randolph knew he needed to take the livestock back to Evergreen Manor. When Baker's son returned from the war, he could get his livestock back. Baker's crops were damaged slightly, so Randolph would pick them and keep a ledger for Baker's son.

Randolph told his people to get more wagons, so they could bring the dead livestock back, butcher them, and smoke the meat. The meat was valuable, so they couldn't let it rot.

Now, the men had the difficult task of digging graves for the Baker family and their two house servants.

Sally asked, "Poppa, can I take the jewelry to save for Robert?"

Her father answered, "Of course, he'll appreciate that."

The men buried the family, and Randolph prayed the family and servants had found peace in paradise.

Later, he decided to return and look through the rubble for anything Robert could use and cherish.

Randolph shook his head and thought, "I came today to help my friend and family, but instead, I'm standing by their graves. My family and workers are very lucky to be spared death or injury during the terrible storm."

CHAPTER 21

After the Battle of Kennesaw Mountain, the two armies remained entrenched opposite each other for a few days.

A sergeant told Austin and a few others to gather up firewood for camp. He warned, "Be careful on the trails, because the rains have loosened up a lot of the ground."

Austin started out ahead of the other men. He thought, "I hate this detail, because slaves did this on our plantation. When this war is over, I won't be cutting firewood!"

One soldier shouted, "Slow down, Waverly. Remember what the sergeant said!"

Austin yelled, "Shut up! Don't tell me what to do, you dumb cracker!"

"Alright hardhead, do whatever you want. Just remember, don't whine if you fall and rip your pants, planter boy!"

Austin stomped up the trail cussing the soldier. Suddenly, the ground gave way, and Austin started sliding down the hill hitting rocks on the way down. He slid into a crop of rocks and stopped. He yelled, "Oh God, help me!" He fell into a nest of copperheads and one snake after another struck Austin as he tried to beat them off and get away. He yelled, "Help me! You have to get the snakes off of me!"

The other men rushed up the trail, stopped, and looked over the side. "Sweet Jesus, I ain't going down there to git bitten by all them copperheads. They be poisonous!"

"Me neither! I can't stand him, anyway!"

Another one commented, "I ain't going down after his sorry body, either. He can rot down there as far as I'm concerned."

Austin thought, "This can't happen to me, because Evergreen Manor is mine! I'm going to be a rich planter! You have to help me!"

He couldn't fight the snakes or move anymore. His lips

were numb, his eyes wouldn't focus, and he was having trouble breathing. He tried to take a deep breath, but he couldn't. He started to spin in a black hole, his lungs wouldn't work, he was cold, and his mind wouldn't concentrate. He gasped one more time, and then there was nothing.

One soldier said, "I think he's dead, because he ain't running his mouth. I ain't going after him, neither, because the copperheads ain't getting me!"

Another one remarked, "I never liked that spoiled, planter boy. He had a big mouth and a mean streak all the time!"

Another one commented, "He was always complaining about something. In my opinion, he was crazy! I say good riddens!"

One soldier suggested, "Let's git out of here and tell his brothers what happened."

When Albert and Michael were told the news, they were dumbfounded.

Michael admitted, "I can't cry for Austin, because he turned into a mean, evil person when he beat up Kramer."

Albert responded, "I can't cry either. Austin was a bitter, angry person, and he was really starting to scare me most of the time."

Michael commented, "I never thought something like this would kill him. Now, we have to leave his body with the snakes."

Albert asked, "What do we tell Poppa and Mama?"

Michael answered, "We tell them the truth, because I won't glorify his life or death."

Albert replied, "I agree. They deserve the truth."

Gen Sherman side stepped Gen Johnston's Army on July 2nd and moved closer to Atlanta. Union pontoons came on July 8th, so Gen Oliver Howard's troops could cross the Chattahoochee River. Later, Gen Sherman crossed the river forcing Gen Joseph Johnston to withdraw behind Peachtree Creek just three miles from Atlanta.

On July 17th, Gen Johnston was relieved of his command by President Jefferson Davis. The political leadership of the Confederacy was fed up with Johnston's defensive tactics. They wanted aggressive tactics, so they replaced Johnston with Gen John Bell Hood. He had served with Gen Longstreet in the Eastern Theater proving he was a hard fighting, brave soldier. The Confederate leadership wanted the army to attack, so they could save Atlanta and the heartland of the South.

The 10th Kentucky along with their brigade crossed the Chattahoochee River and camped on the south side on July 17th.
Gen Thomas' Army of the Cumberland was ordered to march straight to Atlanta. Gen William Sherman ordered the Army of the Ohio commanded by Gen John Schofield and the Army of the Tennessee commanded by Gen James McPherson to march east and destroy the railroads that were supplying the Confederate army.

On July 19th, the 10th Kentucky set up their position south of Peachtree Creek on their division's left.
Gen John Bell Hood learned that Gen Sherman had divided his army, so Hood saw an opportunity to attack Gen George Thomas' Army of the Cumberland. Hood believed Thomas would be vulnerable when he had to cross Peachtree Creek several times. Gen Hood planned to attack Thomas, drive his army westward, and Gen Sherman would be forced to rescue the Army of the Cumberland. Gen Sherman would have no other choice but to pull away from Atlanta.

On July 20th, Gen Thomas' Army crossed Peachtree Creek and started putting up fortified earthworks. Gen John

Palmer's XIV Corps was positioned on the right while Gen Hooker's XX Corps was positioned in the center. Gen John Newton's Division was assigned the left flank. The rest of the IV Corps was reinforcing McPherson and Schofield east of Atlanta.

Confederate Gen Hood ordered Gen William Hardee's Corps to attack the right and Gen Alexander Stewart to attack the left. Hood held Gen Cheatham's Corps out to keep an eye on Gen Sherman's forces east of Atlanta. The attack was scheduled to begin at 1:00 pm. However, the attack didn't start until 4:00 pm, because there was confusion in orders and miscommunication between Hood's corps commanders.

The 33rd Alabama was under Hardee's Corps, Cleburne's Division, and Lowrey's Brigade. The 33rd Alabama was held in reserve and didn't take part in the battle.

The 10th Kentucky was part of Gen Palmer's XIV Corps, Gen Absalom Baird's Division, and Col Este's Brigade. Gen Palmer's XIV Corps position on the right would be attacked by Confederate Gen Alexander Stewart's Corps.

Gen Hardee's men attacked, but couldn't make any headway on the Union left while suffering heavy casualties. Gen Stewart's men plowed into the Union right.

Matt watched the gray wave swarm towards their lines. He had his musket ready along with his friends. The skirmishers fell back into the trenches ready to meet the onslaught.

The lieutenant yelled, "Steady! Don't waste a shot! Fire!"

Matt and his friends fired, reloaded as quickly as possible, picked a target, and fired.

Squire shouted, "They're falling back!"

Henry yelled, "Here they come again!"

The lieutenant ordered, "Fire!"

Volley after volley was poured into the Rebel wave, and

artillery shells screamed across the sky and dropped deadly shrapnel and canister shots. A couple of Union brigades gave way and retreated.

The lieutenant yelled, "Hold your positions! Don't show the white feather!"

The 33rd New Jersey Infantry was overrun and most of the men were captured along with their battle flag.

Ben yelled, "The Rebs have captured an artillery battery!"

Union troops mounted a counterattack resulting in hand-to-hand combat and drove the Rebels back. The lines bent, but they didn't break. The Rebels weren't able to break through the Union lines at any point.

Squire shouted, "The Rebs are withdrawing! Chickamauga, boys!"

Matt gasped for air even though it smelled like gunpowder. He drank from his canteen and wiped his sweaty face. He thought, "Lord, it is hot and humid! Will my ears ever stop ringing? I hope the Rebs don't attack again in the dark. Michael are you out there with your brothers? When is this nightmare going to end?"

Confederate casualties at the Battle of Peachtree Creek were around 2,500 men compared to Union casualties put at 1,900 men. Gen John Bell Hood lost his first battle as commander of the Confederate Army of Tennessee.

The area around Collier's Mill was thickly strewn with the wounded and dead attesting to the savage fighting that occurred there.

Gen Hood had to turn his attention to the successful advance of Gen McPherson's Army on the east side of Atlanta. On July 22nd, the Rebels withdrew from their trenches and fell back to Atlanta.

The 10th Kentucky and their brigade moved towards Atlanta and took up a position two miles from Atlanta and a half mile west of the railroad on Turner's Ferry Road.

The day after the Battle of Peachtree Creek the 33rd Alabama lost their regimental commander Col S. A. M. Adams. He was inspecting his men's front lines when a Union sharpshooter got Col Adams in his sights and pulled the trigger. The colonel was shot in the chest and died sitting by a tree. He was replaced by LtCol Robert Crittenden.

Gen Hood withdrew from his outer lines of defense to his inner lines. Gen Sherman moved forward just like Hood had hoped he would. Hood sent his cavalry to attack and raid Sherman's supply lines. Hood ordered Gen Hardee's Corps, including the 33rd Alabama, to march 15 miles east of Atlanta and attack the left and rear of the Union. Hood ordered Gen Cheatham's Corps to attack the Union position head on.

The Union would lose Gen James McPherson when he was killed riding along his lines observing the fighting. Gen John Logan assumed temporary command of the Army of the Tennessee.

Gen Alexander Stewart   Gen John Logan

On July 22nd, the 33rd Alabama attacked a wooded area and captured many prisoners and all kinds of supplies. The regiment stopped to fill their canteens at a creek. When the regiment came out of the creek area, the Union boys attacked them. The regiment had to retreat and some of them were captured.

Around July 28th, Gen Sherman ordered Gen Oliver Howard to move from the left flank and march behind Union lines to the right flank. Their orders were to cut Hood's railroad supply line running from Atlanta to East Point.

Gen Hood was in high spirits, because he predicted Sherman would send troops to the right flank. Hood ordered Gen Stephen Lee and Gen Alexander Stewart to destroy the Union forces at a chapel called Ezra Church.

What Hood didn't count on was Gen Howard knowing him from their days at the West Point Military Academy. So, Howard's men were waiting in their trenches when the Confederate forces attacked, because Howard figured Hood would pull this kind of maneuver. The Rebels couldn't break the Union lines, but they did stop Howard from reaching the railroad.

Battle of Ezra Church

The Union cavalry failed to cut the railroad, and in the process lost the commanding officer of the Cavalry Corps Gen George Stoneman who was captured.

Confederate casualties at the Battle of Ezra Church were around 3,000 men compared to Union casualties numbering around 640 men.

On August 3rd, the 10th Kentucky and their brigade were relieved from their present position and moved four miles to the southwest where they set up earthworks to the right of the XXIII Corps. This put them near Utoy Creek. Their pickets were under constant fire from the Confederate skirmishers on August 4th.

The 33rd Alabama and all the units manning the trenches found out quickly that they were safer staying in their trenches at all times. Sniper and artillery fire made it dangerous to be in the open.

The 33rd Alabama was ordered to keep moving their fortified trenches further to the left every day. The men already hated the hard, red clay, because they had to use bayonets, picks, or spades to dig into it.

Very seldom were the men able to wash their clothes or bathe in a creek, so they became infested with every insect on the planet.

Albert complained, "If we keep digging to the left, we're going to end up at the Gulf of Mexico!"

Michael added, "That's fine with me! At least, we can jump in the Gulf and bathe. I don't mind drowning the lice and insects camped out on my body!"

Albert fired back, "Amen brother!"

Pvt John Wyatt shot back, "I hate the red ants and chiggers! They drive me crazy!"

Albert added, "All of us scratch constantly from all the bites we have. I hope the Yanks are having as much fun as we are scratching like a dog full of fleas!"

All the men laughed like hyenas full of fleas and chiggers.

Pvt George Peacock added, "The heat and sun be baking my skin into leather!"

Pvt James Metcalf continued, "All of us look like cherries walking around."

Michael chimed in, "I could eat a basket full of cherries, right now!"

Pvt Sam Stevens teased, "Lord boy, you be ending up with dia-ree for a month!"

Michael replied, "On second thought, I'll eat a hand full."

Pvt William Dykes teased, "Ya boy, don't be a pig!"

Pvt Green Burgess complained, "I feel like a rat living in these dirty trenches all day and night!"

Albert commented, "I wish for one whole night's sleep with no snipers and artillery firing at anything that moves!"

Pvt Peacock agreed, "Amen to that ya'll!"

Gen Sherman wasn't happy that he couldn't get around Hood's left flank at Ezra Church, so he decided to try again. This time Sherman sent the Army of the Ohio under Gen John Schofield to his right flank near Utoy Creek.

On August 4th, the Army of the Cumberland's XIV Corps and the Army of the Ohio's XXIII Corps crossed Utoy Creek. The first attack failed against Gen Patton Anderson's Division.

On August 5th, Gen Schofield attacked and the 10th Kentucky with their brigade advanced towards the Rebel rifle pits under fierce fire. The regiment captured the Rebels skirmishers and took over their rifle pits. This advanced the brigade's main line over 100 yards closer to the Rebel's works.

On August 6th, Schofield attacked again, but failed to break through to get to the railroad. Gen William Bate's Division inflicted heavy losses on the Union forces, capturing 200 prisoners, and three battle flags.

On August 7th, the Union forces started extending their lines to the right and putting up earthworks.

From August 4th to August 7th, the 10th Kentucky and their brigade lost 73 men killed or wounded. The commanding officer of the 74th Indiana, LtCol Myron Baker, was killed.

The 10th Kentucky had 250 men fit for duty when they crossed the Chattahoochee River. Now, that number was dropping.

CHAPTER 22

Sgt Warren Taylor read the last letter he received from his fiancée, Laura Waverly. Oh, how he wished he could hold her in his arms in Louisville. Instead, he was abroad the *USS Lackawanna* which was a Union screw sloop-of-war. The ship was assigned to the West Gulf Blockading Squadron and placed off Mobile Bay, Alabama.

On June 14th, she captured the *CSS Neptune* trying to run the blockade carrying 200 tons of cargo. Later, she captured the steamer *CSS Planter* loaded with resin and cotton trying to run the blockade to get to Havana, Cuba.

During March-April 1864, the *USS Lackawanna* was assigned to the Texas coast near Galveston.

In May, she was called back to Mobile to keep the Confederate ram *CSS Tennessee* from breaking out of Mobile Bay.

CSS Tennessee

Warren knew Admiral David Farragut was preparing for an assault on Mobile Bay, because the port was the last one open on the southern coastline. Warships were starting to gather, so he knew it wouldn't be long. He prayed he would survive the war, so he could marry Laura and start their life together.

The Confederate government and navy knew they couldn't defend their entire coastline, so they decided to defend the most vital ports and harbors. The Confederate army was ordered to strengthen Fort Morgan at the entrance of Mobile Bay with 46 guns and 600 men. Fort Gaines at the entrance to Mobile Bay received 26 guns and 600 men. Fort Powell at the western end of Mobile Bay received 18 guns and 140 men. The forts had one major flaw; they weren't protected from an attack from their rear. Gen Richard Page was the local commander of the forts.

The Confederates placed 67 torpedoes (naval mines) across the bay entrance allowing one area for friendly vessels to enter and leave the harbor. The gap was on the eastern side of the channel close to Fort Morgan. Of course, the torpedo field was marked by buoys.

Confederate Admiral Franklin Buchanan was in command of the Rebel flotilla in Mobile Bay which consisted of the ironclad ram *CSS Tennessee* and three side-wheeler gunboats named the *CSS Selma, CSS Morgan,* and the *CSS Gaines.*

Union Admiral David Farragut's flotilla was made up of 18 vessels. Eight were wooden-hulled warships with a large number of guns, three were small gunboats, four were ironclad monitors, and three were called double-enders that could navigate treacherous channels on inland rivers and waterways.

Fort Morgan batteries

Signal corpsmen were put on the major ships of the attacking flotilla, so the flotilla could communicate with the landing forces assigned to attack the forts.

On August 3, 1864, fifteen hundred men landed about 15 miles west of Fort Gaines and marched to within a half mile of the fort where they entrenched. The troops were from the 77th Illinois Infantry, the 34th Iowa Infantry, the 96th Ohio Infantry, and the 3rd Maryland Cavalry commanded by Gen Gordon Granger.

Admiral Farragut ordered his 14 wooden-hulled ships lashed together in pairs. If a vessel's engines were damaged her partner could keep her moving. The monitors would lead the way into Mobile Bay in a column and head close to Fort Morgan. The other ships would form a double column and move on the port (left) side of the monitors, so their wooden hulls would be protected from the guns at Fort Morgan.

Admiral Farragut ordered his monitors to attack the Confederate ram *CSS Tennessee,* and his other ships would attack the Rebel gunboats.

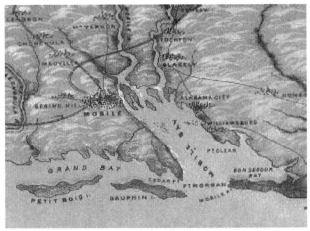
Mobile Bay

Sgt Warren Taylor stood on deck on the *USS Lackawanna* and knew August 5th would be a perfect day for the attack. The tide was coming in, so that would give them more speed. The brisk breeze would blow their gun smoke towards Fort Morgan. He watched the four ironclads with *USS Tecumseh* in the lead heading into Mobile Bay towards Fort Morgan. The *USS Brooklyn* lashed to the *USS Octorara* led the second column, because she was fitted with a device to remove mines called a cowcatcher. The *USS Lackawanna* was lashed to the *USS Seminole* and stood fourth in line to enter the harbor.

The *USS Tecumseh* fired off the first shot around 6:45 am, and the forts answered with a salvo of their own. *USS Tecumseh* moved past Fort Morgan and headed towards the *CSS Tennessee.* The captain of the *USS Tecumseh* took his vessel directly across the minefield, and no one knows if he forgot the instruction to remain east of the minefield, but his ship was doomed. One of the underwater naval torpedoes (mines) exploded under the hull, and she sank in less than three minutes. Ninety-three members of her crew were killed, including the captain, and only 21 crew members were saved.

Admiral Farragut's 14 warships passed into the middle of the bay while his gunboats went after the three Confederate gunboats. The *USS Metacomet* captured the *CSS Selma*. The *CSS Gaines* was badly damaged and was beached to keep it from sinking. The *CSS Morgan* sought protection by Fort Morgan and managed to escape to Mobile the next night.

USS Tecumseh sinking

The *CSS Tennessee* was very slow, so the Union sloops decided to ram her. Several of the Union sloops rammed her, including the *USS Monongahela,* which was fitted with an iron shield on her bow (front of ship), but none of the ramming collisions damaged the ironclad. The *CSS Tennessee's* shells were plagued by misfires and inferior powder.

Two of Admiral Farragut's monitors arrived as the *CSS Tennessee* began to take one lethal blow after another. Her smokestack was shot away, so she couldn't maintain boiler pressure. She couldn't steer, and some of her gun ports were jammed closed and the crew couldn't get them open which meant the guns behind the gun ports were useless.

Sgt Warren Taylor heard the explosion from the *USS Tecumseh,* and he asked, "Sweet Jesus, did the *USS Tecumseh* hit a mine?"

Landsman Louis Chaput shouted, "She's going down, but she's not in the east channel."

Sgt Taylor shouted, "She's going down fast, so it must have split her hull open!"

Chaput replied, "We'll have to pick up survivors! Our guns are ready to fire a broadside at Fort Morgan! Get ready!"

Quartermaster Daniel Whitfield's gun fired along with the rest of the gun crews at Fort Morgan. The gun crews quickly reloaded for another broadside (all guns on one side of a ship fires).

The *USS Lackawanna* started taking heavy fire, and a shell exploded on deck severely wounding Seaman John Burns.

Sgt Taylor yelled, "You must go below to the surgeon! Warren helped Seaman Burns get below and quickly took Burn's place at his station. Later, Burns returned to his station and helped the powder division for the rest of the battle.

Sgt Taylor was blown off his feet by another explosion which knocked down some rigging, and when he got up he saw that Landsman Louis Chaput was badly wounded. Sgt Taylor grabbed Chaput, got him below, and he took Chaput's station until the landsman could returned to his gun.

An enemy shell exploded in the shell room, and Armorer George Taylor who was already wounded rushed into the room and extinguished the fire with his good hand.

Seaman Adam McCullock was wounded when an enemy shell exploded close to his station. Sgt Taylor got to him and told him to get below.

McCullock answered, "I'm not leaving my station until this battle is won!"

Suddenly, another shell exploded causing some of the rigging to fall on the deck. Another shell struck the vessel and several men in a gun crew were killed.

Sgt Taylor and several marines took the place of the dead

and continued to fire the cannon.

When the enemy disabled the powder box at his gun, Landsman Patrick Dougherty kept a supply of powder available throughout the battle for his gun.

Confederate batteries fire on Union warships

The *USS Lackawanna* headed for the Confederate ram *CSS Tennessee* at full speed, and Warren heard someone yell they were going to ram her. Warren and the gun crew braced themselves for the collision.

Quartermaster Daniel Whitfield stood by his gun and waited for the right moment to fire his shot that entered her port side. The two vessels hit, and Warren was still knocked off his feet.

One marine yelled, "She's starting to list!"

The *USS Chickasaw* came up on the *CSS Tennessee's* stern (back of a ship), and the *USS Manhattan* started pouring shells from her 15 inch guns into the Rebel ironclad. The heavy shells bent the iron shield causing the oak backing to shatter, and several men were killed or wounded by the fragments. Admiral Buchanan suffered a badly broken leg from the oak timber.

The *USS Lackawanna* tried to ram the *CSS Tennessee* again, but ended up colliding with the *USS Hartford*, instead.

Adm Franklin Buchanan   Adm David Farragut

Shortly, the *CSS Tennessee* surrendered and her crew was taken prisoner.

Admiral Farragut at Mobile Bay

Another shell struck the *USS Lackawanna* and exploded

near the gun Warren's marines were manning. The last
thing Sgt Taylor remembered was a hot flash and flying
through the air. Sgt Taylor was taken below to the surgeon
unconscious, and the surgeon worked feverishly to get
Sgt Taylor stabilized before he was moved off the ship, later.
Sgt Taylor had suffered a broken arm and leg, plus he was
burned on his left side from his thigh to his neck. Sgt Taylor
drifted in and out of consciousness for several days.

The naval battle at Mobile Bay lasted for three chaotic
hours. Now, Admiral Farragut could concentrate on the
forts, so he sent the *USS Chickasaw* to bombard Fort Powell.
The commanding officer realized the situation was hopeless,
so he ordered his garrison to blow up its magazines and
spike its guns. The men waded to shore to the mainland and
headed for Mobile.

On August 8th, the commander of Fort Gaines surrendered
to Gen Granger and Admiral Farragut.
Fort Morgan was bombarded several times and came
under siege. Gen Richard Page surrendered on August 23rd.

At the Battle of Mobile Bay, the Union fleet suffered 150
men killed and 170 wounded. The Confederate flotilla
suffered 12 men killed and 19 wounded. Fort Morgan
suffered one man killed and seven wounded.
The Union victory at Mobile Bay helped boost northern
morale and President Lincoln's re-election campaign.

The *USS Lackawanna* would have 12 sailors awarded the
Medal of Honor for their bravery at the Battle of Mobile Bay.

Landsman Michael Cassidy
Landsman Louis Chaput
Landsman Patrick Dougherty
Landsman Samuel Kinnaird

Seaman John Burns
Seaman Adam McCullock
Boatswain's Mate William Phinney
Armorer George Taylor
Quarter Gunner James Ward
Quartermaster Daniel Whitfield
Captain of the Forecastle John Smith
Captain of the Top John Edwards

Landsman Michael Cassidy & Captain Top John Edwards

CHAPTER 23

Dr. Mills received advanced information on a group of new patients headed to the clinic from the Navy and Marine Corps. The wounded were coming from the Battle of Mobile Bay. When he got to the last patient sheets, he dropped down on his office chair.

He responded, "Sweet Jesus, how am I going to tell Laura! Warren is in serious condition."

He stepped out of his office and asked Myrtle to come over.

Myrtle could tell by Dr. Mills' demeanor he was upset. She asked, "What's wrong, Doc?"

He handed her Warren's patient sheets and said, "Please read this Myrtle, because I need your advice and help."

Myrtle took the sheets and read them. "Sweet Jesus, the boy is going to need a lot of serious care. Doc, you can take care of his broken arm and leg, but burns are difficult for any doctor. We can't let the burns get infected."

Dr. Mills commented, "Laura can't fall apart on me, because Sgt Warren Taylor needs her love and support; not her sympathy."

"I agree, so I'm going to sit her down and have a heart to heart talk with her."

Doc remarked, "There are three more marine burn victims besides Warren, and I want to put them together in the same area. Two of the marines have facial burns, so we'll have to watch their moods carefully. Myrtle, Sammy will need to work his magic and keep them laughing."

"You bet Sammy will be very important!"

Mills added, "I wish Kramer was here, because he knows how combat injuries affect the soldiers and sailors better than I do."

Myrtle put her hands on her hips and blabbed, "All of us working together will meet this head on and get those men back on their feet! If they want to give me some crap, I'll spank their behinds good!"

Mills laughed and asked, "I know he's from Louisville, but can you tell me about his family?"

"Warren's mother is dead, his father is a steamboat captain, and he has two sisters that are age 19 and 16. As Warren says, his sisters take care of his father when he's home."

Mills continued, "That's good, because the sisters can help in his care when he's able to leave here."

"Do you want me to get Laura and bring her to the office?"

He answered, "Yes and bring Sammy in, too."

When Laura read the patient sheets, she grabbed ahold of Myrtle and sobbed.

Myrtle ordered, "Honey child, you have to be strong for Warren and give him your best care. Don't fall apart and be a blabbing idiot! All those burn patients will need a lot of care."

"I know, but I'm crying, because I know he's in a lot of pain and suffering so!"

Sammy chimed in, "Doc Mills, I'll keep those marines laughing, and I won't let you down!"

Myrtle blabbed, "Laura dear, now that you have cried my bosoms wet I want you to get ahold of your emotions, so we can come up with a care plan for each one."

Dr. Mills said, "We have to set aside an area for them, and we need to get ready and supplied. Laura, you can't fall apart when you see him. Keep telling him how much you love him and that you'll take real good care of him."

Laura sniffed and replied, "I'll try my best!"

Myrtle suggested, "If you have to cry, do it in the office, honey child."

Dr. Mills ordered, "Let's get busy!"

Nurses helping the wounded

Hypodermic needles

chloroform

CHAPTER 24

Gen John Bell Hood ordered Gen Joseph Wheeler's Cavalry on August 14th to capture the Union garrison at Dalton, Georgia, destroy Union supplies, and destroy the railroad tracks at Dalton. Hood hoped this action in Gen Sherman's rear would cause him to pull back towards Dalton. However, Gen Wheeler was unable to defeat the garrison, so he withdrew.

Gen Sherman ordered his cavalry commanded by Gen Judson Kilpatrick on August 18th to destroy supplies and track on the railroads leading into Atlanta. The cavalry hit the Atlanta-West Point Railroad and tore up some tracks.

On August 19th, the cavalry attacked a supply depot at Jonesborough on the Macon-Western Railroad and burned a huge amount of supplies. The cavalry moved on to Lovejoy's Station on the Macon-Western line and started tearing up tracks.

Confederate Gen Patrick Cleburne's Division attacked the Union cavalry, and they fought into the night before Kilpatrick had to retreat or be surrounded.

The track destroyed by the Union cavalry at Lovejoy's Station was quickly repaired and the line was ready in two days.

The 10th Kentucky skirmished with Confederate forces at Sandtown and Fairburn on August 15th. They skirmished with Confederate infantry and cavalry at Camp Creek on August 18th, at Red Oak on August 19th, at Flint River on August 19th, at Jonesborough on August 19th, and at Lovejoy's Station on August 20th.

Between August 26th and September 1st, the 10th Kentucky fought skirmishes at the Chattahoochee Railroad Bridge, Pace's Ferry, and Turner's Ferry. On August 29th, they skirmished with Rebel infantry near Red Oak. On August

30th, they clashed with Rebel forces near East Point and the Flint River Bridge.

Gen Sherman was aware of the Union victory at Mobile Bay. If he could capture the Confederate railroad supply lines, Gen Hood would be forced to evacuate Atlanta. Sherman would have to hit the railroads in force, so he decided to use six of his seven corps. He started moving his troops on August 25th with orders to attack the Macon-Western Railroad between the towns of Rough and Ready and Jonesborough.

When Gen Hood learned Sherman was moving, he knew his railroad supply lines were vital to the army and the population of Atlanta. He ordered Gen Hardee to take two corps and attack the Union forces near Jonesborough, but Gen Hood wasn't aware that Gen Sherman was moving six corps at this time.

During the night of August 30th, the 33rd Alabama was ordered to move to the left. Every time the regiment stopped men dropped from the heat and exhaustion. The regiment got to Jonesborough the morning of August 31st where the men were able to eat and rest for a while.

Gen Oliver Howard's men were entrenched on the east side of the Flint River. Gen Logan's XV Corps was entrenched on high ground near the Macon-Western Railroad. Gen Thomas Ransom's XVI Corps set up on Gen Logan's right at a right angle. Gen Frank Blair's XVII Corps was west of the Flint River in reserve.

Confederate Gen Hardee ordered Gen Cleburne, including the 33rd Alabama, to attack Union Gen Ransom's line. Gen Stephen Lee was ordered to attack Union Gen Logan's position.

Gen Thomas Ransom

Gen Frances Blair

Gen Stephen Lee

Gen Judson Kilpatrick

At this point, the 33rd Alabama's beloved Gen Patrick Cleburne was in command of the corps, Gen Mark Lowrey commanded the division, and Col William Wood commanded the brigade.

Gen Cleburne's lead division, led by Gen Lowrey was attacked by Gen Judson Kilpatrick's dismounted cavalry hiding behind fence rails.

"Company B deploy in front of the regiment!"

Albert wondered as he watched the company deploy as skirmishers, "Will this be my last battle? I'm so very tired.

Help me get through this day."

Michael started walking down a small hill into the woods and to a clearing with the regiment.

Albert commented, "The Yanks are behind rail breastworks, and they have artillery."

Company B skirmished, hotly, with the Union line, and then fell back to the left and took up their position with the regiment.

Capt Smission yelled, "Fix bayonets! Charge!"

The regiment charged the rail breastworks and came under heavy fire.

Albert yelled, "Sweet Jesus, it's cavalry with repeating rifles!"

Lt Baldwin shouted, "Charge the works, men!"

The regiment gave the Rebel yell and plowed into the Union line. The Yankees broke and started retreating towards the swamp to set up a second line of defense.

LtCol James Dunklin hugged the two cannons they had captured and said, "We sure can use you two black devils!"

Pvt John Stevens yelled, "Look at the Yanks skedaddle!"

Michael shouted, "They're being reinforced!"

Capt Smission ordered, "Fall back to our line."

Albert was panting when he jumped into the trench. Sweat was pouring down his face as he gasped for air.

Michael was next to his brother gasping, too. He commented, "God is it hot! I wish we had head logs in this trench. Sweet Jesus, we're in single file and not touching elbows. If the Yanks come at our line, we'll have to do two men's work with the muskets!"

That afternoon Lt Baldwin shouted, "The Yanks are coming, again! Fix bayonets! We must hold the line!"

Michael remarked, "There are two or three columns coming at us!"

Pvt William Snell commented, "That's infantry, not cavalry!"

Albert chimed in, "Good, they won't have Spencer repeating rifles."

Capt Smission ordered, "Aim low! Don't waste a shot!"

Pvt John Stevens remarked, "We ain't had Yankees in our trenches ever, so let's keep them out!"

The blue waves advanced as the 33rd Alabama and its brigade fired volley after volley as each man entered his own world with his musket. The Union forces got to within about ten feet of the Rebel line when another volley sent them staggering back several yards.

Michael slipped out of the trench and dragged a dead Yank to the edge of the trench.

Albert asked, "What are you doing?"

He answered, "This dead Yank is going to be my head log."

Albert replied, "Why didn't I think about that?"

Several of the men did the same thing before the Yanks attacked, again.

Shortly, the Yankees charged them again, but they couldn't break the Rebel line. Soon, men from Gen Cheatham's Corps jumped in the Rebel line to reinforce the sector.

Albert chimed in, "Boy are we glad to see you!"

A private responded, "We had to march at the double-quick for a mile to get here!"

Cheatham's men were panting and gasping for air from the exertion and the heat.

Pvt George Peacock mentioned, "Firing is real heavy to our right, so our boys must be in a real dustup."

Michael continued, "The Yanks in front of us are just firing at us. They seem content to stay where they are."

A lieutenant rushed up and ordered Cheatham's men out of the trenches to plug the hole on the right flank.

Albert asked, "What's happening, lieutenant?"

He answered, "The Yankees have broken our line on the

right, and they captured Gen Govan and 600 of his men!"

Michael thought, "Please don't attack our lines, again."

Michael's wish was granted, because the Union troops in front of them just sniped at them until dark.

Around 9:30 pm, Lt Baldwin ordered, "Form up in regular formation, men. We're moving out."

As the men marched away, they could see flashes of light in Atlanta's direction.

Albert heard an explosion and shouted, "That's coming from Atlanta!"

Michael added, "Just look at the sky! There are fires raging all over Atlanta. My God, our men are evacuating Atlanta!"

Albert said bitterly, "At least, we aren't leaving them supplies. May the Lord help the people in Atlanta!"

Pvt Robert Phillips with his head wound wrapped asked, "Where is the army going?"

Albert answered, "Fate only knows that answer."

Privately, both Albert and Michael wiped tears, because they knew victory was slipping away from them.

Meanwhile on a different part of the battlefield on September 1st, the 10th Kentucky was formed on the right of its brigade in the front rank 300 yards from the Rebel works. At this time, the 10th Kentucky only had 152 men fit for duty.

About 5:00 pm the captain yelled, "Fix bayonets! Hold your fire until we reach the woods!"

As the ranks advanced, Matt licked his parched lips, wiped sweat, and prayed he would survive this day doing his duty.

Next to him were Pvt Henry Grant and Pvt Squire Roberts. They, also, wiped sweat from their eyes, because it was so hot.

As soon as the brigade entered the woods, the Rebels fired a murderous volley of musketry. Leaves and branches were ripped from the trees, and bullets ricocheted off trees with a thud. The brigade stopped and fired off a volley as the 74th Indiana closed up with the 10th Kentucky.

Cpl Orville Young, the color-bearer from the 10th Kentucky, ran forward with his flag, planted it on the enemy works, and yelled, "Rally around the colors, boys!"

The color-bearer from the 74th Indiana, Sgt Joseph Benner, rushed towards the enemy works yelling, "Boys, follow me!" Sgt Benner fell dead, but Sgt Gould grabbed the flag and urged the men on.

Matt's heart pounded in his chest as the regiments charged forward at the 6th and 7th Arkansas Infantry regiments from Gen Cleburne's Division.

Pvt Ben Estes yelled, "Give them the bayonet!"

Over and over again, the four friends fought the Rebels hand-to-hand using their bayonets or musket butts.

The color guard of the 38th Ohio stood gallantly and strong even though Sgt Oscar Randall and Cpl Darius Baird were killed, and Cpl George Strawser was badly wounded.

The color-bearer of the 14th Ohio, Pvt Joseph Warner, was shot while planting the colors on the enemy's second line of earthworks. Cpl John Beely grabbed the colors, but was severely wounded, so Cpl John Snook grabbed the colors and planted them on the works and remained there until the attack was over.

Pvt Henry Mattingly from Company E of the 10th Kentucky captured the colors of the 6th and 7th Arkansas regiments. Later, he would be awarded the Medal of Honor for the capture of the flags.

When the brigade captured the enemy's line, they had no protection on their right flank. The 10th Kentucky and 74th Indiana started taking enemy fire from the right. The two regiments wheeled to the right and poured heavy fire at the enemy for about ten minutes before the Rebels fled.

When the firing stopped, Matt turned to say something to Pvt Henry Grant.

Matt yelled, "Henry! Talk to me! Open your eyes!" He looked at Henry's blood soaked shirt with tears in his eyes. "It's not fair! Why you, instead of me? You were a good friend, and I'll never forget you!"

Matt caught sight of Pvt Squire Roberts, grabbed him, and held him in his arms. "No, Squire, you didn't have a chance!" Matt looked to the heavens and asked, "Why did you take him, too? When is this madness going to end?"

As Matt sobbed, he heard Pvt Ben Estes cry for help. Matt rushed to find him and when he got to him he knew his friend was badly wounded. Matt grabbed him up and rushed to the hospital tents. "Don't you dare die on me, Ben! I'm getting you to Dr. Waverly as fast as I can. You're my best friend, and you got to hang on!"

Ben suggested, "You know that redhead you keep talking about? Marry her the next chance you get."

Matt smiled and replied, "I sure will. I promise you!" He caught sight of Jupiter and yelled for his help.

Jupiter grabbed hold of Ben and rushed towards the hospital tent. Kramer was operating on another soldier, so Jupiter put Ben on a cot. He cut Ben's pant leg and examined the wound.

Ben asked, "Jupiter is it real bad? Am I going to lose my leg?"

Jupiter replied, "I ain't no doctor, but I don't think so. I'm going to wrap it up real good, so you won't be a losing no more blood. Is you hit any place else?"

Ben answered, "I don't think so."

"I'll be looking jest in case you is."

Finally, Matt caught his breath and collapsed by Ben's cot. "Please Jupiter, don't let Ben die!"

"Dr. Kramer be finished operating on his patient in a few minutes. I has a good bandage wrapped on his wound, and it be working, so far. Sit with Mr. Ben while I be talking to Dr. Kramer."

Jupiter came back and told Matt, "Dr. Kramer says for you to gits a good meal while I gits Mr. Ben ready for surgery."

Ben ordered, "Matt go git something to eat, I'll be fine."

He responded, "Alright Ben, I am starving."

Ben looked at Jupiter and said, "Git me ready, good friend!"

In about fifteen minutes, Dr. Kramer was ready to fix up Ben. He looked at the wound, carefully.

Ben ordered, "Tell me the truth, Doc. Am I going to lose my leg?"

Kramer smiled and answered, "The bullet missed bone, and you're a lucky man, because it's a spent bullet. Alright Ben let's go night night, so I can remove the bullet, because you'll be walking in no time!"

Siege of Atlanta

Casualties during the Atlanta Campaign for the Union numbered 31,687 men compared to Confederate casualties numbering 34,979 men. Gen Sherman's Army still had 81,000 men. When Gen Hood evacuated Atlanta, he only had about 39,000 men to oppose the Union forces.

The fall of Atlanta and the Union victory at Mobile Bay boosted northern morale enough to help President Lincoln get re-elected for a second term.

Atlanta burning

The war in the Western Theater would end up going in two different directions. Right away, the Union troops had to pursue Gen Hood's Army during the start of the Franklin-Nashville Campaign. After President Lincoln was re-elected, Gen Sherman made his March to the Sea from Atlanta to Savannah, Georgia.

The 10th Kentucky was ordered to Ringgold, Georgia after the fall of Atlanta and remained there until September 30th.

The regiment was stationed at Chattanooga during the month of October and part of November. On November 14th, they were ordered to Kentucky and mustered out on December 6th.

During the regiment's service, two officers and 70 enlisted men were killed or mortally wounded. Five officers and 144 enlisted men died of disease. Their total casualties during their service were 221.

Gen Hood collected his army at Lovejoy's Station after his defeat in the Atlanta Campaign. Hood moved his army to Palmetto, Georgia where he met with President Jefferson Davis to discuss the Confederate army's next move and plan of attack.

President Davis reassigned Gen William Hardee, the 33rd Alabama corps commander, and replaced him with Gen Frank Cheatham. The two men decided the army would march to Chattanooga destroying Union supplies and tracks as it advanced. They hoped this would force Gen Sherman to follow the Confederate army. Then, Hood would march into Tennessee and destroy Gen Thomas' Army of the Cumberland before it could set up strong fortifications. Next, Hood would capture Nashville, Tennessee and march into Kentucky.

Gen Sherman chose to delay his March to the Sea and sent Gen Thomas to Tennessee to defeat Gen Hood. Gen Thomas would have the IV Corps in the Army of the Cumberland commanded by Gen David Stanley and the XXIII Corps from the Army of the Ohio commanded by Gen John Schofield. A Union division commanded by Gen James Morgan was sent to Chattanooga.

On October 3, 1864, Gen Hood's Army reached Kennesaw, an old familiar battlefield. Much to the men's horror, they could see the decaying feet, arms, and legs of the Confederate dead sticking out of their shallow graves. The men spent a day reburying their dead comrades before marching through Dallas and camping at Cedartown. That night the lightning cracked across the dark sky and rain pelted the soldiers. One soldier was hanging his haversack over stacked rifles when he was killed by lightning. Albert commented to Michael that this was a bad omen.

While the men marched, several soldiers would raid sugar cane fields and eat their fill when they camped at night.

Gen Hood bypassed Resaca and marched into Alabama towards Florence. Here, Gen Hood would join up with his cavalry commanded by Gen Nathan Bedford Forrest and wait for supplies. At this point, Gen Sherman stopped chasing after Hood's Army and began his March to the Sea. Sherman decided to cut his army off from his supply lines and live off the land. This way he wouldn't have to guard hundreds of miles of supply lines under constant raids from enemy cavalry. Sherman really didn't think Gen Hood would invade Tennessee, but when Gen Thomas realized Gen Hood was going to do just that, he ordered Gen John Schofield's Corps to Columbia on the Duck River halfway between Nashville and the Alabama line.

Kramer walked into the general's headquarters, stood at attention, and saluted.

"At ease, Dr. Waverly. As you know, Gen John Bell Hood's Army is marching into Tennessee. What happens in Tennessee is vital to the Union cause. Gen Sherman's Army is stabbing a dagger into the Confederate heartland, and we must do the same in Tennessee killing Gen Hood's Army. We know he's a reckless, aggressive fighter, and we want to turn that against him."

"I know the three year enlistment for the 10th Kentucky is up on December 6th. I have a special place in my heart for your regiment, because of their courage at Chickamauga and Missionary Ridge. Will you stay as one of my brigade surgeons, if I promise to have you home by Christmas?"

"General sir, do you promise to have me home by Christmas as a civilian?"

"Yes, I guarantee you!"

"General sir, I would like to bring two men along with me as an orderly and a stretch-bearer under the same conditions."

"You have my permission."

"General sir, I accept your offer. I guess my clinic can wait a little longer."

"Good! Now, you are promoted to colonel and bring those men back here, so I can talk to them."

"Yes sir, General, but don't you mean lieutenant colonel, General?"

"I mean full colonel, now scoot!"

"Yes sir, General!"

Jupiter, Matt, and Kramer returned to the general's headquarters, stood at attention, and snapped off a salute.

"At ease, men! Thank you for accepting my proposal. I have ordered my aide to get you men settled in quarters near the hospital area. Both of you enlisted men have been promoted to sergeant. My aide has your stripes and Col Waverly's epaulets. I'm a man of my word, and the three of you will be home for Christmas. Now, scoot!"

"Yes sir, General!"

Faces of the Civil War

CHAPTER 25

The 33rd Alabama was in Gen Frank Cheatham's Corps, Gen Patrick Cleburne's Division, and Gen Mark Lowrey's Brigade when Gen Hood's Army marched northward on November 21st. Hood sent his army in three columns screened by Gen Forrest's Cavalry. Cheatham's Corps was on the west, Gen Stephen Lee's Corps was in the middle, and Gen Alexander Stewart's Corps was on the east side. Hood's men marched 70 miles in freezing rain, sleet, and brutally cold winds toward Mt. Pleasant. Once they reached Mt. Pleasant, the three columns joined up and continued to march together toward Columbia.

Gen Schofield's forces retreated and marched northward from Pulaski to Columbia in the same brutal weather. Schofield's men reached Columbia before the Confederate army, started erecting fortifications, and secured the bridge over the Duck River.

Gen Thomas ordered Schofield's Army on November 28th to get ready to withdraw to Franklin.

The Confederate cavalry, artillery fire, and demonstrations by part of Hood's men allowed him to cross the Duck River and side step Columbia. He wanted to get between Schofield and Thomas, so he could defeat Schofield north of Columbia.

Gen Schofield rushed part of the IV Corps commanded by Gen George Wagner to hold Spring Hill and guard their 800 wagon supply train until Schofield could get there.

On November 29th around 11:30 am, the Confederate cavalry reached the crossroads and were surprised to encounter Union forces. The cavalry dismounted and engaged, because Hood ordered them to hold on until the infantry arrived.

Gen Cleburne's men got to Spring Hill in the afternoon just as the cavalry was running out of ammunition.

Cleburne staggered his brigades with the 33rd Alabama in Lowrey's Brigade on the right. Albert, Michael, and the regiment crossed a slope and field driving the Yankees out of their rail defenses, around a barn, and down another slope. The brigade stopped to reform their ranks. The Alabama boys, personally led by Gen Cleburne, were supported by Gen Govan's Arkansas Brigade. The Yankees were routed and Cleburne's men headed towards the Columbia Pike to meet Schofield's forces. The Union artillery poured heavy fire at the Confederates stopping their advance.

By 6:15 pm, the battlefield was dark and the Confederate generals decided to wait until morning to deal with Schofield. While the Confederates slept, Schofield's Army passed through Spring Hill on their way to Franklin.

The next morning Hood was furious to find out Schofield's Army had escaped during the night.

The Battle of Spring Hill was a minor conflict as far as casualties were concerned. The Union lost 350 men compared to Confederate losses numbering 500 men.

Gen Schofield's Army reached Franklin safely on November 30th only 12 miles away from Spring Hill. The Union forces started building strong fortifications around the deteriorated ones built the year before. They included six to eight feet breastworks with a four foot wide trench in front, and thorny branches from osage-orange trees filling the trenches and placed all around the area.

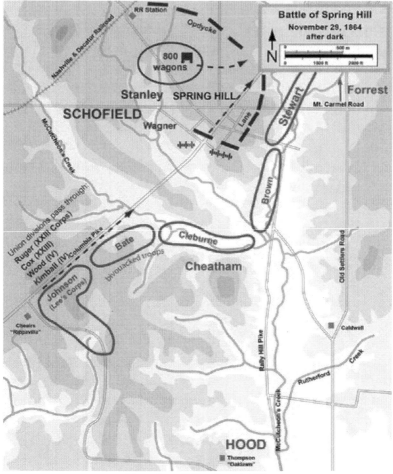

Battle of Spring Hill

Gen Schofield was faced with a monumental task to get Franklin ready to defend against Hood. He had to leave his pontoons behind in Columbia, because he lacked wagons to carry them. The pontoons Gen Thomas ordered weren't in Franklin yet. Across the Harpeth River was a burned out wagon bridge and an undamaged railroad bridge. Schofield's engineers worked feverishly to repair the wagon bridge and placed planking over the railroad bridge, so his wagons and men could cross the river.

By noon, most of the wagons had crossed the river, and

the Union fortifications were ready. Schofield placed his back to the Harpeth River. His fortifications formed a semicircle around Franklin. Where the Columbia Pike entered the town there was a gap in the lines. Schofield had his troops build a barrier 150 yards behind the gap made of rails and dirt. He placed the guns of Battery A of the 1st Kentucky Artillery where they could defend the gap.

Gen Hood's Army got to Winstead Hill just two miles south of Franklin around 1:00 pm. Sunset would be around 4:30 pm, so Hood decided to attack Gen Schofield's fortifications immediately even though his artillery, one corps, and other support troops were far behind his infantry. Hood's subordinate generals protested the decision, but Hood wouldn't wait for most of his artillery and Gen Stephen Lee's Corps to arrive. Hood's 27,000 men would have to march across two miles of open territory with just two batteries of artillery to support them.

The 33rd Alabama in Lowrey's Brigade and Gen Cleburne's Division formed up in a second rank behind the brigades of Gen Govan and Gen Granbury. Gen Cheatham's Corps was ordered to the west side of the Columbia Pike, and Gen Stewart's Corps was placed on the east side of the Columbia Pike.

Two Union brigades were about a half mile ahead of the main Union fortifications. Gen George Wagner's Division was the last to arrive from Spring Hill, so Schofield ordered him to hold Winstead Hill until dark, but Wagner ordered his brigades to dig in halfway between the main fortifications and Winstead Hill. One brigade commander, Col Emerson Opdycke, considered the order ridiculous, so he marched his men behind the gap where the Columbia Pike ran. This left two brigades commanded by Col John Lane and Col Joseph Conrad numbering about 3,000 men out in front of the rest of the Union army.

Gen George Wagner   Gen Emerson Opdycke

Around 4:00 pm, Albert looked at Michael and asked, "Did our boys at Gettysburg feel like this right before Pickett's Charge?"

Michael answered, "I'm sure they did."

Pvt Metcalf remarked, "We got to cross two miles before we gits to the Yankee lines!"

Pvt Dennis Lindsey commented, "Why ain't we waiting for all the artillery? Besides, Gen Pickett had lots of artillery at Gettysburg."

Pvt Ambrose Lindsey chimed in, "The Yanks have strong entrenchments, not a low stone wall like at Gettysburg."

Pvt William Snell predicted, "If we don't win this here battle, we ain't going to win this here war."

Pvt Peter Brown said, "I ain't going to survive this charge!"

Michael asked, "How do you know that?"

He replied, "I jest know."

Pvt Metcalf added, "I ain't either. Tell my folks I did my duty."

Albert suggested, "If I die today, tell my wife, son, and parents I loved them very much. Michael take care of my family and tell Kramer I'm so sorry for beating him."

Michael replied, "I will, Albert. If I should die, tell our family I loved them dearly."

The order was given to advance, and the men stepped forward with heavy hearts.

The troops in the two brigades out in front of the main Union line commanded by Gen Wagner fired a single volley of musketry and two cannons from the 1st Ohio Artillery fired canister. Many veterans from the two brigades retreated on the Columbia Pike to the Union's main breastworks. Those who didn't retreat were captured, so seven hundred of Gen Wagner's men were now prisoners.

The 33rd Alabama with its 285 men and her sister regiments marched over those two miles through brutal artillery fire. They stopped briefly to fix bayonets, because they were ordered not to shoot until they reached the Union breastworks. The regiments moved towards the Carter House cotton gin. Lowrey's Brigade would attack the Union sector defended by the 100th and 104th Ohio Infantry, the 6th Ohio Battery, Battery A of the 1st Kentucky, Battery A of the 1st Ohio Artillery, the 16th Kentucky, the 12th Kentucky, the 8th Tennessee (Union), and the 175th Ohio Infantry.

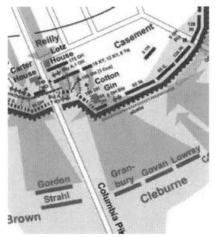

Gen Cleburne's position along Columbia Pike, Franklin

A shell exploded near Albert, and he saw Pvt William Matthews drop wounded in the hip. He saw Pvt William Wiggins lying on the ground mortally wounded.

Michael's ears rang, his eyes burned, and his heart pounded. "Please Lord help me!"

Albert yelled, "I can't see, because the smoke is so thick! We're taking musket fire!"

Capt Smission yelled, "Double quick, men!"

The 33rd Alabama ran towards the Union line yelling the Rebel yell. Albert and Michael struggled to get through the abatis. Pvt John Wyatt was next to them when he was wounded in the left arm.

Gen Lowrey yelled, "Carry both lines, men!"

His brigade drove the Yankees out of their first line of trenches and fought across the parapet of the second line.

Pvt Metcalf fell dead in the first ditch, and Pvt William Snell fell dead before he could reach the parapet. Pvt John Stevens screamed when he was shot in the hand, and Pvt Peter Brown fell mortally wounded trying to gain the parapet.

Many of the Union troops were forced to retreat to the Carter House. By this time, the Rebels had driven 50 yards into the Union lines. Savage hand-to-hand combat broke out between Rebel and Union soldiers using muskets, axes, hatchets, and knives around the trenches.

Albert fell into a ditch full of dead and wounded soldiers, but he managed to fire his pistol before he was bayonetted. The Yankee fell on him, and Albert struggled to get free.

Gen Patrick Cleburne ran towards the Union breastworks with his sword in one hand and his cap in the other. Two horses had been shot out from under him, and he managed to get within 50 yards of the Union breastworks before he was shot dead.

The South had lost one of their best generals known as the "Stonewall Jackson of the West."

Michael saw a Yankee trying to strangle Pvt George Peacock, so he jumped the soldier stabbing him in the back.

Lt John Baldwin rushed towards the parapet waving his sword to urge his men on. He yelled, "Follow me, boys! Give them the Rebel yell!" He waved his sword one more time before he was shot dead.

Michael saw a Yank rushing at him with an axe, so he hit him with his musket butt knocking the axe out of his hand. The two struggled for the axe until Michael seized it and planted it in the soldier's shoulder.

Color Sgt Cornelius Godwin planted the regiment's colors just over the breastworks. He yelled, "Rally around the colors, men! Charge the parapet!" Pvt Andrew Batchelor walked over a ditch filled with dead and wounded soldiers

to reach the colors where six men were. Sgt Godwin waved
the colors and was shot dead. Shortly, Pvt Batchelor was the
only one left alive. He ran up to the corner of the old gin
house and was jerked over the works.

The brigade was ordered to fall back in the coming
darkness. In a daze, Michael carried a wounded soldier from
another company with him when he retreated. Albert freed
himself from the pile of dead and wounded and carried a
wounded comrade with him.

Three hundred and fifty Union troops from the 12th
Kentucky and the 65th Illinois near the Carter House fired
16-shot, lever-action Henry rifles that could fire 10 shots per
minute. Many Rebels fell back to the first line of the Union
defenses and were pinned down for the rest of the evening
in the dark, because those Henry rifles kept them from
raising their heads let alone trying to get out of the trenches.

 Gen Walthall's Division got mingled in with Cleburne's men,
and they all had trouble getting through the osage-orange
thorny abatis. To make matters worse, they were taking fire
from Fort Granger across the river, too.

Confederate Gen John Adams galloped his horse upon the
Union earthworks to rally his men, but he and the horse
were killed as he tried to seize the flag of the 65th Illinois.

Gen Schofield started pulling out his infantry at 11:00 pm
to cross the river. Gen Hood didn't destroy Gen Schofield's
Army or keep him from joining up with Gen Thomas at
Nashville. Franklin was left to the Confederates, but that
came at a cataclysmic cost.
The Confederate army suffered 6, 252 casualties,
including 1,750 killed and 3,800 wounded in just a few
hours. About 2,000 men suffered wounds that were treated,

and they were returned to duty. The Confederate military leadership in the Western Theater was seriously decimated. Six Rebel generals were killed or mortally wounded, one general was captured, and six generals were wounded. Among the casualties were, 55 regimental commanders.

Union casualties were 189 killed, 1,033 wounded, and 1,104 missing or captured.

The 33rd Alabama lost two-thirds of its 285 men, so they were consolidated with the 16th and the 45th Alabama regiments to form a fighting unit, again.

Gen Hood decided to march his 23,000 man army towards Nashville, because he was afraid his army would desert if he retreated.

Michael found Albert and the brothers walked into each other's arms and wept. Both brothers were spattered with blood and tissue that came from their comrades. They were exhausted physically and mentally, and all they wanted to do was sleep for a month after they got something to eat.

Albert commented, "I thought I was going to suffocate in that ditch full of dead and wounded. Every time I tried to get out of that ditch somebody would fall on me. Oh God, Michael, I felt like I was in a coffin."

Michael said, "I'm so tired! When I grabbed an axe from a Yankee who was trying to split my head wide open with it, I went crazy swinging at one blue uniform after another. I don't know how I ended up with a group of our men on the ground in the dark. I don't remember carrying the wounded soldier either."

Albert admitted, "We're losing the war, and I don't know why I'm not full of holes."

Michael agreed, "I should be dead! I know all my body varmints are dead!"

Albert smiled and said, "My varmints are dead, too!"

The tall soldier chimed in, "If my varmints ain't dead, they sure is stone deaf!"

Michael added, "We don't have a regiment left."

Albert predicted, "If we keep this up, we won't have an army left."

One soldier asked, "Did you hear that Gen Cleburne is dead?"

Albert reacted, "Sweet Jesus! He's our best general!"

Michael added, "We have lost our Stonewall Jackson!"

Albert continued, "There isn't another general like him. What are we going to do?"

One soldier responded, "I ain't following jest anybody!"

Michael suggested, "I guess we'll wait and see who takes his place."

Another soldier asked, "What is Gen Hood going to do now?"

Albert suggested, "You know Hood is all about charging no matter what, so he'll have us marching towards Nashville in no time."

Michael chimed in, "He better let us eat first and rest some. I wish I had a glass of Poppa's wine in my hand while soaking in a warm bath."

The tall soldier laughed and said, "I wish I was in bed with my wife all cuddled up under several blankets."

Albert blabbed, "I'll go for that, too. What are you going to be doing under the blankets, boy?"

He replied, "What Mother Nature tells me to do, boy!"

The men laughed, because it was better than crying. They knew it was another brutal day in the life of a soldier they managed to survive.

CHAPTER 26

The Battle of Nashville would be another nail in the Confederate army's coffin in the Western Theater. The Union army spent two years building strong fortifications to protect Nashville. There was a seven mile semicircle dotted with forts to protect the south and west sides of the city. The north and east sides of the city were protected by the natural barrier of the Cumberland River. Also, there was a strong Union fleet of tinclad and ironclad gunboats protecting the city.

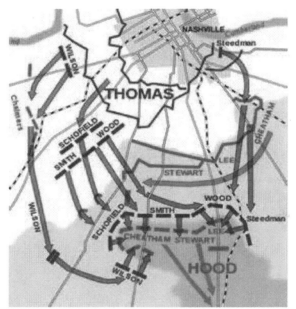

Battle of Nashville

On December 2nd, Gen Hood's Army made it to Nashville, and he started building his own entrenchments. This time, Hood decided not to attack Gen Thomas' fortifications, because he wanted Thomas to attack his line. The Confederate left flank contained five redoubts (enclosed defensive barrier) sort of like a small fort with cannons and 150 men in each one.

President Lincoln and Gen Grant were worried about Gen Sherman being in Georgia and Gen Thomas not seeming to want to attack Gen Hood's Army. So, President Lincoln and Gen Grant kept up the pressure on Gen Thomas to defeat Hood's Army.

Gen Cheatham's Corps, including the decimated 33rd Alabama in Lowrey's Brigade, manned the extreme right which stopped at a railroad cut that was part of the Nashville-Chattanooga Railroad. line.

On December 8th, the region was hit by a brutal ice storm and below freezing temperatures that lasted through December 12th. The Rebel soldiers suffered badly, because they didn't have warm overcoats, gloves, and scarves to protect them.

On December 14th, Hood added on his right a four gun lunette (fortifications made up of two sides forming an outward projection in a trench line and two parallel sides) manned by the Texas Brigade commanded by former Gen Granbury who was killed at Franklin. The lunette was concealed by brushes and trees.

Gen Thomas put his plan of action in motion on December 15th. He planned to hit the Confederate right hoping Hood would send troops to the right to reinforce his troops. Then, Gen Thomas planned to hit the Rebel left in full force.

Two Union brigades from Gen Steedman's Division were ordered to attack Gen Hood's right flank. One brigade was made up of bounty jumpers, convalescents, and new draftees, and the second brigade was made up of United States Colored Troops.

The two brigades marched towards the Confederate trenches in the cold, crisp air.

Albert yelled, "The Yanks have overrun our skirmish line!"

Michael shouted, "Our battery west of the railroad is pouring shells down on them!"

The tall soldier added, "They're getting close to Granbury's lunette!"

Another soldier shouted, "Sweet Jesus, look at them pouring enfilade (gunfire in a lengthwise direction) fire into the ranks! Let them have it, boys!"

A lieutenant yelled, "Keep up your fire! Aim low!"

The Union brigades broke under the furious fire and retreated back to the Confederate skirmish line. From there the brigades continued to fire into the Confederate works pinning them down until sunset.

Around 2:30 pm, Gen Thomas's forces attacked the five redoubts defending the Rebel left flank. The Rebels in Redoubt No. 4 and 5 fought desperately, but they were overrun by four Union brigades. Another Union brigade captured Redoubt No. 3, but in the action Union Col Sylvester Hill was killed by a Rebel sharpshooter. Redoubt No. 2 fell quickly from the Union onslaught, and Union troops coming from three different directions captured Redoubt No. 1. Confederate Gen Alexander Stewart's Corps was decimated and had to retreat over a mile to a new line of defense.

Gen Hood ordered Gen Cheatham's and Gen Lee's Corps to

retreat and set up in line with Gen Stewart's battered corps. Hood established a compact line starting on the east at Peach Orchard Hill, the center ran along a series of stone walls, and the west flank ran along small hills to Compton's Hill.

Gen Hood placed Gen Stephen Lee's Corps on the right, Gen Stewart's battered corps in the center, and Gen Cheatham's Corps on the left. This time the Confederate fortifications were shallow trenches with no abatis . Simply, the Rebel troops were too exhausted to dig them deeper or cut down trees after the day's savage fighting.

The 33rd Alabama found itself on the Confederate left close to Granny White Pike.

On December 16th, Gen Thomas used the same tactics as he did on the previous day. This time, Thomas sent four brigades against Peach Orchard Hill around 3:00 pm. The brigades marched into a wall of musket and artillery fire. The 13th United States Colored Troops battled their way to the Rebel parapet while losing 220 officers and men, and a flag in the process of combat. The regiment lost 40% of its men.

This time, Gen Hood did send two brigades from Gen Cheatham's Corps to reinforce the right.

Gen Thomas ordered Gen Schofield to attack the Rebel left and capture Shy's Hill. Schofield requested more troops and when the division arrived he still didn't order his men to attack.

A division commander from Gen Andrew Smith's Corps named Gen John McArthur saw the pounding the Confederate lines were taking from artillery fire from almost every direction. He sent a message at 3:30 pm to Gen Smith and Gen Thomas saying that he was going to attack Shy's Hill and the Rebel line to its east in five minutes if he didn't hear from them.

At 3:40 pm, Gen McArthur's Division attacked capturing Shy's Hill and rolling up the Rebel lines all the way to Granny White Pike.

Albert saw the blue wave rushing towards them, and the brothers fired and reloaded as quickly as possible. Albert ran out of ammunition, so he took some from one of the dead.

Michael yelled, "We can't hold them back. They're swarming like hornets!"

Albert shouted, "Where are our reinforcements?"

The tall soldier answered, "There are none. They ain't coming!"

Just then, Albert screamed and grabbed his shoulder, because the shot had knocked him back in the trench. He yelled, "Help me, Michael, I'm hit!"

An artillery shell exploded close by, and Michael felt a hot searing pain in his hip and side. The tall soldier fell dead from shrapnel that almost decapitated him. Michael fell across the tall soldier's body, and he couldn't crawl to Albert.

Albert crawled to his brother and shouted, "Don't you dare die, Michael! Stay with me! God take me, not my brother! Do you hear me, God? I was a bad person for a long time, but Michael has a kind spirit. Do you hear me, God? Take me! Talk to me, Michael!"

"The pain is bad, and my hip is on fire! Run, Albert, so you can get away! You have a wife and son, so run! Get away from here! You have to run! Now go!"

Albert yelled, "I'm not leaving you behind! I'm not going!"

Michael pleaded, "Please, Albert, you have to run!"

Albert replied, "I'm not going, you hardheaded cuss!"

Michael fired back, "So are you! Save yourself and run!"

Suddenly, three Yankees stood on the trench and pointed their muskets at them.

Albert yelled, "We surrender! Please don't shoot! My brother needs help! Please get him to a surgeon!"

One Yank replied, "Your army is running down Granny White Pike and Franklin Pike, so they done left you behind."

Albert pleaded, "Please don't shoot us!"

Another Yank shot back, "You sure was shooting a lot before you gots wounded!"

The third Yank commented, "I've had a belly full of killing! We don't shoot prisoners, so let's get them to the hospital tent area!"

The young Yank added, "If you Rebs try to pull something, I'll be shooting you stone dead."

"Shut up, Jasper! Help us git these Rebs to a surgeon!"

The other Yank scolded, "Ya, Jasper, this could have been us, you fool!"

Albert and Michael fought the pain as they drifted in and out of consciousness. They could vaguely remember being on stretchers and being put on something.

The young Yank commented, "You Rebs sure look and smell awful!"

Matt looked down at the two Rebs just brought in. He looked again and yelled, "Sweet Jesus, Jupiter help me!"

Jupiter rushed over, looked down, and shouted, "Sweet Jesus in heaven! We gots to help them, so Dr. Kramer can fix them up!"

Matt patted Michael's face and he opened his eyes. Matt said, "It's me, Michael! You sure are a mess!"

Michael grabbed Matt's arm and pleaded, "Please help Albert and me, Matt!"

"Jupiter and I will get you ready for Kramer!"

Michael looked at Jupiter and asked, "How are you, good friend?"

"A lots better than you and Mr. Albert be a doin'!"

"Albert has changed a lot, so he's a much better person. Take care of him, good friend."

Matt asked, "Where is Austin?"

"He's dead on Kennesaw Mountain."

Jupiter said, "I'll be right back. I gots to get Dr. Kramer."

Matt ordered, "Take it easy while I work on you."

Albert groaned, Matt leaned over him and asked, "Albert can you hear me?"

"Oh God, is that you, Matt?"

"Don't worry, cousin, we'll take good care of you. Kramer and Jupiter are here!"

Albert whispered, "Thank God there is mercy on the battlefield."

Kramer rushed to the stretchers and saw his two brothers for the first time in years. They were so gaunt, pale, and dirty. Tears filled his eyes and his chin quivered, but he knew he needed to get control of his emotions.

He leaned over Albert and said, "Don't worry, Albert, I'll take good care of you."

Albert grabbed Kramer's arm and pleaded, "Please forgive me for what I did to you, because that was an evil thing I did. It has been haunting me every day since then."

He leaned over Albert and said, "You're already forgiven." Kramer wiped tears from Albert's eyes and kissed his forehead. "Now, let me take a look at your shoulder."

Kramer went over to Michael and took his hand. "You look more like me every day! Let me see about your hip and side."

Kramer gave Matt and Jupiter instructions to get them ready for surgery.

Michael commented, "I never thought I'd see you again. You were right about the plantation, and you'll be proud of the changes Poppa has made."

"We'll talk more after I take care of your wounds."

Matt pulled Kramer aside and said, "Albert and Michael are so thin and look a fright."

"They've been walking through hades like so many other

soldiers. Matt, burn their uniforms, because they're rags. We have a long road ahead of us to get them well."

On the night of December 16th, Gen Hood's battered army retreated south on Franklin Pike and Granny White Pike headed for Columbia. Union cavalry pursued the Confederates to Columbia attacking the rear guard division causing many casualties on December 17th and 18th. The cavalry was forced to stop, because they were almost out of supplies.

The Rebel artillery and infantry crossed the Duck River at Columbia on December 19th destroying the bridges behind them.

When Gen Thomas' pontoon train arrived, the cavalry was able to cross the Duck River on December 23rd. The Union cavalry fought rear guard actions at Sugar Hill, Anthony's Hill, and Richland Creek for three days.

On December 28th, the Confederate army crossed the Tennessee River near Bainbridge, Alabama. The Union cavalry couldn't stop the Rebels from crossing the Tennessee River, but they were able to capture many supply wagons and a pontoon train on December 30th. The Union pursuit ended here.

Gen Hood retreated as far as Tupelo, Mississippi some 220 miles away from Nashville. Hood resigned his command on January 13, 1865. The Battle of Nashville ended the life of the Army of Tennessee.

The Army of Tennessee entered Tupelo with less than 15,000 men.

Confederate units only issued a few reports concerning casualties suffered at the Battle of Nashville. Union Gen Thomas reported 4,561 prisoners captured at Nashville. This total didn't include troops captured during the retreat. The best guess concerning Confederate casualties puts it at

2,500 killed and wounded. During Hood's campaign, the army suffered around 2,000 desertions.

Four Minnesota regiments lost more soldiers at the Battle of Nashville than at any other battle during the Civil War.

CHAPTER 27

Matt and Jupiter refused to leave when they were relieved, because they were sitting with Michael and Albert waiting for them to wake up from surgery. Kramer had them put in a special area by themselves away from the other prisoners. Kramer had to perform very delicate surgery on both brothers. Now, he'd have to make sure infection didn't set in and ruin all his excellent work. He made up his mind to take his brothers to his clinic when he left the army before Christmas.

Albert moaned and opened his eyes. Matt leaned over and took Albert's hand.

Albert asked, "Did I lose my arm?"

"No, Kramer did his best work to save it. I want you to know your brother is a fine surgeon."

Albert admitted, "He's a fine person I didn't have sense enough to see or appreciate."

"Austin had a lot of influence on you back then."

"He turned into a mean, bitter person no one liked. When he died, no one cried, including me and Michael."

Matt suggested, "Looks like you have a new start in life."

Kramer went inside the general's tent, stood at attention, and saluted.

"At ease, Col Waverly, I'm a man of my word. Sgt Burdette, Sgt Green, and you are ready to go home, so you'll be home for Christmas."

"General, sir, thank you very much. I would like to take two wounded Confederate prisoners to my clinic in Louisville."

"Why on earth would you want to do that?"

"General, sir, they are my brothers."

"Holy smokes! What kind of shape are they in?"

"General, sir, the war's over for both of them. They are weak, malnourished, and they need a lot of special care to regain their strength and recover. My family will help them all the way."

"Col Waverly, because I trust and respect you I'm going to grant your request."

"General, sir, thank you."

The general came around his desk, shook Kramer's hand, and said, "Good luck to you, Waverly. You have served me well, but stay in uniform until you get to Louisville."

"Yes sir, General!"

"You can send a telegram to your family letting them know you're coming home."

"Yes sir, General. I'm proud to have served with you, sir."

Kramer asked his family to meet them at the clinic, because Michael and Albert needed to stay as warm as possible. The clinic had an area set up where his brothers could have privacy away from the other Union wounded. His Uncle Edwin assured Kramer the family was excited to see Albert and Michael. As he said, it was time for the family to heal the wounds. Poor Albert and Michael hadn't heard from their family since early 1863. Very little mail got through to the families and soldiers in the South. At least, mail on the Union side usually got through.

The train stopped at the Louisville station and ambulances were waiting to carry the wounded to the Louisville hospitals and the clinic. Kramer was pleased his brothers made the trip fairly well. The brothers were loaded onto an ambulance and transported to an excited clinic.

The whole family waited with pounding hearts in the room set aside for Albert and Michael. When they entered the room, many of them burst into tears of joy. Once the boys were in their beds, the hugging and kissing frenzy started and tears flowed like rain.

Kramer wrapped his arms around his dear Maddie and kissed her crazy. Rosie ran into Jupiter's arms, and they kissed each other silly. Eleanor grabbed Matt in a bear hug as she wept. Edwin let the women have their tearful reunion, so he went over to Albert and Michael.

He said, "Welcome home boys, we're so excited to see you after so many years!"

Albert replied, "Uncle Edwin, please forgive me, and I'm so glad to see you."

"Uncle Edwin, please help us recover, so we can go home one day," Michael responded.

Edwin continued, "We'll make sure you get home when the war is over. That's a promise!"

Zeke came over and said, "Welcome home Mr. Michael and Mr. Albert."

Albert responded, "Zeke, please forgive me for all the wrong I did to you and your family, because I'm a different person, now."

"Mr. Albert, we forgive you, because we wants your heart to heal as well as your wounds," Zeke remarked.

Michael continued, "It's so good to see you, Zeke."

"We's going to git you well and put some meat on your bones," Zeke teased.

Sophie came over and hugged both boys and said, "You be gitting lots of home cooking, now!"

"I can taste your buttered biscuits already," Michael teased.

Laura grabbed Kramer and showered him with hugs and kisses. Finally, she said, "Warren and I were married during the Thanksgiving holiday."

"Congratulations, Sis, I know Warren is a fine man!"

Warren commented, "Your clinic saved my life, and

they're helping me get my strength back. Shortly, I'll be able to join my father on his steamboat, because he is so busy carrying supplies up and down the river."

"I'm glad to hear you're recovering."

Laura and Warren went over to her brothers fighting back tears. She hugged and kissed Michael and said, "Welcome home! We're going to help you recover. You sure do look a lot like Kramer!"

"I've been told that. It's good to see you and feel your hugs and kisses.

She introduced Warren to her brothers, and both boys shook his hand and welcomed him into the family.

Laura went to Albert and wasn't quite sure what to do. When she left Evergreen Manor, Albert had helped his twin brother beat the tar out of Kramer.

Albert reached out his good arm and said, "Please forgive me, Laura, because I'm not that same man anymore."

Laura buried her head in Albert's good shoulder and they both wept, because they had been granted this precious moment to make right a wrong deed from so many years ago.

Both brothers were shocked at how pretty a young woman their cousin Tess had grown into. Matt's redheaded sweetheart showered him with lots of love and wouldn't let him go. That greeting told Matt all he needed to know about her feelings. When they had some privacy, he was going to propose to her.

Myrtle walked into the room and shouted, "Sweetie Pie, I have to give you a big bear hug!" She grabbed ahold of Kramer and planted a big kiss on his cheek while hugging the stuffing out of him.

"Be careful, Sweetie Pie, you don't want to crush your

bosoms!"

"To hades with my bosoms, I've missed you something terrible!"

"I have missed you, too, Sweetie Pie!"

"Now, introduce me to your brothers since I'm going to be taking care of them."

She looked at Michael and blabbed, "Lord sakes, you look a lot like Kramer. Is you as ornery and no account as that brother of yours?"

"Maybe a little like him, darling."

"I thought so! That makes another ornery cuss I'll have to put up with." She looked at Albert who broke out in a big smile. "Just what I thought; you are another ornery, worthless cuss. What is wrong with your family, Sweetie Pie? Laura is the only good egg in the basket, and the rest of you are a bunch of rotten eggs!"

Albert blabbed, "We'll try to do better, sweetheart!"

"Don't try to sweet talk me! I'm your nurse, so you better do what I say, or I'll find me a mess of chiggers and put them in your drawers!"

Michael begged, "Please don't do that! I'll be good, because chiggers are like a plague of locust!"

Albert added, "It'll be real hard for me to scratch chiggers, right now, sweetheart!"

"I'm glad both of you understand. Now, I'm going to bring you something to eat, and I better not hear any complaints coming out of your big mouths. Do you two pests understand what I mean?"

"I'll eat any kind of food you bring me, sweetheart," Albert replied.

"Bring all the food you want, Darling," Michael shot back.

"Lord deliver me! Sweetie Pie, darling, and sweetheart coming out of your mouths is making me dizzy. I can't keep up with all these names!" Myrtle stomped out talking to herself while the room broke out in laughter.

Over the next several months, Michael and Albert recovered from their battle wounds. Albert lost some motion in his shoulder and arm, but he knew that might happen. Michael ended up with a noticeable limp, but he could manage without a cane.

Matt married his redheaded sweetheart and found a home for them to live in. Jupiter married Rosie, but they couldn't find a home anyone would sell to them. Of course, they weren't surprised to run into that problem even in Louisville. Kramer and Maddie talked it over and decided that Jupiter and Rosie could live upstairs in the big house Kramer had left to him. Maddie and Rosie got along well together, and if the neighbors had anything to say about it, Jupiter and Rosie were paid to help cook, keep the house clean, and help Kramer at the clinic.

Michael and Albert helped do the lighter work at Edwin's freight company, and nothing was ever said about the brothers being former Confederate soldiers.

When Gen Robert E. Lee surrendered at Appomattox, and Gen Johnston surrendered his battered army at Bentonville, the family started discussing how they were going to get Michael and Albert home, safely.

Randolph and Alice were desperate to find out where their sons were. There had been no word from them since early 1863, because there had been savage fighting in 1864 where the 33rd Alabama would have been. Only a few casualty lists had trickled through, and they weren't always complete. They did find out that Robert Baker, the son of their deceased neighbor, was a prisoner of war.

They knew Gen Patrick Cleburne had been killed at the Battle of Franklin. News about the Battle of Nashville and Gen Hood's retreat to Tupelo was horrific, so they wondered if their sons were dead on one of those battlefields.

Randolph had reassured his colored workers nothing had changed concerning them. They would continue to work together and share the profits, because times were going to be very difficult after the war.

Faces of the Civil War

Chapter 28

Edwin sat in his living room near the end of May and said, "It's about time you boys go home. My sources tell me we can travel by rail as far as Montgomery, safely. I have arranged for carriages and wagons to take our group to Evergreen Manor. A military escort is standing by in case we need them."

Albert commented, "I appreciate everything your family has done for Michael and me. You have helped us heal in many different ways."

Michael smiled and remarked, "We are thankful to have had the opportunity to meet dear Ms. Myrtle, because she kept us on our toes!"

Matt blabbed, "Amen to that!"

Edwin announced, "Zeke, Sophie, and Jupiter realize they will be better off staying here. After President Lincoln was assassinated, I fear Radical Republican Reconstruction will be very hard on the South. There's just too much hatred still around."

Kramer agreed, "We want them to be safe."

Eleanor asked, "Do you think we need a military escort?"

Edwin answered, "They'll let us know when you get there, because a lot depends on local activity such as bands of deserters or just plain hoodlums roaming the countryside. Kramer, Warren, and Maddie's father, Carl, will be carrying concealed pistols in case there's trouble. Remember, no weapons for Albert and Michael unless there's serious trouble."

Carl asked, "Have any of your contacts gotten word to Randolph and Alice?"

"Not yet!"

Albert asked, "When do we leave, Uncle Edwin?"

"Three days from now."

The family arrived in Montgomery and got into their carriages and wagons headed for Evergreen Manor. Laura and her brothers were so anxious and nervous. As they traveled through the countryside, the boys and Laura pointed out familiar things to the others.

Freddie saw several carriages and wagons headed his way, so he ran like his britches were on fire to spread the warning. He wondered if a bunch of carpetbaggers were going to cause trouble for Mr. Randolph. Freddie knew Mr. Randolph was repairing the chicken house, so he headed there first.

He ran up and shouted, "There are wagons and carriages headed up our lane. They might be the no account carpetbaggers you been hearing about, sir!"

"I'll go to the house, and you spread the word, and tell the men to come armed, because we might be in danger!"

"Yes sir!"

"Were there any soldiers with them?"

"No sir!"

"Alright Freddie, scoot like the wind!"

Randolph ran to the mansion, went inside, and yelled, "Everybody come quickly!"

Alice inquired, "What on earth is all the commotion about?"

"Wagons and carriages are headed our way, so they could mean trouble! Asa, Leroy, get your weapons and take your positions upstairs!"

"Yes sir, we be on the way!"

Beulah blabbed, "Daisy and me will gits our pistols, Mr. Randolph. Ain't no carpetbagger goin' to mess with us!"

Alice added, "I'll get my pistol. Where's Freddie?"

"He's spreading the alarm!"

When they could see the mansion, Laura and her brothers wiped tears from their eyes, because their beloved home they grew up in still stood strong and beautiful.

The plan was for Warren and Carl to get out and approach the house first. Randolph's children wanted to surprise their mother and father right out of their britches.

Warren and Carl walked towards the mansion's steps as Randolph came out on the porch carrying his gun. He ordered, "That's far enough! State your business."

Carl responded, "My name is Carl Sawyer, and this is Warren Taylor. We have something in common, but I'd feel better telling you what, if you'd lower that gun you have aimed at my chest."

"That's not the only gun aimed at both of you, so state your business before I pull my trigger!"

Carl answered, "We have brought you a very big surprise!"

"Listen Mr. Sawyer, I'm losing my patience!"

Warren said, "Well, I guess we better tell him before he really gets mad. I'm your son-in-law."

Carl announced, "One of your sons married my daughter, sir."

"What in tarnation are you talking about?"

Laura stepped out of her carriage and started towards her father.

Randolph yelled, "Sweet Jesus! Then, he fell to his knees as Alice came rushing out the door. Laura ran up the steps and into the arms of her parents. They hugged, kissed, and held each other tight as they wept. Warren joined them, and Randolph grabbed his hand and said, "Welcome to the family!"

Shortly, Daisy and Beulah rushed out on the porch and hugged Laura senseless.

When Laura managed to get some control back, she

announced, "That's not all, Poppa!"

Maddie and Kramer got out of their carriage and ran to the steps. The scene was repeated with tears, hugs, and kisses.

Randolph pleaded, "Forgive me son, because you were right all those years ago, but I changed life on our plantation because of you."

"Michael told me about the changes you made for the plantation, and I'm proud of you, Poppa!"

Asa and Leroy ran out and hugged Kramer and Laura. "All of us has missed you! We prayed you'd come back to see us."

Kramer told his parents about the Battle of Nashville, but he didn't let the cat out of the bag. Albert and Michael stepped out from behind the wagon and bolted towards their parents as fast as they could move. Again, the scene was repeated with hugs, kisses, and lots of tears. Everybody managed to cry a river of tears.

A lot of the workers came running to do battle, but when they saw Laura and Kramer they rushed towards them, because they were long lost friends. Everybody took part in the tearful reunion.

Albert commented, "I'm a different person, Poppa! What you have done here is important and wonderful."

Alice asked, "Is Austin in one of the wagons?"

Michael answered, "We're sorry mother, but Austin is dead on Kennesaw Mountain." He went on to explain what happened to Austin. This time, his parents shed tears for his tormented soul.

Albert blabbed, "There's one more surprise for you, Father!"

Eleanor stepped out of her carriage and rushed towards her brother. They held each other tight and wept, because they hadn't seen each other for over ten years.

Sally heard all the commotion and when she reached the house she didn't believe what her eyes were seeing. She screamed and launched herself at Laura, and then, at the boys. When she saw Albert she pulled back, but Albert rushed into her arms. Albert had to let the people who made up Evergreen Manor know he was a different person.

Asa suggested, "All you fine folks go inside to visit, and we'll take care of your things."

"Thank you, Asa."

Leroy added, "We'll take care of the horses and wagons real good."

"I appreciate that, Leroy."

Daisy and Beulah flapped their jaws and blabbed, "We goin' to cook you folks the best meal ever, and it will be a feast from heaven!"

Freddie ran like the wind when he realized the group wasn't hoodlums or carpetbaggers. He and Michael always cared about each other before Mr. Randolph changed life on the plantation. Michael grabbed him up in his arms and tickled the daylights out of him.

As the group visited, Randolph and Alice were very sad to hear the news that Gordon had been killed in action.

Daisy and Beulah breezed in with trays of warm honey cornbread and apple cider.

Albert stood up and said, "This cornbread cake stayed in my mind from one battle to the next. Ladies, this kept me goin' during the desperate times, and I'm going to savor every bite. From now on, I want to live in the present and not the past. My journey will be complete when I see my wife and son."

315

Beulah replied, "Thank you, Mr. Albert. That's what all of us be a wantin'."

Alice mentioned, "I thank the Almighty for giving me my family back! I want our nation to heal and change for the better for everyone."

Asa rushed in and shouted, "Mr. Randolph come quick!"

All the men rushed out to see Robert Baker collapse on the steps.

Albert shouted, "My God, he's in awful shape!"

Kramer told Asa to get his medical bag and said, "He's exhausted and nothing but skin and bone. Let's put him on the couch, so I can examine him!"

Sally grabbed Robert's hand and pleaded, "Wake up, Robert, it's me! Talk to me!"

He looked at her and smiled, "Sally, my parents are dead and my house is destroyed. Help me, because I don't know where to go or what to do."

She ordered, "You're coming here and get well. Poppa is going to help you, Robert!"

Albert offered, "We'll clean you up, feed you lots of good food, and put some clean clothes on you. You're about my size, so you can have some of my clothes."

The boys got busy cleaning Robert up and burning his tattered uniform. Of course, the honey cornbread and cider put a smile on his face. When he looked at Sally close up, he couldn't believe what a fine looking woman she had grown up to be.

After dinner, Randolph gave Robert a ledger showing him exactly what Robert owned and how much money his crops had made last year.

"Mr. Waverly, you've planted cotton, corn, tobacco, and all sort of vegetables on my land last year and this year. You've repaired all my fencing, barns, and chicken coops. I don't know what to say, because thank you just isn't enough."

Randolph added, "I have a lumber mill and gristmill, so we can cut wood and build you a new home. It won't be as grand, but that's how it is. My colored workers are free and have been since 1862. They own land, have homes, they help me run Evergreen Manor, and we split the profits."

"That's incredible! It sure looks like it works!"

"Robert, we have to change and heal our nation. We must do whatever it takes to make life better for all of us. Hate and prejudice are deadly diseases we need to stop!"

"Mr. Waverly, I don't understand everything you are doing, but I'm willing to try and change. I want to make my parents proud."

"Alright Robert, we'll help you get back on your feet."

Randolph's children looked at their father and mother in a different light, now. They were truly remarkable people with a vision and dream for the future. They were willing to change in order to heal a battered nation and heal the scars so many soldiers were carrying.

Coming Next
Trans-Mississippi Theater
96th Ohio Infantry Regiment
"Shut the Backdoor"

Dr. Ryan Braden, along with several of his relatives and friends, join the 96th Ohio Infantry Regiment in 1862. All the men believed they would either fight Gen Robert E. Lee in the Eastern Theater or the Confederate forces in Kentucky and Tennessee. Little do they know, they will be assigned to the Trans-Mississippi Theater and become part of the Union army's desperate struggle to control the Mississippi River and close the backdoor of the Confederacy.

ABOUT THE AUTHOR

Faye M. Benjamin was born and raised in Virginia where she still lives with her husband and black cat "Spooky." She enjoys creating her stories and wants to share that joy with those people who love to read.

Readers can visit her website at www.fayebenjamin.com for the latest information on her current and future releases.

So, readers sit back, relax, laugh, and enter her Freestone Investigations and Security's world of murder, mystery, intrigue, humor, and the paranormal.

For those readers who enjoy Civil War novels, she is writing a series of human interest stories about the Civil War that are historical fiction.